Walking in the Sun

Ruth Adams

This book has been written in memory of a little Tunisian boy who gave me his very own gold bracelet seventeen years ago, and with thanks to another boy (Ryan) who took the time to publish it.

Prologue

35, Avenue de la Republique

Salma watched Omar fasten the chain around their baby boy's tiny wrist. He had been with them for an anxious three months, although she had lost two of them. The labour had lasted days, and the bleeding took a long time to stop. She was still bed-ridden, and too weak to stand. She raised her head off the pillow and looked at the bright sky. It could have been home, but the voices on the street below were not speaking a language she knew, and there were no smells of her mum's tagine. She collapsed back down and put her hand on her empty chest.

"You are missing her, aren't you?"

Her eyes filled. Omar leant closer to her, their baby in his arms,

"Look my love: your family is right here."

Salma could not look. She just reached up and touched the bracelet, shimmering in the Mediterranean sun, set in a sapphire sky.

Ann set the last box down and straightened up, hands on her hips. It was really happening now; her long-hoped for dream was right here. She glanced over at the white canvas, already propped up, waiting to be filled. A baby cried in the room above, and she heard the sound of a man hushing it. She hoped that wouldn't turn into a problem. Silence was important to her now, after all those years of responding to every call, day and night. Those times were done. They were both gone and no-one needed her any more. Especially not him.

Alberto sat at the end of his dying wife's bed, and gripped her hand, willing her to live. His two daughters were asleep in chairs nearby and he kept watch alone. They said it was a matter of days, or even hours. He looked at her troubled face, and knew this was the end. And then what? He called softly to rouse the girls to watch his precious Mia make her final journey.

The door to nothing slammed in his face as he leant back, empty.

Francois stood with a smile fixed on his face and watched his Nationalist dad standing on a podium, embracing his wife in front of an air-punching crowd. He hadn't told them he'd enrolled in the university to do music, not the politics they had tried to push him towards. He also hadn't told them that his political beliefs were the polar opposite to theirs. Nice did not need more segregation, it needed to celebrate its diversity. But there was no way he was going to share that either.

CHAPTER ONE

Leaving

The delicate gold chain sparkled on deep blue velvet and Rachel tried not to cry. The sounds of home - a pressure cooker hissing, dad grinding coffee beans for his ten o'clock break, the dog barking up and down the garden, the local news shouting nasally from the radio - they all retreated as she touched it and avoided looking at Charlie.

He cleared his throat,

"It's just something to remind you of me. When you're living it up in France."

She nudged his leg with hers,

"As it I needed help, silly." She glanced over at his jiggling leg, his flushed face. He reached up and pulled at his chestnut hair with both hands.

"How long have we known each other now, Rach? Fifteen years?"

Rachel looked through her window at the fast-moving clouds, thinking,

"You hit your ball into my sandpit, and I took it back to you?" Rachel winked at him.

"No, *I* came and got it, remember?"

She laughed, "Of course I remember. You know me Charlie, I don't forget things. Or people."

She met his dark eyes.

"Especially you."

They sat in heavy silence.

"Nervous?"

Rachel shook her head then nodded, laughing at herself.

"I don't really want to go - the thought of being in France, with a heap of people I don't know, and speaking a language I'm better at reading and writing. It's scary, you know?"

There it was - the feeling she had been trying to push down. Trust Charlie to get it out of her.

"You'll be fine - you always are."

He squeezed her round the shoulders for a brief second, then shifted away. He sighed and then mumbled,

"I'll miss you, you know."

Rachel stared at her hands,

"It's only nine months, and then I'll be back."

Nine months echoed and pounded around the room. The packed bags leaning against the door frame pushed stubbornly into their consciousness. Charlie sat forward and gripped his knees.

"Rach, there's something I - "

At that moment Pepsi the family Springer bounded into the room knocking over the bags, his lead in his mouth.

"Rachel!" Mum was calling,

"Can you take him out?"

Rachel sighed,

"I guess we'll have to say our goodbyes now then." She looked at Charlie's pale, serious face as he stood up.

The two best friends hugged each other awkwardly and pulled away, each forcing a smile. Charlie turned and said over his shoulder,

"A bientôt, Rachel. Don't forget to phone me."

"How could I ever forget you, you big eejit?" She got close again and punched him lightly on his arm.

Charlie pushed his hands into his carpenter trousers and left, not looking back. Rachel crouched down and put her arms around Pepsi, watching her best friend walk away. He was tall now, and handsome, she noted with surprise.

What had he wanted to say to her? She'd ask him some other time.

✤

Rachel looked down at the credit card dad was holding out.

"Dad, I don't need it - I have my own, remember?"

"I know that. This is only for emergencies. Keep it somewhere different to your wallet, and then you'll never be stuck."

"It's Nice, not a war zone in the Middle East. I won't need your card."

Dad kept pushing the card towards her, and eventually Rachel took it, rolling her eyes.

"I'm telling you, I'll be fine."

Dad lifted his hands in surrender, but then said,

"You have to plan for the worst case scenario when you're travelling. I'm sure you'll be alright, but it would make me happier if I knew you had a back-up. I know, I know, you don't think you'll need it, but you've got to humour your old dad this time."

He gave her a hug then, and she went out to the car with her last bag. She was about to sit down when she noticed a gift bag sitting on the seat. She lifted it and got in.

"What's this?"

Mum started the engine and pulled out of the driveway.

"Oh, it's just a few wee things that might come in handy. You can put them in your pockets if you've no free hands."

Thinking of her bags already packed to bursting point with mum's everything but the kitchen sink mentality, Rachel shot her a sideways look and started putting as much as she could manage into her coat.

"You're fussing, mum. As bad as dad,"

"We are just both going to miss you Rachel."

Rachel felt tightness in her throat. She stared out the window, willing herself not to cry.

❖

The leave-taking had been strained, but the flight was on time, so there wasn't much chance of drawing out the goodbyes. Rachel checked in her two massive bags, willing them to arrive in the right place. She leant over and pushed her tiny teddy further into the side pocket, the only friend that she could bring with her. She turned round and waved cheerily to her mum. She knew she would stay there until she was out of sight.

The queue going through security was slow. Rachel had to empty all the things her mum had given her out of her pockets, her cheeks burning. Once out of the line, she put her head down and shifted her bag on her shoulder, trying to look nonchalant. She knew she could put her walkman on but she might miss an announcement, so she left the headphones hanging round her neck. The hard seats in the departures lounge were nearly all taken by time she'd got there, so she just leant against a wall watching everyone. There were a couple of men dressed in dark suits, sitting together but reading newspapers and not speaking. A red-faced man was bouncing a screaming baby on his knee, waiting for his similarly harassed wife to come back with their toddler from the toilet. A couple of Goths were standing a metre away, their arms draped lazily round each other.

When it was time to board Rachel reached for her passport. Wrong pocket. With sweat prickling her armpits, she handed it over with her boarding pass and tried to smile at the air hostess but she was already focusing her heavily made-up eyes on the person behind Rachel. There was the usual rush to get pre-booked places, as if there weren't enough for everyone. A few people did sit in the wrong seats, but it was politely resolved. Rachel sat down, nursing her bag, feeling her stomach clench. This was really happening. She reached up to tidy her hair, and saw a glitter of gold out of the corner of her eye: Charlie's bracelet.

She closed her eyes and pressed her arms to her body to stop the shaking panic building inside. Cold air pumped down on her head. She could already smell the unappetising 'fresh' egg and onion sandwiches. She dutifully paid attention to the air hostesses criss-crossing flat life-jackets and tapping the inflation tube. She craned to look out the tiny window then leant back again. It was not helpful watching her homeland shrinking away from her. She reached forward and pulled out the mundane in-flight magazine. A cheerfully plump Stelios grinned at her from his orange photo. She flicked over to the irrelevant duty free offers, and didn't even try to read the articles on the other pages. With every moment her heart thudded, wishing she was not flying away from the only place she had ever known.

There was a bit of a wait in Luton airport for the second flight to Nice but Rachel barely noticed. She just sat in the same seat, checking her ticket and the departures screen every other minute. She felt someone's eyes on her, and looked up to see an older swarthy skinned man in a turban watching her. He smiled. She busied herself with her bag, trying to look like she had done this a hundred times before. She saw air hostesses rushing out with their wheelie suitcases, shifts done for the day. She envied all the people who were going back to their own beds, and wondered what hers would be like that night.

After an uneventful but slow flight, the turquoise Mediterranean finally came up closer and closer and the pilot announced their approach, in English and French. Rachel put her headphones on and turned up the volume of Counting Crows' *This Desert Life*. The red-faced dad was cheerily singing 'we're going home' to his baby girl, still bouncing her on his lap. Rachel wondered if it was helping them both.

She was not going home, she was leaving it.

She shifted in her seat and leant her head against the tiny window to take in the long pebbled beach, the smooth

Promenade des Anglais running alongside it, the city rising gradually from the burnt orange roofs and yellow walls of the Old Town, along the pink buildings of the city centre, to the grander white-washed houses settled in the hills above. The wealth was easy to spot from the air: countless yachts were moored at the harbour, small deep blue squares of swimming pools sparkled in the sun, the pink and blue tipped dome of the Negresco hotel stood proud above the shore-line. Rachel looked down at her crumpled clothes and worried. This city was already making her feel under-dressed and she was still in the air.

A few dicey metres beyond the sea, the plane touched down and ferried across the sweltering runway. Many of the other passengers were taking off their coats and jumpers in preparation for the heat that was waiting to grab them as soon as the doors were opened. Rachel kept hers on, unable to figure out how she was going to carry all the just-in-case paraphernalia her mum had insisted on giving her at the last minute. Why on earth was there a Yankee candle bulging in her coat pocket and when would she need a plastic cutlery set? She smiled and shook her head, pushing the ache back down. It kept trying to get out and make her cry, but she wouldn't let it - once out it would expand to a size so big it would never fit back in.

After squeezing between the bouncy-backed seats, and smiling her way through elbows, sweaty arm-pits and painted toe-nails, she finally got out.

Well, hello Nice, home for the year.

Rachel looked down to her socks and trainers. She should have worn flip-flops like everybody else. She looked so inexperienced. Standing waiting for her luggage she watched a breezy group of skinny girls flicking their long glossy hair, and fixing their Dolce and Gabbana sunglasses. There were at least ten less glamorous people fussing around them and the Hermes cases at their feet. Models. Couldn't even carry their own handbags.

Heavy bags retrieved, sweating in far too many layers, Rachel made the slow walk through 'Nothing to Declare' and into the cream-tiled, squeaky airport foyer. She scanned the name cards being waved by taxi-drivers, business men and long-lost relatives. Then she spotted her: a plump, serious-faced lady in a floral dress walking towards her holding a sign with 'Rosemary' scribbled on it.

"Well, hello. Are you Rosemary?"

Rachel stopped searching the faces and stared at her.

"I'm Rachel, not Rosemary, but I think you've got the right person - Margaret, is it?"

"Oh shoot, I'm sorry. Must have got our wires crossed, and here we are speaking the same language. You see, it can happen so easily. We've such a crowd of folk passing in and out of our little congregation it's hard to keep track. Bill thought you'd be more relaxed with me, but he only said your name when I was already in the car so it was hard to hear - these manual engines are much noisier than the ones we drive in the States."

As she was chatting, the pastor's wife picked up one of Rachel's bags and walked towards the exit. Rachel hoisted her rucksack onto her back and hurried after her. The wide hall was buzzing with people speaking mainly French, with other languages bubbling up as she passed them. Once outside, there was a queue of white taxis, and several dark-skinned men weaving in and out of the crowd, flashing their white teeth. All of a sudden Rachel was stopped by a man pulling on her sleeve, grabbing at her rucksack and talking all the time. She guessed he was speaking French, but his thick accent made it almost impossible to understand him. She shook her head and tried to step away, but he stuck to her like a persistent child.

"Hey! Leave her be! Get lost!"

Margaret pulled Rachel's other arm and rushed her away.

"You'll get used to them, don't worry. Just be firm and they'll get the message. This city is crawling with men like that one, more's the pity."

Rachel turned back to see her persistent man quickly home in on somebody else, doing the same things to her. She looked at him, met his eyes and sped up.

"Who are they? And why are they here at the airport?"

Margaret spotted her car, and stopped to get her keys out.

"They're mainly North African, seeking a better life than they left behind. Trouble is, they have no qualifications or permit to work here, so they spend their time harassing people to get money. They are a nuisance, and all we can do is try to get out of their way. Thankfully they live in the banlieue, but they do wander around the centre during the day and sometimes late into the night too."

"Why don't they just go home?"

"They don't want to. Seems like here is home for them now. I suppose the wild hope for a lucky break keeps them here."

Rachel took off her rucksack and threw it into the boot. Clearly, she had much to learn.

As they drove away from the centre and climbed the hills into the suburbs, Rachel began to relax. The streets got wider, the houses further apart, trees more frequent. She shifted in her seat to catch a glimpse of the bright blue Mediterranean, the earthy tones of the Old Town and the numerous apartment blocks behind her.

"We're nearly there now, and you'll see your friends."

Rachel fiddled with her bag.

"Actually, I don't think I know anyone who's coming here; it's just a random collection of students working as classroom assistants in the same city."

Margaret nodded once. She parked up outside a somewhat dilapidated building which Rachel guessed was the hostel, pulled the hand-brake, turned and smiled.

"As it happens, a girl who went to the church has just moved out of a cute little bedsit we own to return to South Africa, and it's lying empty. You could live there, if you liked?"

Rachel tried to process this out-of-the-blue offer.

"It's a one bedroom flat, but don't worry - we've got to know some of the neighbours after the seven years we've had the studio, so you wouldn't be alone."

Alone. Rachel glanced down to her wrist and held onto the bracelet there.

"That is very kind of you, can I have a think about it?"

"Sure thing, you can call me tomorrow, if you're interested." Margaret got out a pen, scribbled down her number and the studio address on a bit of paper and handed it to Rachel,

"I'll help you out with your bags and then be on my way."

"Thank-you for bringing me, I don't know how I would have found here otherwise."

"You are most welcome. All part of the service!"

Margaret got back in, started the engine, stalled, laughed and wound down the window. After she'd turned she waved and called,

"Think about that flat, Rachel - it might be a good opportunity for you."

Then she was gone: the only person that Rachel knew in Nice. She took a deep breath, gathered up her things and headed inside.

When she had checked in, she followed the hostel volunteer upstairs to a crowded, noisy corridor. He turned, raised his dark eyebrows and asked her where she wanted him to carry her rucksack to.

"She'll come with me, Jean. We have space in our room."

A brightly dressed girl with massive bead earrings and messy hair skipped over, batted her eye-lids at Jean and stuck her hand out.

"I'm Laura. Who are you?"

This question was posed in English, which made the French she had spoken before sound impressively fluent.

"Hi. I'm Rachel."

"And you're Irish. Que c'est mignon?!" She smiled at Jean-Paul again for some reason.

"Northern Irish, actually, but I'll take Irish here."

Laura laughed and looked at Jean again.

"Come on then, let's get you to your room! Nearly everyone's here already - there's Nick (he's from the States, well Mexico really which is so much more interesting don't you think?), and there's a ton of people from my part of the world in York, and a few from more exotic places than icky England. Who do you know that's here? Maybe I've missed a heap of folk out. Have I Jean?"

Jean shrugged his shoulders under the rucksack straps.

"Here we are! See, there's an empty bed right by the window. Quelle vue, non?"

Rachel was beginning to get used to Laura's easy way of slipping from her native English into French but it was still slightly unnerving. Jean set down her luggage, nodded and left with Laura at his heels, still chirruping.

Rachel walked over to the bed, pushed her rucksack to one side and sat down, facing the glass sliding doors, barred on the outside to waist level. She stood up again, pushed the windows open and leant against the bars to take in the view. There was a racket of cicadas in the trees below, horns blasted intermittently from the streets and the air smelt of hot plastic, garden herbs, car fumes and swimming pool chlorine. The city was there in one expansive sweep, bordered by the rugged hills and underlined by the blue strip of Mediterranean along the coastline. The sky was cloudless and the sea was flat. The earthen toned houses close to the beach looked like they were pulsating in the choking heat, while the more modern white ones further up were cooled by surrounding trees and neighbouring pools with sun-shades strategically placed round the edges. There was the sound of jazz music coming up from below her. Rachel looked over to see the source, and caught a glimpse of a grungy looking boy about her age playing a clarinet. The bars clattered and he looked up, meeting her stare. He didn't smile, just shrugged and went back to his music. He was good, if a touch impolite.

You should be happy, Rachel told herself. Who would be sorry to be in this dazzling place, so close to the sea, kissed by the sun? She turned away, and dug in the side pocket of her rucksack. The small photo album was her most valued possession; it held everyone she loved, everyone she'd left behind. She turned the pages slowly, feeling the tightening in her chest with every face, every place that was in there. Home. That was the view she longed for. Not this one.

"Rachel! Que fais-tu? Everyone is downstairs on the terrace, waiting for dinner. Oh, what have we here?"

Laura took the album out of Rachel's hands and wagged her finger at her.

"Don't be doing that. I will not tolerate home-sickness - the year is meant to be fun, and those photos will not help."

Laura collapsed down on the bed beside her and flicked through the album.

"Ooh, who is this? Pretty hot, isn't he?"

Rachel flushed,

"That's Charlie."

"Boyfriend?"

"No, just a friend."

"Good. You're better to not have any ties holding you back this year. Me, I'm planning a few dalliances of my own while I'm here - nothing serious, mind. There's no-one to miss back in England, so I'm free as a bird." Laura held out the album. Rachel took it back and put it away, trying to hide her annoyance.

She found her hand gripped, and was off the bed speeding down the stairs before she'd had time to change her shoes, or take off her superfluous layers.

A group was gathered around the edges of an outdoor pool, chatting, smoking, sunbathing with their eyes closed.

"Everyone! Je vous presente Rachel!"

Only a few people turned round to look at this red-faced, blond haired, wide-eyed girl. Most of them were hunched over, talking in small groups around tables placed beside the outdoor pool. Rachel looked for somewhere to sit, but Laura beat her to it and grabbed the last chair. She shuffled back to lean against an ivy-covered wall and watched the confident group talk easily to each other. What to do when you have nothing to pretend you're busy with, and no-one to speak to. She tried looking nonchalant for a while, then searched for someone else on their own.

"Well, well. A new person. And who are you?"

A very scruffy fellow with a smoke behind his ear, a once-white sun hat, cut-off faded blue linen trousers and what looked like a book stuffed into his waistband sidled up to her.

"Oh hi. I'm Rachel. From Northern Ireland."

"Well hello Rachel from Northern Ireland. I'm Nick. From the United States of America."

His eyes were laughing, his mouth was twitching. Rachel felt ridiculous.

"Want a smoke?"

"No thanks, I don't."

Nick shrugged his shoulders and moved on, clearly having lost interest.

Laura came back, looking excited about something and dragging another poor person with her.

"Rachel!"

She nudged her latest victim forward.

"Here's our new flat-mate."

She was beautiful: swarthy-skinned, dark hair and eyes, white teeth, petite.

"This is Francesca. She's from Brazil. She speaks perfect English."

Francesca laughed and shook her head.

"I can speak for myself you know. Hi, Rachel, is it?"

Rachel could not keep up with this - she had never said she would share a flat with Laura, never mind a glamorous Brazilian, and yet here she was, apparently doing just that, She put her hand out and quickly retracted it when she realised this action was not a common one for Francesca. She kissed her on both cheeks instead.

"Yes, nice to meet you, Francesca."

Laura and Francesca stared at her expectantly. Rachel heard herself making the decision without realising.

"Actually, I already have plans for somewhere to live."

There were disappointed sounds from the other two.

"How did you find somewhere already? We're going in to look tomorrow, but have no clue how to start."

"It was a pastor's wife from the International Baptist here - I contacted them before I left, and they've been really helpful."

"Well, good, but we'll not leave you alone, whatever your plans. Tell us where you're going to be, and we'll come see you." Laura linked arms with Francesca and smiled brightly as Rachel wrote out the studio address for them.

Laura took it and pulled a map of Nice out of her bag to find the street.

"That's not far from Jean Medicin. Let's meet up there tomorrow lunchtime?"

"What time is that? One o'clock?"

"Yeah, that'll do. See you."

The pair walked away, giggling and chatting, leaving Rachel to wonder if she had just made a big mistake.

Dinner that night was an unfamiliar cold pasta/mussels

combination with slices from an already hardened baguette and a tossed salad with olives. She sat on the end of one of the long benches and forced herself to eat at least a quarter of the food. Francesca and Laura came over with their plates and sat opposite. They talked away, and had no trouble eating their dinner.

"You not hungry, Rachel?"

Rachel shook her head, a mouthful of cold pasta stuck in the back of her throat.

Laura patted her on the back and pulled a face.

"It will get easier, believe me. I've been here a week, and already it feels almost *chez moi.*"

Francesca nodded sagely.

"On s'habitue a tout, as Albert Camus once wrote."

Rachel nodded, feeling slightly patronised. What if she didn't ever feel like it was home? What if she never got used to it?

✣

Everyone else was still downstairs - drinking, smoking, talking, laughing. Rachel was already in bed, clutching her teddy to her chest, staring out at the city lights, feeling achingly hollow. The nerves had subsided, but now she just felt numb. She squeezed her eyes shut, willing herself to not bring up images of her mum and dad, Pepsi the dog, her cosy bedroom, her familiar house. Her bed now was hard, and one of a dozen lined up along two of the walls. The rest were uninhabited, but covered with all the detritus of hurried unpacking. She propped herself up on her elbow and looked at her neatly stacked, practically untouched bags. It was hard to believe that it was less than 24 hours since she was at home, staring at them, feeling nervous. She dropped back on the pillow and sighed. What was the point of taking everything out when she was leaving again tomorrow or the day after?

Slowly, a couple of hours later, the girls started coming up, whispering and giggling, fumbling their way through the darkened room. Rachel pretended she was asleep, but she had realised early on that sleep just wasn't going to come tonight. It didn't take long for everyone else to fall asleep, and somehow this made her loneliness more acute. She was too tired to form memories or thoughts to feed her homesickness now. She just lay there, gripping her teddy, tearless and empty, staring out at the twinkling lights of the city, the black, blank space of the sea beyond.

The sun rose early and she watched it with relief. The night was over, the sky was getting back to its cheerful blue hues. She looked at her watch and wondered how acceptable it would be to get up for her shower now, at seven. Her room mates were all still sleeping off their revelling from the night before.

After what felt like an age of waiting, she grabbed her things and tiptoed out. The shower was freezing, either because it was too early for hot water, or because she hadn't figured the knobs out. Still, it was refreshing and gave her a reason to move quickly, washing off the misery she'd been indulging all night.

Maybe today would be better. Maybe she'd find something to be happy about.

❖

Rachel sat on the immaculately made bed and looked at her watch. Charlie's chain winked at her. It was eight now and still no-one else was up. She stood and smoothed down her sundress. Then, her flip-flops slapping into the quiet, she left the room and made her way down the stairs. The clattering of pots and crockery welcomed her. She hovered at the kitchen door. Jean looked up from his coffee, and nodded to her,

"Bon matin. You're the second up today. Cafe or chocolat?"

Holding her hot bowl of steaming hot chocolate, Rachel took careful steps across to the dining room. Nick was sitting at the top of a long, empty table eating a torn off chunk of baguette. He saluted her with it. She stayed standing.

"Have a seat, Irish girl."

She sat at the other end of the table, facing him. He cupped his hands round his mouth and called to her,

"That close enough for you?!"

She opened her mouth to explain but was stopped by his laughter.

"Just yanking your chain. Sit where you like, no skin off my nose."

She sipped her drink glancing over at Nick, who'd pulled a dog-eared book out of somewhere, possibly his trousers?and was seemingly engrossed in it. Once she was done, she headed out to the payphone to tell Margaret she wanted her studio before she changed her mind. She would move in in three days' time.

That day and the next, the assistants met for preliminary training in teaching English. Laura and Francesca always sat with Rachel for some reason, but she welcomed their company. She was learning that when you're abroad everything happened a lot faster - friendships forged after the first hello, decisions that normally took weeks made in a flash. Laura had already wheedled Rachel and Francesca's back-stories out of them, but said little of her own. She didn't have much time for any of her old class-mates from York, but was intent on forging new links with everyone else. She baffled Rachel, but challenged her own dependency on home as well.

CHAPTER TWO

New digs

"Well. Here we are."

Rachel shifted the heavy weight of her rucksack and took in the battered terracotta front door. She glanced up and down the street then looked up to the much more appealing blue sky. It had been like that since she'd arrived - constant, unfailingly bright. The side of the street that housed her new bedsit was in shade, and did not look as reassuring. It was all situated not far from the port, and within walking distance to the main shopping precinct. Margaret had driven them, so it was hard to judge distances. Rachel had taken in the small supermarket on the crossroads at the top of her street, Avenue de la Republique, and as they drove slowly along, she saw a hairdressing salon, a risqué lingerie shop, a bakery full of tall baguettes and croissants, a patisserie with delicately arranged delights, a delicatessen with golden, glistening chickens turning on a spit, tiny, dark cafes and one doctor's surgery. It had everything she might need, apart from friendly faces, and these were becoming increasingly more vital to her.

Now that she was out of the car, the heat and smells hit her.

She wrinkled her nose and took a step back as she registered the burst bin bags lined up just outside the door. One of them was moving. A rat burst out and pitter-pattered across the street, dodging the angry cars as it ran.

"Oh dear, how disgusting! The perils of living in the city I suppose. I've never seen them up near us. The odd Maghreb, but no rats."

Rachel looked up at Margaret to see if she was joking, but she was deadpan.

"Shall we go in?"

They climbed the three flights of stairs and let themselves in only to be faced with another short climb to the bedsit. The recently painted lounge/tiny kitchen/bedroom were lit up with the sunshine streaming in through two skylights and it was chokingly hot. Margaret went over and opened one of the windows as wide as it could go, but there was no relief from the heat. She laughed,

"Nothing like fresh, hot air to cool you down! Do you like it?"

It was so high up, so closed off from any human contact.

"Yes. This is great, thank you."

"Now, don't you worry about company - as my south African friend told me, the building is full of people from different parts of the world and they're friendly enough."

Somehow, Rachel did not find this reassuring.

Margaret noted her worried face, but kept on talking.

"I think there's a family just below and then there's an Italian gentleman called Antonio, or Alessandro, or Alberto, something like that anyway!" She laughed then looked solemn.

"His is a sad story from what I can make out." She told Rachel all she knew about him. Once finished, she shook her head in concern, but turned brisk seconds later. She fished her keys out of her bag and hooked it over her arm again.

"You're all set now, aren't you. I have to rush off, errands to run before lunch. So, I'll leave you to get settled."

She put her hand on Rachel's arm.

"You look a little worried. Don't be, it will be great. And remember: everything happens for a reason."

With that unreassuring platitude, Margaret gave her a quick hug and left.

Rachel put her rucksack on the floor, and sat down on the futon. She pulled out her walkman, turned it on, lay back and let the words of *Amy Hit the Atmosphere* wash over her:

If I could make it rain today/And wash this sunny day down to the gutter/
    I would/Just to get a change of pace/Things are getting worse but I feel a lot better/And that's all that really matters to me...
    We've waited so long for someone to take us back home/It just sinks like a stone/Waiting for mothers to come

Rachel had woken early, as the sun shone through the blinds above her head. Just like it had been the past two mornings, it took a moment to realise she was not in her bed at home; the walls were not lilac, and the room was not cold. It was hot, white and tiny. She shifted up onto one elbow and looked over the low wall that separated the sleeping quarters from the rest of the flat - two doors - one for the way out, one for the bathroom. The kitchen consisted of a two-burner gas hob with a small oven underneath, a scratched red counter, white sink and a bar with two high stools pulled into it. Her sitting space was a navy blue futon, a pine coffee table and a huge, ancient TV on wheels. The floor was tiled throughout, with brightly coloured rag rugs scattered over it. She got out of bed and walked the five steps to the bathroom. It was a marvel in sunshine yellow with a black mosaic tile finish. There were no windows there, but, as with the rest of the space, many light-reflecting large mirrors had been mounted to the walls. Rachel looked in one and stuck her tongue out - her hair was a spiky, greasy, faded blond mess, her pale blue eyes were surrounded with dark rings, and her skin was dull.

She stood there staring for a minute, willing herself to cry. The pain stuck in her chest but no tears would come. She turned away to get washed.

Once showered, hair washed and dried and face spruced up, she squirted on some Tommy Hilfiger, pulled on her blue sun-dress, chunky beads and flip-flops and headed out.

A wave of hot sun, wheezing bus engines and new smells hit

her. She had two more days to get used to Nice before her work in schools began, and she wasn't intending to waste them. A door on the first floor clicked shut as she walked past. She stood still for a moment, wondering if the person watching would come out and say hello, half hoping they wouldn't. There was just silence. She lifted her chin, and headed out into the sunshine.

As it was so early, the bakery had plenty of fresh bread and she bought two warm pain au chocolat - one for now, one for later. She went into the underwear shop but left as quickly as she could after seeing the risqué corsets with a hole cut in the crotch, thongs and fish net tights. The middle-aged owner with bobbed black hair had just glanced up from her till and looked away again. Nothing, it seemed, would surprise her - she'd most likely seen it all before. Rachel smiled at the audacity of the French, and their lack of shame about sex.

Further on, she paused at the hairdresser's and looked for prices. She needed to get her highlights done - she'd been too busy packing and organising to do it before she left. There were no signs anywhere. She looked in at the two tall, glamorous hairdressers. One of them started walking over towards her. Rachel frantically tried to recall the word for 'highlights' in French but drew a blank. The door opened and the woman spoke to her. By mime and broken French/ English they got to the point, and she found herself leaving, appointment made.

Once off Avenue de la Republique, she walked until she reached Avenue Jean Medicin, the main shopping street in Nice. She browsed through the clothes racks in Zara, got mesmerised by the cosmetics in Sephora and lifted up a couple of the bags in Galeries Lafayette. She realised now that in Nice, there was no excuse for slovenly appearances; almost everyone she passed was dressed smartly. Looking about her, she crossed the road and went in to a shoe shop on Rue Massena. There she saw a pair of turquoise leather court shoes, with a strap and small heels. She surprised herself by buying them - not her usual trainers/flip-flop look, and yet she knew it would help her to fit in so it was money well spent.

Heading back, she caught herself finishing the 'one for later' pain au chocolat. She'd leave the Old Town for later with Laura and Francesca - it deserved a full afternoon. She took a right turn off her street and followed the road until she reached the port. It was packed with huge white yachts bouncing on the vibrant blue sea, sparkling in the hot sun. There was so much wealth here - and so many rich tourists having their holiday on La Cote d'Azur. Rachel felt out of place walking alongside the boats. She knew she didn't belong there. She felt lost all of a sudden, and imagined the fun she would have if Charlie were there. He would not be intimidated by the people here, or their ridiculous displays of opulence. In fact, he would laugh at it all and make her laugh too. He was the best of friends. She threw a stone into the water, and looked out beyond the boats to the horizon, wondering what he was doing right that moment.

"Why did you close the door again, papa?"

Omar put his finger to his lips and Mamoun copied him. They stood like that, waiting for the footsteps to retreat.

"I didn't want to scare her, that's all."

"Who?"

"The new girl."

"Why would you scare her?"

Omar sighed and looked down at his nine year old.

"Because we look different, sometimes people get frightened."

Mamoun frowned.

"Why?"

"They think we might be bad people."

"Why do they think that?"

"Because some people with dark skin have been bad, and they think we're all like that."

There was a snort and a tut.

"That is the stupidest thing I've ever heard."

Omar rumpled his son's hair.

"Let's get you to school mon fils."

"Bye Maman!"

They opened the front door again, and hurried out.

✣

Rachel looked at her watch - the girls had said they'd be there at one, but it was two now, and they still hadn't showed up. She felt her stomach rumble and started to gather her things to go out again by herself. There was a knock on the door. Rachel opened it to Laura and Francesca. Francesca was taking off her stilettos and moaning.

"I thought we were heading straight out. I've been waiting for you two for over an hour."

Francesca just pushed past her and went up the stairs on all fours.

"What's the matter with her?"

Laura rolled her eyes,

"She wanted to glam up, so we've walked most of the way with her in heels. Dodging the dog business was the best part."

Francesca called down the stairs,

"Do you have any foot soak?"

The other two girls burst out laughing.

"No, but I do have Yves Saint Laurent body cream."

"Oh. Well. That might help."

They laughed more and then went up after her. She was sitting with her feet up, not looking as though she would ever get up again.

"Sorry for teasing, Francesca."

She pouted.

Rachel went over to her sleeping space and dug out another pair of flip-flops.

"Wear these for now, so we can all enjoy ourselves."

Francesca lifted the shoes up with a look of distaste on her face. Still, she put them on, stuffed her strappy sandals in her bag and stood up.

"Better?"

"I suppose."

When the girls got to the edge of the Old Town it was lunch time. They stopped at one of the many roadside cafes and ordered lunch. Laura and Rachel had a baguette sandwich but Francesca ordered the oyster platter. She made a show of eating it, while the other two, finished with their lunch, looked on.

They stopped for ice-cream then and wandered around the cobbled lanes, the hot afternoon sun beating down on their heads. The Baroque streets were narrow, and the tall houses almost blocked out the sun. There were numerous boutiques, cheese mongers, butchers, delicatessens, eateries and shops selling hand-woven baskets, jewellery and scarves. Most of the shops had an external awning over their best wares, making the path through even more awkward. There was a heady smell of spices, fish, cheese and charcuterie. They went into a hand-crafted merchandise shop and bought some reasonably priced rings. At Place Rossetti, they went inside the cool, dark Cathedrale Sainte Reparate, mainly because they were all sweating with the heat.

"I'm spent. You think we can head back now?"

Laura was slumped on a church pew, spraying Evian water on her face and neck.

"You ladies light-weights? It's hardly too hot."

It was Nick from the hostel, looking enviably chilled out.

Laura sat up straight and glared at him.

"We are fine, thank-you."

"I'm not sure your Brazilian friend would agree."

Rachel and Laura looked down the pew at Francesca; she was bent double and groaning.

"Francesca! What's wrong?"

She managed to mumble 'oysters' before she bolted out the door, hand over her mouth.

Nick smiled and shook his head.

"Well, well, the foreigners can't hack the food."

"Shut up, Nicolas. Nobody asked for your opinion."

Laura stood up and marched after Francesca.

"Still not want a smoke?"

Rachel shook her head at him and left too. She found a grey and shivering Francesca lying on the church steps, sweat sticking her black hair to her forehead.

"I think we'll need to call it a day Rachel. I'll help her back to the hostel now."

"Not the best sightseeing afternoon, was it?"

"We've got months to do it, anyway. And we'll find somewhere to live tomorrow. Right, Francesca?"

The Brazilian girl moaned and the other two exchanged resigned looks. Rachel took her leave, suddenly thankful she lived alone.

When she got back, she stood in the kitchen considering what to make for dinner. She wondered if she'd ever lose that lonely feeling when she walked into her empty rooms.

There was a knock on the door. She stood still and listened. Another knock. She stood up.

"Allo?!" The sound was inescapable - it echoed round the stairwell, hitting Rachel's heart and ears two times.

It was a child's voice. She clattered down the stairs and opened the door a crack. He was tiny and dusky brown with a flash of little white teeth. His clothes were too small for him, and had faded in the sun. He was wearing black leather sandals, dusty from the streets. His fists were up, as if he was expecting a fight. Rachel reckoned she could take him, if it came to that. She fought the urge to close the door and race back upstairs.

"Hi."

He grinned, opening his fists to reveal a Lipton teabag in one hand, and a paper twist of sugar in the other.

"Maman says welcome to our building!"

"Oh, how nice of her. Thank-you." He stared at her, mouth open. She ploughed on,

"I'm Rachel. What's your name?"

"Mamoun. I am nine." He bowed, pressing his hands together like a sultan.

Rachel nodded, trying to match his seriousness and not laugh. She took the teabag and sugar, thanked him again and watched him leap down the stairs back to his own flat. She'd forgotten to ask him which flat was his, or what school he went to, or if he had brothers or sisters, but she had a feeling that it wouldn't be long before he told her. She went back in, set the gifts on the counter and started to unpack. She caught herself smiling, the mists of homesickness had lifted. Maybe there would be friends here after all.

Mamoun skipped down the stairs, whistling. At last, a neighbour who looked at him, and spoke to him. Sure, the Italian guy Alberto would speak if he could, but he was always so sad looking. And the English lady just looked too scared of him to be friendly. This one, though, this one had beaten them all. He wondered why she was there, what she worked at, where she came from. He knew she wasn't French, and she wasn't Maghreb like him. She was white as white could be, with golden hair and pale blue eyes. Heaven. He burst in his front door,

"She says thank you, maman!"

Mamoun crashed in to the kitchen where Salma was cooking. She gave the tagine one more stir, stepped back and put her hijab back on. Her hair was still a lustrous black, and today red jewelled clips sparkled above her ears. Mamoun thought she was the most beautiful woman he had ever seen, but not many would know that, as she always covered everything up when they went outside their home.

"Did you say welcome, Mamou?"

"Oh yes. She is very lovely, maman, with light hair and blue eyes. Her skin is almost white."

Mamoun stuck his finger in the bubbling tagine and got his hand slapped away.

"Wait! If you're hungry, have some bread, or an apple. Little boys do not put their dirty hands into the dinner being cooked for them."

"Just a little bowl now? It looks like a lot, anyway."

"No! This'll do us two days at least so leave it be!"

Mamoun pulled a face, which got him another slap, and ran off to his room.

Salma watched him go, and sighed. He looked so lonely sometimes. The front door opened, and her husband Omar came in, shoulders hunched, head cast down.

"Bad day, my love?" Salma approached him and took his hands. He lifted her hands to his lips and kissed them.

"Nothing that you can't fix with that delicious stew." He stuck his finger in, and was licking it when Mamoun walked in.

"Maman maman - papa put his finger in too!" Salma turned and waved her wooden spoon at them both with mock anger.

"Mamoun met our new neighbour today - I sent him up to welcome her. She's all on her own, miles from her home Omar. Just like I was."

"Ah, but you had me, didn't you? So not completely alone."

Omar put his arm round his wife's shoulders and kissed the top of her head.

"We will do all we can to help her, my dear. If she will let us that is. What's she like Mamoun?"

The little boy beamed. "She is like a princess. Maybe one day I will marry her."

His parents laughed, then stopped when they saw he was serious.

"Sometimes, Mamoun, people are too different to be together. You are young, she is grown up. You are Maghreb, she is British."

"So, you want to welcome her, but you are telling me she is too different to belong here?"

"I know. It is complicated, but one day you will understand, I promise."

Mamoun folded his arms.

"Maybe I don't want to understand. Maybe I will show you."

Salma pulled a face at Omar, prompted the one sentence of thanks to Allah, and started serving out the lamb into warmed clay bowls, leaving the bread in the centre of the table for them all to share. Her son forgot his indignation and rushed to start eating. The argument could wait for another time.

Salma ladled out the lamb tagine, thinking about what she had just said. She knew her duty was to be a hospitable neighbour, but it was a terrifying idea. Imagine knocking on one of the doors to ask a total stranger into your home! She'd sent Mamoun up because she couldn't. Always, she expected hostility and rejection. She saw it every day when she went out to get the groceries. A kind of blank look, or, worse still, averted eyes. It was the head covering that put them off. The fact that they couldn't see her face. At least, she hoped it was fear that made them turn away, and not hatred.

"Maman! The dinner!"

Salma realised she had been holding the ladle suspended over an empty bowl. She shook her head, and got to serving again. She looked over at Omar, who had a concerned frown on his face. Mamoun's babble distracted them all, and her moment of dark reverie passed.

"So, Omar, was it a worse day than usual?"

Omar put down his bread.

"It wasn't. I didn't sell any, but there are days like that. At least my night job is a regular wage."

He started to dip his bread in the tagine, using the crust to spoon it into his mouth. `He stopped again,

"I was thinking how Youssef would have coped with this life, had he stayed. He was right to leave. Maybe we should have gone back as well." He rubbed his hand over his face.

"Don't let yourself think like that. Look at the opportunities Mamoun is getting: the good education,"

ʲun snorted and put his fingers on either side of his
ı. to make horns.

"With the devil teacher," he laughed. He got a sharp slap on
the wrist for that.

"She's only for a year, and then there'll be somebody better.
But Omar, have you heard his French? He sounds like any
Nicois. It's his ticket to a good job, a secure future."

"Unlike me, you mean," Omar said in a gloomy voice. Salma
chose not to respond. She couldn't let thoughts of despair
grab hold of her, or Omar.

It had been a pleasing mix of familial arrangement and love
at first sight when Salma and Omar married in Morocco
eleven years ago. Omar had come from Nice to finish his
education, and was staying with his uncle who was a
business associate of Salma's father. The two men had got
their heads together, and agreed the dowry terms before
speaking to either party. It was a small sum, demanded with
the understanding that Salma would be leaving her family
home and settling in France. Salma's mother could not be
persuaded, but the deal was arranged despite her misgivings.

The next day, Salma and Omar were introduced. She was
covered head to foot, with only her terrified eyes on show.
Omar looked into them and whispered, "Don't be afraid," as
the two older men loudly congratulated each other and her
mother sobbed. Salma met her future husband's kind eyes,
and knew everything would be just fine.

They married three months after that and left for France to meet his parents the next week. They had not been able to come to the wedding because Omar's father was unwilling to leave his business and reluctant to accept the payment for their flights from his brother. Salma said goodbye to her two older sisters and their families, and fought against the urge to cling onto her weeping mother.

As she stepped off the plane in Nice airport, her heart was a whirl of wild hope and terrible fear. Omar seemed at ease amongst all the white Westerners, and walked past their closed expressions with his head held high. Salma tipped hers down and let the hijab fall over her face. This would always be her view of Nice: snippets framed by dark cloth. She felt the heat of stares burning into her back and the rush of cold air as people stepped further away from her. Then there was Omar's strong hand reaching for hers and leading her through the airport crowds and onto the bus.

When they reached the flat on Avenue de la République Omar let go of her hand and opened the door for her to step in. Her eyes stopped at the tiles on the walls along the stairs, and she smiled at the familiar geometric patterns - a little whisper of her home country right there for her to see every day. Her heart pounded with every step as they climbed up to the second floor. The door was flung open as soon as they stopped at it, and a frail but smiling woman stepped out to greet them. Her head was uncovered, and she was wearing Western clothes. She shuffled over to Salma and found her hands.

"Maman, this is Salma. My wife."

Omar kissed his mother and smiled as he put his hand on

Salma's back.

"Welcome to our - your home - my daughter."

Salma tried not to look too closely at the faded furniture, the dripping tap, the propped up cupboard doors. The smell of age was almost disguised by the bubbling tagine sitting on the hob, but not quite. It struck her then that Omar's parents were a lot older than hers, and that her job would most likely be compensating for their elderly inadequacies. His mother hugged her and studied her with kind eyes.

"You will be happy here, I hope."

And she had been. A year after her arrival, Omar's mother had died, swiftly followed by her broken hearted husband. Omar had squared his shoulders and stepped easily into his sonly duties in his father's business. Salma had fallen pregnant then, and life had shifted its focus away from death and onto new life. Her mother had come for the final months, and stayed for the first sleepless weeks after Mamoun's arrival. As Salma's recovery from a traumatic labour took longer than usual, her mother postponed her departure. When she did leave, she took her daughter's confidence with her. It took a further year before Salma ventured outside. During this time Omar concealed his struggle with the business, and persevered until it became impossible. It was the same day that Mamoun took his first steps that he told her he was giving up. He brought in a case and opened it up on the kitchen table. It was full of sunglasses. She frowned,

"What are these for?"

Omar's smile did not reach his eyes as he answered.

"These are my new business."

There was a tense silence as Salma's head raced with questions.

"How did you pay for them?"

"I had a little money left from the shoe repairs."

"And you thought these would be a good investment?" Salma picked up a couple of pairs and read the mis-spelt brands emblazoned on them. Mamoun toddled up and got lifted onto her knee.

"Why, Omi?"

Omar put his head in his hands and then looked up,

"I had no choice. No-one I spoke to was interested. Not a single one. Until I thought to ask at the school to see if they had anything - they've offered me a job in the evenings."

"Doing what?"

"Cleaning."

Salma heard herself whisper,

"Can we live like this?"

Mamoun was trying to pull off Salma's scarf and eat her hair. She pushed his little hand away and rubbed at the tears threatening to spill over.

"We will be ok, my love. I will work hard, and our life will improve. I promise."

CHAPTER THREE

New friends

Francois pulled his sleeping bag out of the bin-bag and threw it onto the lumpy mattress on the once ornate, now chipped and faded four-poster bed. He dropped down onto it and watched the dust rise in clouds around him. He looked up and saw overlapping circles of damp. He sniffed the old person smell. He got up and went to open the shutters, but they had expanded in the heat and were stuck. He pulled harder and looked down at the shutter now off the wall and in his hand. He propped it against the filthy window pane and moved into the tiny kitchen, carrying his bag with him. He opened the cupboards and counted two small plates, two coffee-stained cups, one saucepan. He whistled through his teeth, then dug into the bag to retrieve a set of plastic cutlery he'd found on the floor of the girls' room in the hostel. He turned the kitchen tap on, and after a loud bang, a trickle of water came out, making drips of white in an otherwise grubby sink. He dropped onto the sagging, stained armchair and pinched the bridge of his nose with his thumb and index finger. He mumbled into the air,

"I know you said basic, but seriously man?"

The fact of the matter was, Francois was broke. He was still enrolled at the university, but had skipped so many classes, flunked so many exams, he doubted they'd let him back in next year. His past-times of jamming jazz on his clarinet with his 'friends' anywhere they were allowed and the usual late nights of drinking that followed had put him here, in this dump, on this damn uncomfortable chair. It was his band-mate Jean who had hooked him up with a part-time job in the hostel up the hill and now the digs - it had belonged to his granda before he popped it, and the family couldn't shift it. And I wonder why? He chuckled to himself, and moved over to get out his stereo. This hole needs music. He put a jazz CD in and turned up the volume.

As Rachel went slowly down the stairs, a door opened and a hesitant, typically Italian craggy face poked out.

It had to be the Italian, but what on earth was his name? She smiled and dredged up the only Italian she knew.

"Buongiorno?" Her voice echoed round the stairwell, mocking her.

Uncertain or not, her feeble attempt prompted a gush of the foreign language, until Rachel held her hands up in laughing surrender.

"You don't speak Italian. Che peccato!" He shook his grey head slowly.

"I'm sorry - which is better for you -English or French?"

"They are both difficult for me. So?"

He shrugged, his eyes filling.

Rachel looked at him, and resolved to learn some Italian. She knew what it was like to feel isolated by language.

"Ok then." She pointed to herself,

"Rachel."

She raised her eyebrows and pointed to him,

"Alberto."

Rachel nodded and ploughed on, "Let's see what I know - cornetto?"

He started to smile.

"Spaghetti?"

"Ferrari?"

He laughed.

"Bello?"

Rachel stopped, stuck.

"Bella?" They both looked at each other; they had reached the end of the line. Rachel felt her cheeks getting hot as

Alberto stood and stared at her, a fixed smile on his face.

Suddenly, he seized her by the arms and kissed both her cheeks.

"Thank-you, mia amica. Thank-you."

He turned back to his door, hiding his face from her. Rachel stepped further into the hall. What else did she think would happen? They couldn't speak to each other.

"Bye Alberto, nice to meet you," Rachel said to the closing door.

Alberto let himself back in to his apartment and stood still in the dark hallway for a moment. Then he angrily wiped his eyes and shuffled in to the kitchen. He groaned when he looked in the small fridge and saw one slightly mouldy lump of parmesan, two forlorn tomatoes and three shrivelled olives. 'Buon appetito," he sighed. This was one of the times of day when he missed his family the most - the bitter-sweet memory of his wife's comforting home-cooking, bunches of garlic and fresh herbs hanging above the ever-busy cooker, wood crackling in the open fire. Two years after cancer had taken his beautiful Mia, the financial situation in the south of Italy had made his jewellery business no longer tenable and he knew he had to do something drastic. Maria, his eldest, had tried to scrape together the same amount of food, but when he realised she wasn't eating herself so that the rest of the family could be fed, he made his decision. The next week, he packed his case, and set out for France. They had all cried at the parting, and his younger daughters had begged him to stay, but Maria said nothing - she knew he had no choice. "It won't be for long, I'll be back in a few months,' he'd promised.

That was seven years ago. He had thought at the beginning his skills and experience in jewellery would assure him a decent post in one of the opulent stores on Rue Paradis and Avenue Verdon, but they turned their noses up at him - his foreign-ness, his poor French, his age. After a day of rejections from snooty French sales assistants - they never once called in their manager- he realised he was going to have to try for a more manual, non-speaking job. When he was a young man starting out, he'd worked as a welder on building sites for a year. He was going to have to go back to that now, for the money he needed. The money his family needed. It was easier approaching builders for work the next day, and that afternoon he started work. The pay was half what he had been getting in Italy, but it was weekly, and enough to survive on. He posted his first cheque back home with an apologetic letter, smudged with tears. He knew how his family would silently feel, but hoped they would understand. The frustration of not being able to provide or recoup what his business had lost ate away at him, shutting him down, blocking everyone else out. He saw his neighbours most days, but rarely spoke -what was the point. They weren't the people he wanted to be living beside, they didn't speak the language he wanted to speak. The little boy had tried at first, saying "salut!" every time they passed each other on the stairs, but when there was never a smile, a nod or anything, he'd stopped. Alberto knew he should feel sorry about that, but he had no room in his already heavy heart. He closed his eyes and thought of Italy, but shook his head seconds later - no point dreaming of home, when he had to be here. In this apartment, in that tedious, back-breaking job. He got the vegetables out, and started chopping. He'd just have to imagine he was eating one of Maria's pasta bolognese dishes. He could smell the curry cooking upstairs, and grimaced at the tomatoes on his chopping board. Buon appetito indeed.

✣

Ann waited downstairs until the sound of footsteps stopped with a door bang. She didn't want to see or speak to anyone. She slowly made her way up the one flight of stairs with her shopping bag of mince, tomatoes, onion, fresh herbs and spaghetti. She'd had a craving for Italian cooking today, and so she would indulge it. Why not? She had no-one to answer to, no-one at all.

There had been a time when solitude was not an option, as she cared for her ailing parents, answered every ring of their bedside bell, bit her tongue when they demanded the impossible, and cancelled social meetings at the last minute when the unexpected demands of old age rose up. She didn't resent it at the time - they had cared for her all her life, so why should she not repay them? They had died within a week of each other, as often happens, and after a respectable year of mourning, Ann had upped sticks and moved to the French Riviera, the beloved region of Matisse and Picasso, Monet and Cezanne. She was the struggling artist she had always dreamed of being, back in her restricting carer days. She sold a painting a month, and that was enough to get by here.

She walked into her flat, and heard light steps running past.

That must be Mamoun. She smiled. He seemed to be a very innocent, friendly child, but she couldn't for the life of her think of anything to say to him. Children were an unknown entity to her. She had thought about motherhood once, a long time ago, but when everything went wrong, she had eventually accepted that door was closed now. Besides, she raised her chin, art was her child, her companion, her escape into a more beautiful world. She stopped pacing, and hurried to the studio - the urge to paint had risen up again, and she needed to harness it.

Ann gathered her brushes, put her arms into a paint-splodged smock, sat down at the easel and began to mix the azur blue she had seen today, and did encounter nearly every day. Oh the joy of living near the sea. It was hard to think of anything else. Just as well. She sighed and shook her head. She looked at the beach scene she had already stared for a long time, and then found herself painting something, somebody into it. After an hour had passed, she sat back and looked. Her cheeks were wet; she hadn't even realised. Why could she not forget? She lifted her brush again, and covered over the image with more stone-coloured paint. It was happening all the time these days - long-gone memories taking over the present life. Painful memories.

But what was that racket? Loud jazz was pumping through Ann's roof, thudding into her chest. She took off her smock and hurried over to the door. She opened it a crack, and saw another door open across the hall. She closed hers again, and went hunting for ear plugs.

When she went to cook her dinner, she realised she had forgotten the garlic. Of course a neighbour might have some, but she would just go back to the shop, save her having to look anyone in the eye.

As she was walking back, she saw a woman, head and face covered with cloth, bending over to rub her shoe. Ann watched as she looked round, eyes darting from side to side. Then she dropped her bag, and oranges started rolling towards the road. In a tiny act of bravery, Ann approached her and asked if she needed help. Eyes as terrified as her own looked up at her and then the woman fled. Ann slowed her pace and watched as the cloaked lady hurried towards Ann's apartment block and let herself in.

Could it actually be that someone else as secluded as she was lived only a few steps away from her door?

The music had pushed in the walls around her. The pounding drums, the moaning saxophone and the repetitive melodies, had only served to further exacerbate her feelings of panic, claustrophobia, helplessness. She guessed that most of the day she had been the only one suffering it - the heavy front door had banged several times throughout the afternoon, signalling people going out to enjoy their Sunday. Omar had taken Mamoun up to the castle but Salma had not felt like going with them. She said it was a headache, but really it was the feeling she got every time she went anywhere. Terror. Of what, she couldn't quite say.

Most days she hoped that Omar would see how she felt, but most days she also tried to hide it. She wanted someone to rescue her, but if they tried to, she would probably run away. She had locked herself into a prison and the only person who could free her was herself. It didn't help that they lived in a predominantly white part of Nice, far from the banlieue where most of her kind existed. It made her feel as though there was no-one else who was like her - with the same skin, language, clothes and history. She had tried to explain this to Omar, but he was so defensive of his father's decision to move there on Avenue de la Republique that it was no use.

She walked over to the cooker, and saw that everything was ready for dinner. She looked at the spotless floor, ran her finger along the dustless surfaces, patted the pile of ironed clothes. She wandered from one room to another, smoothing down the beds, adjusting the blinds. She sat down on Mamoun's little bed and sighed. There was nothing for her to do.

Oranges. She could go and buy some oranges. She stood up and got her purse and shopping bag. It was something that would please Omar. He loved oranges. She headed out in a mixture of nervousness and excitement. The shop was quiet and she was able to buy them without drawing much attention to herself.

On the way back she kept her head down, let the scarf fall across her face and focused on placing her feet one in front of the other on the littered pavement. Although it was fairly crowded every day, she never walked into anyone. They always side-stepped around her, going onto the road where necessary to avoid acknowledging she even existed. That suited her. Mostly. There was a part of her that craved human interaction, just somebody to find her eyes and say 'hello', or 'I see you', or 'are you OK?' But they were never going to do that, not in this part of the city.

She had walked this street of white faces in Nice for more than ten years, and aside from the grocer telling her how much money she owed, no-one had ever spoken to her. Not even once. At the beginning it had taken her a huge amount of courage to even step out of her front door. But when she had managed it and realised that people were always going to pretend she wasn't there, it became slightly easier.

Every day when Mamoun got back from school and her husband from work, her loneliness was forgotten, her empty life filled up again. She just had to survive those hours without them.

She stopped and looked down - dog dirt was squelching beneath her shoe. There was nothing to be done but to walk gingerly on. Stopping and looking for grass was futile after the hot spell they'd had, and would draw too much attention. Sweat pooled between her shoulder blades and her breathing quickened. She was nearly back, just two doors to go. She held onto a lamp-post and tried to rub off the dirt on the edge of a concrete slab. It wasn't coming off. Her bag of fruit fell from her other hand and started rolling towards the road. She started grabbing at them.

"Here, let me help you."
    It was a white-skinned woman with a concerned face. Salma put back her last orange, lowered her eyes again and walked round the stranger.
    Just like everybody had always done to her.

❖

The bass was thudding against the outer walls of the

apartment building. It had been going all day, on a Sunday no less. Alberto knew that the neighbour opposite had been bothered, as she had opened her door at the same time as him. She was a mystery - he'd only caught glimpses of her eyes as she looked out to check the hall in front of her door. She had been there when he had moved in, and yet he had never seen her face, or heard her voice. Her door clicked shut again, when she saw his was open.

He stepped out into the hall and stood trying to figure out the source of the racket. It was definitely coming from upstairs, and couldn't possibly be the Moroccan family - they had always been very respectful. He started up the stairs, unsure as to what he would do, never mind say, when he reached the culprit. But Sundays were his only day at home all week, and he needed them peaceful. Everyone in the building did. Everyone apart from this person. He put his hand to the pulsating door, and knocked. No answer of course. He made his hand into a fist and thumped it repeatedly. After at least twenty bangs, the door opened to reveal a grimy young man with bloodshot eyes.

"Oui?"

Alberto took a breath. He put his hands to his ears and made a face.

"Musica."

Francois raised his hands, pretending not to understand.

"Forte."

Another blank look.

Alberto grabbed him by the arm,

"Stop it please."

Francois shrugged off his hand and backed away,

"Ok, ok, I'll turn it down Mario."

"Alberto."

"Whatever."

Alberto stood waiting, making sure Francois went over and turned it off. He turned it down slightly, and Alberto shouted "More!" until it was sufficiently quiet.

"Grazi". He nodded at the still sullen young man and offered his hand. It was ignored, and soon Alberto was standing looking at plywood again. He nodded once and walked back down to his flat. He heard the opposite door closing again and he was eighty per cent sure there was a whispered 'thank-you' before it clicked shut. Was she English? Interesting.

CHAPTER FOUR

Another challenge

Rachel ran around the flat, getting ready for her first day as language assistant. She had not slept well - someone in one of the flats below was playing jazz at full volume into the early hours. She grabbed a stale croissant from the bag she'd bought the day before and headed out her door. Locking up, she heard someone on the landing one floor below, and hesitated. A little voice called up to her "salut!" and she looked over the wrought iron bannister to see Mamoun standing there looking up at her. She started down the stairs towards him, hoping he was alone. He was.

"Where are you going?" he asked in French.

Rachel kept walking, and he hurried behind her.

"Why are you in a hurry?"

He had somehow managed to wriggle in front of her and was standing blocking her way with his arms folded across his 80s football shirt. He scratched his dark curls but didn't move, starting to awkwardly tap his foot. Rachel sighed,

"Good morning, Mamoun. I'm going to school."

That was met with peals of laughter.

"School! But you are too old!"

"No, no. I'm going there to teach English."

"Ah, so am I."

Rachel must have looked confused, because he laughed again.

"I am not a teacher! I am a student, at your service."

He bowed like a grown man, but didn't straighten up again. Rachel side-stepped and got past, carrying on down the stairs. As she reached the front door, she heard breathing beside her.

"Wait! What is your school called?"

Rachel was beginning to feel as though there was no escape. She stepped out onto the street.

"I can't remember its name; I just know where it is."

"Is it in the Vieille Ville?"

"Yes."

"That is my school! Quelle chance!"

Mamoun started skipping beside her, babbling mostly incomprehensibly until he stopped dead.

"Which teacher are you going to see?"

Rachel pulled her notebook from her bag and checked.

"Madame Tessier."

Mamoun put his hands over his mouth and groaned.

"What is it? Is she not a good one?"

"Elle est comme le diable!"

"Surely she isn't as bad as that."

"Oh, she is. You'll see. And she particularly hates me."

"Why?"

"Because I'm Beur. Because my skin is like this."

Mamoun started hitting his face, pulling at his cheeks.

"Don't do that. I'm sure Madame Tessier has never told you that."

"Si! She told me to go and wash because my skin looked dirty and when I said no, she shook my desk and roared."

Rachel walked on, horrified.

"It is ok, Madame, she is dirty on the inside. That's what

maman says. And that makes her unhappy."

They turned left into the Old Town then, and conversation became more difficult. Rachel looked down at Mamoun and felt the urge to take his hand so he wouldn't get lost in the crowded streets but his hands were stuffed in his pockets and his head was up, showing he had been there many times before.

They were almost out into the square when Mamoun stopped and pointed.

"Des glaces."

Rachel looked up at the humming van selling a rainbow of different ice-creams. It was the same one she'd gone to before. The smell there was cool and fresh, and the bright sun was glinting on the glass counter, dancing over the tempting display. There were different sizes of striped white and blue pots neatly stacked at one side, and a hand-written blackboard listing all the flavours and prices. The pair must have tarried too long, as the shop keeper shuffled over to take their order. Mamoun looked up at Rachel, raising his eyebrows.

"No way! It's far too early for ice-cream!"

He shrugged his bony shoulders and ran off again, the school in sight at the top of the hill. Rachel hurried after him, got through the gates and then he was gone. She looked for the way in, failed to locate it and then started scanning the playground for a teacher. There was a group of six or seven adults standing talking, their backs to the children. She shifted her bag on her shoulder, and walked over. Most of the children were too busy playing to notice somebody new had arrived. One girl was sitting on a step by herself. There was a little stick propped up beside her, and Rachel saw one of her legs was notably thinner than the other. Caught staring, Rachel moved over and sat beside her.

"Salut."

"Salut."

"I'm Rachel." She gave a little wave.

"I'm Eloine. Where are you from?"

"Ireland. I'm the new English teacher."

Eloine's eyes widened.

"I would love to learn English. I would love to have a pen pal. To have a friend who can't see this." She waved her little hand over her leg and her stick.

Rachel glanced at Eloine's sad face and round the playground.

"Do you not have anybody here?"

Eloine gave a hollow laugh,

"No. They don't like the look of me, and besides, I can't exactly play tag can I?"

"Well in that case, I will be your penpal."

"Really? Even though you've seen me?"

Rachel smiled at her,

"Especially because I've seen you. You know, you're the only person who has spoken to me here in this playground. Now," she stood up, "I need to go get somebody's attention. Nice to meet you, new penpal."

Eloine grinned and nodded.

Rachel went towards the group of adults, trying to find a space to stand in, trying to catch somebody's eye, but they all had their backs to her, and didn't seem to notice. She tried coughing. No response.

"Excusez moi?"

The teachers continued their conversation, so she tried again, but louder. This time one of the men turned round and saw her.

"Oui?"

Rachel said the lines she had been practising since she had first landed in Nice, and waited. A light dawned then; he smiled and beckoned her to follow him inside. They left the noise of the playground and entered a tall ceilinged, dark entrance hall. Rachel met the receptionist and signed in. She was then taken along two corridors and up a flight of stairs. The further away from the entrance they got, the more pictures and colours there were. Rachel looked at the drawings and felt comforted by the universal signs of childhood - how could there be anything terrible here, when there were cardboard butterflies suspended from the ceiling?

"Voila!"

They stopped at one of the primary coloured doors and the male teacher rapped it, then whispered "Courage!" and left.

There was a loud sigh before the door was opened and a blond haired lady appeared. You would have said she was conventionally beautiful with her wavy fair hair, blue eyes, perfect features and slim figure. But then her rose-bud lips tightened and curled, her shaped eyebrows pulled into a frown, and she was changed.

Rachel did her lines again, and tried to look friendly. She was answered with a grunt, and was asked for her papers. As Rachel dug through her bag, her shaking hands slowed her down and she heard the teacher sighing loudly.

"D'ou venez-vous?"

"Oh, I'm from Ireland, Northern Ireland to be exact."

"En Francais!"

Rachel realised too late that her nerves had made her slip into English, so she quickly answered in French - it was a standard GCSE question, she could have kicked herself. As she tried to continue the conversation, a bell rang and she was directed to sit down in a chair at the front of the class, beside the teacher's desk. The chair was a tiny pupil's seat, and set her at least two feet lower than the desk beside her. The class filed in then; no-one spoke until Mamoun came in, spotted Rachel and waved a cheery hello. The teacher, who

Rachel had concluded was definitely 'le diable' Mme Tessier, smacked a metre stick against the table in front of Mamoun, who cowered over to his desk. She turned back to the door, and said in a loud voice,

"Someone come and help Eloine."

Nobody moved. Eloine tried to get through the heavy door by herself, but her stick clattered to the ground and she was left holding on to the door frame. Madame Tessier sighed loudly at the class and then picked up the stick to hand back to the small girl. Eloine made her way awkwardly to her seat, set apart from the others in the front row. By the time she sat down the class had lost interest. Only Rachel saw her trying to hold back her tears.

Madame Tessier marched along the rows of desks, clacking her high heels and repeatedly thwacking her stick against her other hand. Her blond ponytail did not bounce or swing; it just sat there rigid with hair spray and rage. The roll call was a clipped affair, with each child parroting their name back as fast as she had fired it out to them. When they started to talk, the murmur was cut off by the sound of her cracking her long ruler against her desk. Without even standing up, she introduced Rachel to the class in three words, rolled her eyes and waited for them to dutifully giggle. Then she leant back in her chair and gestured for Rachel to begin. Rachel pulled her notes out of her bag and stood up, moving to the middle of the blackboard behind her. She was sweating and the papers were rustling wildly in her hand. Everyone was looking at her, waiting for her to begin, apart from Madame

Tessier who was busy filing her nails into even sharper points.

"Hello. My name is Rachel, what is your name?" She accompanied this English with massive hand gestures to make herself understood. She then repeated it again and pointed to Eloine who looked instantly terrified, and glanced over to Madame Tessier who just threw her hands up and said in a sharp voice,

"Parles-toi!"

Eloine looked at her stick, then at Rachel. Rachel crouched down beside her and gestured for her to speak.

"Allo. Je suis Eloine"

Rachel smiled at her and said in a low voice,

"Hello. My - name - is - Eloine."

She nodded to Eloine to try saying it. As Eloine opened her mouth to speak, Madame Tessier gave a raucous laugh and said in a sing-song voice,

"My- name -is- Eloine." She looked to the class for their appreciation, and after a few seconds they obliged by laughing unenthusiastically.

Eloine did not laugh however, and she whispered to Rachel, "My name is Eloine". They both grinned at each other and Rachel dug a sweet out of her bag to give to her. Seeing the bribery, some of the children put their hands up to have a go. After getting through most of them, ending with Mamoun,

Rachel taught them how to say goodbye, and she finished up the lesson. She was aware of Madame Tessier's narrowed eyes watching her success, but refused to let it bother her. She stood at the end, unsure what to do next. She waited, then after a minute had passed, she turned to Madame Tessier.

"Oui?"

"I'm finished now, what should I do?"

The teacher lifted her head and gave a laugh.

"Go."

Rachel waited again, unsure as to whether it was a joke.

"Go! Go!"

Unwelcome tears pricking her eyes, cheeks burning, Rachel waved goodbye to the class, smiled at Mamoun and Eloine, and stumbled to the door. As she left she caught Mme Tessier saying something about her, and the children dutifully laughing.

She found herself half-running along the corridors, past the pictures, out of the school, down the hill and only stopped when she got to the ice-cream stall. The owner recognised her from before, and also clocked her flushed, determined face,

"Deux boules de passion, m'amie?"

He pointed to the vibrant yellow ice-cream with his scoop

and waited.

Laughing with the surprise of him knowing what she wanted to order, Rachel nodded and got out her money. Ice-cream in hand, she looked at the streets ahead of her, spied a gap and hurried towards it. Again the darkness opened up to a tantalising view of blue sky and sea. She crossed the road, dodged the skaters on Promenade des Anglais and ran down the steps onto the pebbled beach. She picked her way round the tables and chairs of the sea side cafes, skirted the small groups of sunbathers and found a spot to sit. She pulled her cd walkman out, threw down her bag, flattened it out and sat down on it. She balanced her ice-cream on a grey stone and turned on the Scottish tones of Rod Stewart. She ate her tub of passion fruit slowly, not really looking at the other people beside her, just focusing on the planes taking off from the airport at the other end of the beach. She knew it was not healthy, but she just couldn't stop looking at them - feeling the strong wish to be on one, flying away from Nice, heading back to Ireland. She shifted and dug a blank postcard out of her bag.

Dear Charlie. I'm sitting on the beach, the sea is blue, the sun is shining, the ice-cream is delicious and yet I would change it all to be home. `Hope you're well, and studying hard.
    Rach

Would she put an X there? Or just an O? Or nothing? Why was she taking so long to decide?

All at once a shadow blocked her view, and a brown hand waved in her face. He was smiling, and had a richly coloured hat on. He lifted up the folded bag he was holding and let it unfold, revealing a cluttered display of sunglasses, marked with the convincing brands of Versase, Dulce et Gabana and Chanell.

"Des lunettes? Bon prix? "

Rachel shook her head, and when the seller got closer, she put her hand up firmly. He eventually got the message, and moved further down the beach. She would never have been that assertive at home. But she realised that pushy Maghreb men needed to be put in their place.

Now, where was she? She did a smiley face on the card, addressed it and stuck on a stamp. Still holding the card, she put her ear plugs back in and turned up Rod Stewart's *Every Beat of my Heart*, ready to slip back into her home-sick funk.

Seagull carry me, over land and sea
To my own folk, that's where I want to be
Every beat of my heart
Tears me further apart
I'm lost and alone in the dark
I'm going home

He was tired of this - the walking up to white tourists and pestering them with clearly fake 'designer' sunglasses. But what else could he do? He had tried to keep up his father's shoe repair business, but the shop they had rented to his family was in an unfrequented side-street, so business had never recouped the cost of the rent, not even after years of trying to make it work. Even when he was a child, he remembered many times when his father had to pay to replace smashed-in windows and scrub off the racial slurs painted on the door. His parents had persisted after trying and trying to get different premises, but the unfeasibility of their business had worked against them. As the attacks increased with every year that passed, and with both his parents dead and his only brother back in Morocco, Omar had given up, closing the shop with desperate disappointment - he felt he had done the one thing his family before him had never allowed themselves to even consider - give up.

At the start, he had been bitter - knowing he was more skilled, more deserving of a respectable job, but that feeling of entitlement soon fell away, knocked back by the repeated rejections first of the Nicois people with their vandalism of the shop and now by his prospective, more international customers. He knew that when they looked at him, if they even did that, they saw a nuisance, a nobody. He started to believe them. They had made him the way they saw him - nothing.

He shifted his wares under his arm and spotted a potential. Was she that girl from upstairs? It was hard to tell - white people all looked the same. She certainly didn't seem French - her face was too open and uncertain to belong on this beach. Her blond head was bowed over her pulled-up knees as she wrote on a card. Maybe she would be kind. He stepped over the rounded pebbles towards her and began his sale patter. He watched as waves of surprise turned into fear, and then into hostility. It didn't suit her. He wasn't going to push this one though; she deserved better.

Just like me, he thought as he walked away. Just like me.

Rachel waited until the man was far enough away to not come back to her, then stood up, slung her bag over her shoulder and headed back to do her shopping. She was so used to just looking at the shelves and remembering what she needed. But that was at home. This was France - different language, different food. There'd be so many things she didn't recognise, so much that she would have to figure out. What she would give for a packet of Tayto, a bottle of Club Orange, a box of recognisable biscuits, even a bottle of milk that was fresh, not UHT. The food from home just seemed more appealing. She wondered if that would change.

She walked through the old town and along Boulevard Jean Jaures, heading for the *Casino* supermarket on Place Garibaldi. When she got there, she was confronted with shelves of food she did not recognise, or have any desire to try. There were cartons of olives on a stall just outside the entrance, bottles of UHT milk in the fridge, dubiously fresh baguettes and trays of glistening oysters. She sighed as she scanned the shelves for dry pasta, jars of tomato sauce, cheese and ham. The ham was hard to find, and below the numerous packs of salami and foie gras. She wanted mince, but all they had was steak tartare. She wanted chicken, but all they had was whole cooked chickens - too much for one. As for the cheese - there was everything but good ole plain cheddar. She decided to turn temporarily vegetarian and put a handful of mushrooms, peppers and courgettes in brown paper bags. She picked up a tub of Boursin, and decided it would make a nice croque monsieur for tea. She looked at her pitiful collection of food in the basket and steeled herself for the mathematical challenge of paying for it with francs.

Finally, one light shopping bag in each hand, she made her way back to the flat feeling decidedly unexcited about her dinner that evening. She had found fresh milk and a box of an excuse for cornflakes. She knew that she should be eating French, but somehow all she wanted was food like it was at home. She let herself in and slowly tramped up the stairs.

"Madame Rachel Madame Rachel!"

It was a flushed Mamoun.

"Hi Mamoun."

"You must come eat with us tonight! We made enough for you!"

"Oh. Well. I have my own dinner in here, but thanks anyway."

Mamoun eyed her bags with suspicion.

"What is it?"

Rachel floundered.

"Well, I think I'm going to have a croque monsieur tonight. Maybe."

"Pah! What is a croque monsieur when maman has made you curry?! Please come."

Rachel hesitated, and in that second, Mamoun grabbed her bags and ran in the direction of his apartment. She had no choice but to follow him.

The door opened to reveal a striking dark skinned woman, a wooden spoon in her hand, her head covering slipping off.

Salma had a feeling that tonight there would be someone else at their dinner table. She had never done it before, but she had seen there was enough leftover curry to feed more than the three of them and she felt ready to share it. She knew that the smell of her spices would offer an unspoken invitation to the other residents in their building. Before this, she had never considered having someone else into her house, but the arrival of the new girl had forced her to come out of her shell for the first time in years. She stirred the pot and left the kitchen door open. Mamoun was sitting at the set table watching her so she told him her plan.

The building door opened and slammed shut. Salma turned, spoon suspended in mid-air.

"Listen! I hear someone walking past. It might be her. Quick Mamoun, go and see."

A minute later Mamoun returned with a sheepish looking Rachel at his heels. She looked as though she would like to be anywhere else but there. Mamoun pushed her over to a seat and she half sat down.

"I was actually just going back to make my own dinner. I'll leave you to yours."

She started to stand up again, clearly flustered.

"No, no. You don't have to cook today - please stay and eat with us."

Rachel looked from Mamoun to Salma. They were both smiling and nodding.

Salma gestured to the table.

"Please be our guest. A welcome to our new neighbour." She smiled at Rachel.

"Well. Ok. Thank you. You will have to come to me for dinner one day too."

"Oh no, no. This is our pleasure - we don't ask for anything in return."

Salma turned and started to ladle out the re-heated curry over three bowls of warm saffron rice. Her hands weren't steady and some of the sauce hit the edge of the bowls, dripping down onto the table-cloth. She felt Rachel watching her, but just carried on. As she placed them on the already laid table, Rachel was surprised to see that an extra place had already been set, as if they had been expecting her.

CHAPTER FIVE

The catalysts

"Rachel!"

Rachel looked over her shoulder. It was Alberto.

"Ciao, Alberto!"

"Going to work?"

"Yes."

"Be careful."

Rachel looked down at Alberto's worn hand on her arm, and up into his eyes. The look on his face reminded her of her dad.

"You have daughters, don't you?"

He shook his head in miscomprehension and shrugged, smiling.

"Well, have a good day Alberto."

She carried on down the stairs, leaving the awkward moment behind her.

When she got on the bus at Place de la Republique to head up Jean-Medecin, she dropped onto a seat beside a well-dressed auburn-haired lady with a briefcase who re-arranged her stilettoed feet and continued powdering her nose. On the grey pavement just between Zara and Sephora, Rachel spied a woman sitting cross-legged with a baby on her lap. She was dressed in worn, dirty rags, and had one dark-skinned hand held out. Everyone walked past her, looking busy. The baby started to cry and so did her mother. The business woman beside Rachel tutted and leant towards her to mutter,

"That's what they do - nip the child and try to get money. Typical."

Rachel said nothing. She just kept looking at the mother and child crying on the street. Put on or not, you still needed to ask why they were there in the first place. Nice may be a glamorous, beautiful city but right now, it was not coming across as a nice one. Rachel smiled to herself, thinking about how many people said 'Nice!' when she told them where she was going for her year, not getting the pun. Already she had encountered an ugly side to the place, or to its inhabitants at least and she didn't like it, azur sea or not.

When she alighted, she saw that the area was a middle-class one, with comfortable, reassuring detached houses, leafy streets and blue swimming pools. She walked up the hill to the school, feeling more at home there than she had anywhere else. She thought of her house back in Ireland with its huge garden and saw why. This time, she did not hesitate to go in to the playground. The children were already lining up and quietly filing in to their classrooms. Rachel caught the attention of one of the teachers and approached him. He kept ushering the children inside and either didn't notice her, or had nothing to say.

"Excuse me? I'm the new English assistant. I wonder where I am supposed to go?"

He still didn't look round, so she tried again, in a louder voice. He stopped then, said hello and waved his arm towards the last children walking in.

"They are your children now. I will be at the back of the classroom."

Suddenly plunged into her lesson with no introduction, Rachel let the children find their seats and then made an attempt to begin.

"Hello. My name is Rachel. What is your name?"

The laughter rose until the teacher at the back looked up from his book and shouted 'Silence!"

Rachel tried again and was met only with slight sniggers this time. One by one, the children raised their hands to speak, realising the pattern of the lesson. As they tried out the new English words, the others started to chatter - it was just a murmur at first, but quickly turned into a racket where it was impossible for Rachel to hear anything at all. She looked back to the teacher but he was engrossed, and seemed to be expecting her to control the class herself.

"Please be quiet," she tried. Now some of the children were off their seats, standing at each other's desks. None of them paid any heed to her, until she banged both hands on the desk. Then even the teacher looked up. She pointed to the boy who she guessed was the ring-leader.

"Come up here please." She made hand movements to get him to move.

He shrugged his shoulders, rolled his eyes at the class and walked over, hands stuffed in his pockets. Rachel's voice shook a little as she asked the simple question again. After a time of silence, the boy answered. The class cheered and she sat down, feeling as though she had just won her first stand-off. Only then did the teacher come to the front and introduce her properly. There was no thank-you, or sorry, only an unspoken communication that she was an unwelcome nuisance, a bothersome outsider.

As she was hurrying out of the classroom after a highly unsatisfactory first lesson, she crashed against someone going in. Her still open bag was knocked off her shoulder and all her lesson plans slipped out onto the floor. She crouched down to retrieve them and looked up to see a young man down with her, helping her.

"I'm so sorry, I was rushing. I'm late. As usual."

Rachel took in his dark hair, brown eyes and tanned skin. His scent was familiar to her, she couldn't think why. As they picked up the papers, their hands brushed against each other, and they both laughed a little.

"Hello, you're new here aren't you? I'm Sebastian, teaching student here for six months."

"Rachel, English assistant."

Rachel stuck her hand out. After a moment's hesitation, Sebastian shook it.

"Ah, so not French then?"

"No, not French."

"Excellent! I'm always on the look-out for people like you."

Sebastian smiled.

"Why?"

"Nice is too segregated, too hostile to outsiders, so when someone comes from somewhere else, I welcome it."

Rachel realised this was the first time that anyone had said they were pleased she was here. She stared at Sebastian again, lost for words.

"I have to go, Monsieur Bernard will be struggling without me to do all his work for him."

With that, Sebastian rushed off.

Rachel re-traced her steps along the corridor and was half-way across the playground when she heard her name. It was Sebastian, running after her.

"Could you give me your phone number?" He stood waiting, not showing any embarrassment whatsoever.

Rachel dug pen and paper out of her bag and wrote it down. She handed the scrap of paper to Sebastian and he ran back inside.

What would come of that, she wondered.

Rachel got back at four that day and fell into bed, pulling the covers over her head, and putting Counting Crows in her ears. *Perfect Blue Buildings* never failed to get her to sleep. She had no idea how full-time teachers did it, but after only two classes - one in the morning, one in the afternoon at the neighbouring school, she was wiped. It was exhausting trying to teach people to speak a language that is alien to them, and making them see it is a worthwhile thing to do. Maybe if the teachers had been nicer, or more involved. As it was, they had treated her with absolute disinterest.

The only good thing about today had been Sebastian - that was a pleasant surprise. She fell asleep wondering when he would phone her, where they would meet, what they would talk about…

Half an hour later, she threw off the covers, smoothed down her hair, rubbed her face and shuffled in to the kitchen. There was a knock on the door. She opened it to see Francesca and Laura.

"Who is that grungy looking boy that we passed on the

stairs? He didn't say hello, just walked past with a case and a grumpy face." Francesca tossed her hair in disgust.

"I've no idea. He must have been the one playing loud music into the night the other day. Haven't met him yet."

"Well I wouldn't bother yourself."

"He did look familiar, though. Was he not the guy hanging round the hostel, Jean 's bandmate?"

"All the more reason not to speak to him - he is a low-life musician who sponges off his friends."

Rachel raised her eyebrows at Laura and moved over to make the coffee. The two girls were all full of news - about the schools, about Jean, about their new digs.

Rachel told them both about meeting yet another unsupportive teacher, getting a delicious chicken and cheese panini for lunch at a stall just off Avenue Felix Faure and her more wealthy but not necessarily better behaved pupils.

"Oh, and also, a French boy asked me for my number."

There were whoops, squeals and whistles from her friends, as Rachel's face got redder and redder.

Francesca seized Rachel's hands.

"So you'll have your first date here? I'm so jealous of the pair of you, with your French lovers."

Laura laughed and Rachel shook her head.

"Oh no, Sebastian was just being friendly. It's not going to be a date."

"Yeah right. You're a pretty girl, and you're Irish - what guy would pass on that?"

Rachel's surprised face made the other two laugh.

"I'll do your hair for you. Scraped back in a sexy bun, to accentuate your amazing blue eyes."

"No, Francesca, she needs the tousled, cheeky pony-tail look."

Rachel drained her coffee and let them argue. It wasn't going to be a date, he was just being kind. Plus, he hadn't actually phoned yet.

The phone rang. Francesca and Laura screamed and raced over to get it, handing it over to Rachel. She moved over to her sleeping space to get some privacy.

"Allo?"

"C'est Sebastian. Rachel?"

"Hi Sebastian."

Laura and Francesca clamped their hands over the mouths and sat down on Rachel's bed to listen. She glared and shooed them away, but they didn't move.

"Are you free tomorrow after school to go for a coffee?"

"Em, let me just check."

Rachel covered the mouthpiece, the other two were now bouncing up and down on the bed.

"Hello? Tomorrow afternoon sounds good - I could meet you at three at Le Sarao, Promenade des Anglais?"

Rachel said the only cafe/restaurant name she knew, but tried to make her voice sound as though she knew them all. Francesca and Laura gave her a thumbs up.

"Ok, I will see you there. Bye Rachel."

The phone went dead. Rachel looked at it for a moment before she was pulled into a victory dance with the other two.

Later, when the pair had gone back to their own digs, Rachel made her dinner - smoked salmon on top of creme fraiche, rolled up in a bought crepe. She ate and enjoyed it until the last few bites, when the richness made it sickening. Washing it down with tap water, she sat back on the bar stool, and thought. Was it a date? Why did she keep thinking about Charlie when she should be planning for meeting Sebastian? It felt wrong somehow, meeting another boy and she didn't know why. It's not as if Charlie and she had an understanding. She looked at the phone, but resisted phoning him - he wasn't expecting it and would think something was wrong. She'd just have to see how tomorrow goes.

The next day, Rachel rushed home from school, tidied herself a little and set out for Le Sarao. She was just on the edge of the old town when she spotted Sebastian, standing waiting. He was scanning the busy street, his hands in his khaki trouser pockets, his rucksack over one shoulder, his shirt open to reveal a Hard Rock cafe T-shirt beneath. His hair was darker than Rachel remembered it. When he spotted her, he smiled and waved, walking over to meet her. They greeted each other with the traditional French bises.

"Hi Rachel."

Rachel tightened her messy pony-tail, and smiled.

"I was hoping I would catch you before we got to Le Sarao. I know a place that you might like better."

He stepped aside to let a group of loud American sight-seers past. Rachel moved back too.

"That's ok. I mean, that's good. To be honest, I only said it because it's the only one I know here."

"Well, we'll have to do something about that." He gave her a comical salute. "Come on - it's day one of Rachel meets the real Nice!"

Sebastian grabbed her hand, guided her through the narrow streets and turned onto one close to the edge of the old town just beside Promenade des Anglais. He stopped outside an African tea room and finally let go of her hand. He raised his dark eyebrows at Rachel, checking she approved and then held open the jangling door for her.

It was hard to make out anything at first, coming out of the bright sunlight into a shadowy space. All the windows were half-blocked with thick gold and turquoise curtains. The room was lit by tiny mounted multicoloured glass lanterns, strung across the walls. There were no chairs, just dozens of patterned pouffes and low mahogany tables. Two men in traditional Moroccan dress were moving around, carrying trays of elegant burnished silver tea-pots and glass/metal cups. Rachel looked over her shoulder, and Sebastian pointed to the nearest table. After they had sat down on the cushions, a man came to give them their menus. The choice of tea was extensive - green, mint, white, flowering, scented, black, fruit, herbal and many more that Rachel could not identify. A minute later, the man was back to take their orders. Sebastian waited, saw Rachel's consternation and ordered two vanilla teas for them both.

"Sorry about that - I get menu anxiety at the best of times, never mind when it's in French."

When the tea arrived, Rachel started to relax, and found herself chatting about her classes, the apartment, her flatmates, and Ireland. She told Sebastian all about her family, and the place where they always holidayed. He was a good listener, helping her out with some French words, and asking questions.

She stopped to finish her tea, and was aware of him looking at her, with his dark eyes.

"I'm sorry, I seem to have taken over the conversation. What about you? What's your family like?"

Sebastian looked away, shrugged his shoulders, and started to stand up.

"My life is not worth talking about, believe me. We should probably go now anyway. I have five lesson plans to do before tomorrow."

Rachel frowned at the brush-off, but picked up her bag and followed him out into the sunshine. Sebastian turned to her, kissed her on both cheeks and then hurried off, leaving her to wonder at his sudden mood change.

She made her way down to the beach, unable to walk away from the sea when it was so close, unable to stop her self-indulgent moping after the planes taking off and flying away from the city, to places a lot closer to home.

Ann put her paintbrush down and sighed. It was no use - the pain kept coming back, invading her work, making her melancholy. She needed a break, maybe even a conversation with someone else. She stood up, strode to the door, and flung it open. There, on the stairs below her was that new girl who lived in the attic. She looked as though she had been crying. She stopped climbing and they both stared at each other.

"Hello, Rachel is it?"

Rachel nodded and frowned slightly.

"How do you know my name?"

Ann stepped back and gestured to her to come in.

"I may not venture out that often, but I'm not deaf, and your friends the other day were loud enough for me to figure it out."

"I'm sorry about that - they tend to get over-excited. And what's your name?"

Ann smoothed her flyaway hairs back into their bun, and found her smile - she'd thought she had lost it.

"I'm Ann. Originally from Manchester."

"And what brings you to Nice?"

Ann looked a little uncomfortable at the question, and moved on into the kitchen, mumbling,

"The colours, of course."

Rachel glanced at the open doors of the sun-lit studio with its signs of painting in progress, and two, possibly three canvases propped up against the wall. She glanced at Ann,

"May I take a look?"

Ann shrugged, but watched Rachel closely as she bent down and examined each piece in turn.

"I see what you mean about the colours. What's happened here?"

Rachel was pointing to the bottom corner of the scene, which was clearly smudged out. Ann turned away.

"Dinner? Would you like to eat here?"

The query was put so awkwardly that Rachel was unsure how to answer.

"I have chicken and salad? Enough for two." Ann looked surprised at herself, but her wide-eyed vulnerability made it impossible for Rachel to say no.

"That sounds perfect. Thank-you."

As Ann put the dinner together, Rachel took surreptitious glances round the apartment. There were no photographs, no trinkets. It was a very empty looking space, apart from the paintings.

"And what about you, Rachel. What are you doing here?"

"Oh, I'm on a year out, teaching English in primary schools. I'll be home again at the start of summer."

"Do you miss it?"

"I'm trying not to, but not doing very well at it, to be honest."

"There's someone special back there?"

"Oh no, I don't have a boyfriend." Rachel gave a short laugh and went red.

"Are you sure?" Ann gave her a shrewd look.

"Yes. I mean, no." Rachel put her hands up to her face. "To be honest, I just don't know."

"Well then. A year away will straighten all that out for you, one way or the other."

Rachel looked at Ann, wondering where all that wisdom was coming from. She knew better than to ask.

They both ate in silence then and after helping to clear up, Rachel made to leave.

"Thank-you for the meal."

Ann looked embarrassed

"You're my first guest."

Rachel did a second take.

"Have you only moved in too?"

"Oh no, I've been here for nine years, maybe more."

"Well, now I feel privileged. Thank-you, Ann. It means a lot."

They stared at each other. Rachel turned to leave, shutting the door behind her. Ann looked at it for a few moments, not quite believing what had just happened. She had let somebody in. And she'd survived.

She moved back to the two spoiled canvases and began to

paint. Why should he not be in it? Who was going to dare to ask who he was? No-one.

As the sunny, hot September gave way to a more autumnal October, the rain showers started. They were not like the constant Irish drizzle Rachel was accustomed too. No, these were explosive, violent bursts of rain so heavy it felt like hailstones. A number of times she had been caught out in it; no waterproof or umbrella could keep you dry. It was exhilarating - the kind of weather that lifted your heart and made you want to run screaming delightedly through it. Mamoun had done just that the last time they'd walked to school together. He had no coat but didn't seem to care that he was going to sit in wet clothes all day. He told Rachel the next morning that Mme Tessier had taken him to task over it but short of telling him to strip, there was nothing she could do, so he just sat there, making happy puddles on the floor. Every time the teacher passed his desk, she sighed and had to step over the wet floor. That in itself made the whole thing worth while.

As time went past, and Rachel became an expected presence every week, Mme Tessier lost interest and stopped her interfering, mocking ways. Rachel did wonder how she would have been treated if she hadn't been blond haired and blue eyed. Mamoun was still getting either ignored or told off for no good reason. It didn't seem to bother him, or perhaps he was used to it. Either way, he always had a smile for Rachel, and continued to angle for an ice-cream on the way to school. She knew that one day, in the not so distant future, she would relent.

Sebastian had been silent since that day at the tea room. She saw him at the other school, but only as she was leaving and he was coming in. They said hello to each other, but, although she wished for it every time, he never came running after her. She still couldn't figure out why, so after two weeks of nothing, she decided to do something about it. After the usual hellos, and instead of heading home, Rachel decided to walk down the hill, buy something for lunch from the cafe across the street and find a place to sit and wait.

This particular cafe was optimistically called *Dolce Vita*, and was run by an Italian family. It was just opposite the bus stop, so Rachel had noticed it before. The curly haired girl with a red bandana on her head who seemed to be always behind the counter was a bi-lingual Italian and sang with gusto as she walked up and down the high counter, heating food up and serving the customers. Rachel had seen a billboard advertising mochas, and with dreams of chocolate-y coffee topped with cream, she ordered one along with a croque-monsieur. The girl shouted her order back to Rachel (and anyone else within earshot) and got to work, opera singing above the racket of the coffee maker the whole time. When she was done, she shouted the order again. Rachel quickly lifted it down. She carried it to one of the tables set up outside, sat down and looked. There was no tall glass mug with whipped cream, only a tiny espresso cup filled with black coffee. She glanced up at the girl who was watching her.

"Mocha, it's a type of coffee bean. Very strong."

Rachel nodded, took a sip and burnt her tongue. She was going to have to drink it now. She grabbed some sachets of sugar and poured them all in when the cafe girl was serving another customer. Once she had finished her sandwich, she knocked back the heavily sugared, highly caffeinated drink. Not a coffee drinker, apart from when it was disguised in hot chocolate, she felt the buzz almost straightaway. She looked at her watch - the lesson Sebastian was taking would nearly be over, and he would be on his way to get the bus. She pulled her chair round so it faced the way he would come. Her heart was already pounding and her hands were shaking, helped on by the coffee, she guessed. She got out a notebook and pen and pretended to be busy now that her lunch was done but every other second she looked up, watching for him coming.

"Rachel! You're still here!"

Rachel jumped and knocked her book on the ground.

"Will you drop papers every time we meet, I wonder?!" He was smiling, and bent down to pick them up for her.

"Sorry, I was looking for you, but you came a different way. You gave me a fright."

Rachel thudded back down on the seat, pressing her hands into her side to stop the shaking. Sebastian lifted the espresso cup, saw the four empty packets of sugar and started to laugh.

"Not what you expected, was it?"

Rachel explained the polar difference between a mocha at home, and a mocha in France.

"Sounds disgusting, your excuse for a coffee."

He was still laughing.

"Well, that just depends on who's drinking it. Anyway. I was actually waiting for you."

Sebastian's smile faded, but he stayed standing.

Rachel fiddled with the sugar sachets.

"You see, I was a bit confused when you left so suddenly the other day. Did I say something wrong?"

"No. Of course not."

"So, we're ok then?"

Sebastian sat down, and levelled his dark eyes at her. He took her hands in his.

"We're ok, Rachel."

"So would you like to meet up again, and this time, I'll not talk so much?"

"But I like you talking." Sebastian grinned at her.

"Ok Rachelle. Will we try Musee Matisse this time? After school tomorrow, if you can wait for me? And not drink mocha coffee?"

"Stop laughing at me, I'm just an ignorant foreigner. Yes, I can be here tomorrow. We can get the bus up."

"Well then. I'll see you to your bus."

They crossed the road, Sebastian grabbed her upper arms, kissed both her cheeks and waved goodbye.

Once she was on the bus, Rachel looked out and saw him hurrying over to the other side of the road to get a bus going the opposite direction. He didn't look back, and again Rachel wondered what he was hiding from her.

CHAPTER SIX

Beginnings

It had been a terrible day that day - Alberto's boss at the Renault car repairs centre had been in a foul temper, lashing out at whoever was closest, which, this time, was Alberto. He marched over, picked up the clutch plate Alberto was working on and threw it down in disgust.

"What do you call this? It is wrong! You have attached the wrong part here! Imbecile!"

Alberto lifted up his work and began again.

"Do you have no answer? Speak, man!"

"Scusa," he muttered.

"What?! Speak French, only French in this country."

Alberto began to get flustered.

"Sorry, scusa, pardon,"

His boss narrowed his eyes, then raised up his hands, swore, and moved on to find another victim. Alberto wiped his sweaty hands on a rag, avoided the stares of his work-mates and turned back to his work. It was a far cry from being in charge of his own business in Italy. But there was no use in thinking about that now.

He stepped into the phone box close to his flat and dialled.

"Pronto."

"Maria, it's papa."

"Oh, is everything all right? This is not your usual time?"

"I know, I just wanted to hear your voice."

There was a pause and a clatter.

"Sorry papa, I'm in a hurry to get the dinner ready. We are going to a special mass this evening."

"What's it for?"

"To remember all those we've lost. I'm going for mama."

The words punched Alberto in the chest.

"Bueno. Well, I must go. Ciao, m'amie."

He hung up and stared at the receiver until a woman banged on the glass, in a hurry to get in.

Treading slowly up the steps, nearly home, Alberto almost

walked straight past her. It was the woman who lived opposite. She was standing outside her door, looking lost.

Alberto stopped and looked at her. Her dark hair was falling out of its bun, her brown eyes were flying all over the place and she was flushed.

"Ok?" It was all he had in his cross-lingual repertoire.

Ann looked at Alberto's lined, concerned face and began to cry.

"It's my keys. I can't find them."

Reading the actions, Alberto figured it out. He immediately dropped to his hands and knees in front of her, searching the ground. No luck. Next, he politely took her bag and shook it. No jangling there. He patted his pockets, and pointed to Ann's. She reached into hers and shook her head. Alberto held his hand up and lifted her coat again. There was something there. She felt the bottom of her coat and laughed,

"They're here! In the lining!"

Alberto clapped his hands and kissed her on both cheeks, much to both of their surprise. They stepped apart.

"Thank-you…"

Ann raised her thick eye-brows in question.

"Alberto"

"Ann, pleased to meet you." They shook hands and smiled

at each other, forgetting to let go or look away.

After a moment, Ann turned and let herself in to her flat, leaving a bewildered Alberto to cross the landing to his. What had been a terrible day had suddenly got a whole lot better.

Ann leant against her door, and tried to slow down her breathing, her pounding heart. How had she never seen him before? She had been living here for nine years for dear sake. Was he living alone? Married with a family? She didn't have the answers and, for the second time in as many days, she felt embarrassed at her secluded life, her lack of engagement with anyone else. Why had she done that? Her French was passable, she could cook, she had records to play, she could have people in.

But something had happened to her, something which had hurt her so badly, she had closed herself off, to everything and everyone. She had entertained before, but it had been with him by her side, squeezing her shoulders, kissing her neck as she stood over the cooker, making sure their guests' glasses were always full. If she tried to do it now, there would be no ally, no-one to stand beside her as her partner in crime. She didn't know whether she could do it without him now.

Giving Rachel dinner had been a huge step in the right direction. It had shown her that she could do it. On her own. If Alberto was also alone, perhaps he would like to have a meal with her. No, that was never going to happen. Was it?

"I've a question for you, Rachel."

Rachel turned away from the wok and her stir-fry and waited. Laura was sitting at the breakfast bar, sipping her wine.

"Yes?"

Her friend set her glass down,

"Why is it that your wee African friend - "

"Mamoun."

"That's the one - why does he live here and not with the other ones, up in the banlieue?"

"Does it matter?"

Laura flushed.

"No, no, not at all, I was just curious, and Jean -"

She broke off, seeing Rachel's frown.

"I don't know why - it's not something I care about, but I'll ask him, if the opportunity arises. Maybe. But not for Jean, for you."

Laura stood up and went over to the cutlery drawer.

"What do you think - should we have knives and forks, or will we go crazy and get out these chopsticks?"

She held up two sets of intricately painted chopsticks, and clicked them together.

Rachel drained the noodles and poured them into the sweet chilli vegetable mix in the wok.

"Let's do it right. But if I only manage to grab one bean, I'm going back to our good ole British ways!"

After they'd sat down to two steaming bowls of Asian food, Laura asked another question,

"You never really told me how it went with your French lover."

"Sebastian, and he's not my lover. Well, it was strange. He asked me loads of questions and I talked a lot about my life back at home, but then he kind of froze, and made a quick getaway."

"Ah, a mystery man then. You going to try again with him?"

"I think I have to - find out what was wrong, or what I said that was wrong. I waited for him yesterday, and we've arranged to meet again."

Laura reached over and grabbed Rachel's wrist.

"You didn't do anything wrong, you hear? If he wants to cut you out, let him. I don't like the sound of it, anyway. Be careful, Rachel, please."

"I will. I'm sure there was a simple explanation for his

behaviour, and before that, I felt we had a connection. Chemistry."

"Ooo. Well you definitely need to chase after that one then."

Rachel smiled and stopped herself from telling Laura that she hadn't mentioned Charlie to Sebastian once. Why hadn't she? He was a huge part of home to her. The main part really. She looked down at the bracelet he'd given her, and wrapped her fingers around it. She hadn't taken it off since he'd given it to her.

❖

Once she had her eyes done (a new gold eye shadow from Sephora), and her hair deliberately tousled, Rachel threw her light coat on, slipped her feet into turquoise leather pumps (also a new purchase) and left the flat. Mamoun was already outside his door, waiting for her.

"Salut Mamoun."

He grinned at her, opened his front door for a second, called goodbye and skipped down the stairs.

After they had got to the end of Avenue de la Republique, Rachel found herself asking the question.

"Mamoun. Why does your family live on this street, and not further away from the city centre?"

Mamoun frowned.

"Why?"

"I just wondered, that's all."

"Buy me an ice-cream and I will tell you."

His eyes were narrowed, making him look ten years older, but then he made a cheeky face and the moment passed.

Once the chocolate ice-cream was in his hand at ridiculous 8:30 in the morning, he licked it several times, wiped his mouth and began. Rachel found herself having to ask him questions so she could better understand his simple answers.

As it turned out, the apartment had first belonged to Mamoun's grandparents who had moved to Nice from Morocco during the unrest of the 1950s. Mamoun's father, the eldest of their two sons, had returned to Africa and lived with relatives for a while to find a wife, but came back with her to care for his elderly parents until their deaths. His brother, Mamoun's uncle Youssef, had gone to college in Nice, but had left after that to live in Tangiers. He had only returned once to bury their parents. He was married with a family now and had never come back to Nice. Once Mamoun was born, there was never a question of them leaving France to live in Morocco. This was their home now, and they stayed in honour of Mamoun's grandparents and the sacrifices they had made to settle here in Nice.

"Papa says we are not like the other Beurs, we've been here for a long time."

Mamoun finished off his ice-cream and then walked over to put his serviette in a bin.

Rachel got up from the low wall she had been sitting on and brushed herself down.

"Thank-you Mamoun. I am sorry I asked. You have as much right as anybody to live where you like."

Mamoun shrugged, mumbled his thanks for the ice-cream and headed for the school. Rachel watched him run off, his curly head ducking through the oblivious American tourists, his too-short trousers flapping round his calves as he jumped up the yellow stone steps. She thought back to the dread she had felt when the Maghreb man had got too close on the beach. He had probably been just like Mamoun once - happy and care-free, expecting the best of everybody. How long before that innocence would knocked out of him, as the world brutally showed its preference for a different colour of skin, a different religion and culture?

The weak sun was out again as Rachel waited, her hands round a wisely chosen cup of black tea, not the mocha she'd had the day before. She still missed the presence of milk with tea, but she was getting used to living without it. Breakfast cereal, now that was a thing she would never be glad to do without. She had gone to the Marks and Spencer at the top of Jean Medicin and had found scones, but no Shreddies. What she would give for a bowl of them, drowning in milk. Pain au chocolat were great, but she was tiring of them in a way she never had with cereal. She wondered if that would change as the year went on, if Albert Camus was right. Do we really get used to everything? Do we stop missing the things we always had before? Time would tell.

Sebastian interrupted her reverie, collapsing on the seat opposite.

"Well, how are you today Rachel?"

"I'm fine, thanks."

She caught herself,

"You're speaking English to me?!"

"I thought I would give you a present of English today. Am I good?"

Rachel laughed, and decided to nod.

"Will we go?"

They headed for the waiting bus, showed their passes and found a seat. They kept stealing glances at each other, but didn't speak. Rachel looked out the window and Sebastian looked at Rachel. All of a sudden, he grabbed her hand and pointed,

"The fort. Do you see it?"

Rachel looked down at their hands, then searched out the back window.

"Barely. I'm not sure."

"Come on, let's move to the back."

They moved along the rows of seats until they were holding onto a pole at the back. The window gave them a panoramic view of Nice - the Old Town, the airport, the shore, the woods on the hill with the fort set just above them. The sea and sky were a paler blue as the temperatures settled into a more autumnal heat. Sebastian moved behind her and stretched his arm out, pointing straight ahead.

"You see it now?"

"Yes."

She was aware of his breath on her ear, his hand on her waist. Then, as suddenly as it had happened, he moved back from her.

"This is our stop."

Rachel felt her face going red, so she busied herself with her bag, and made her way out of the bus without looking back.

"Can we speak French now, please?"

Sebastian looked sheepish and held his hands up.

Rachel kissed him on the cheek, surprising herself.

"Of course. It was nice of you to try for me anyway."

"Always."

She blushed again as he smiled at her.

It was a short walk through a park of olive trees and past a few small Roman ruins until they reached the pinky/red building which was the museum.

"Do you like Matisse?"

"I don't know much about him, except that he used to canoe."

Sebastian laughed. He told Rachel all that he had learned in school about the artist in three sentences.

"I never thought to check with you if you were interested in this?"

Rachel went over to an olive tree and sat down beneath it. Sebastian joined her. They both looked at the trees, the Roman ruins, and the house where the gallery was.

"I won't know until I see it, I suppose."

"Well then, let's go!" Sebastian gave her a hand up and, just like in the Old Town, he didn't let go. They got in to the art exhibit, and walked slowly round it, stopping from time to time at the most interesting pieces. There was a whole room dedicated to his nude paintings. Rachel stopped at the last one,

"Thank goodness. This one's wearing a white dress. What a relief" she said in a stage whisper. The other couple near her frowned. She started to giggle and hurried out into the corridor, followed by a slightly embarrassed, very amused Sebastian.

"I'm sorry, it's just, well, you can only have so much of nudes you know?" She wiped her eyes.

"Do you have a problem with nudity?" Sebastian looked serious.

"Well, I mean, no, I just…"

Sebastian laughed then, watching Rachel squirm.

She punched him on the arm for teasing her, and moved on.

She stopped at another painting, and turned to look over her shoulder.

"Now I do like this one, have you seen it?"

Sebastian bent to read the name, and then started to walk away.

Rachel saw the title of the piece, *Window at Tangiers.* Why had Sebastian not wanted to look at it? She hurried after him. He looked bothered.

"Didn't you like that one? I think it was my favourite." She looked up to him, waiting for an explanation, or an answer at least. He moved away.

"I think I've had enough of Matisse for today, let's go."

Rachel grabbed his arm,

"Could we just go to the shop for a minute and see if they had a postcard of that one?"

Sebastian looked at her hand on his arm and changed direction, towards the shop.

When they left the museum, they walked in silence back to the bus stop.

"Is this the way we're going to end all our times together? In silence?"

Sebastian sighed and put his arm around her shoulders.

"No, it isn't. I'm sorry, there's just a lot on my mind."

"Why don't you tell me?"

He squeezed her, and kissed her on the head.

"I will. Soon. I think."

Rachel knew better than to probe any further, but her mind was a storm of questions and theories. Who was Sebastian, and why did he not speak about what was bothering him? She would have to wait, she supposed. And she would. He was too lovely to walk away from.

As he saw her onto the bus - he was getting the other one further up the hill into Cimiez, he took her face in his hands and kissed her. It was the first time, and not, Rachel hoped, the last.

Head in the clouds, Rachel skipped up the stairs until a door, Mamoun's door, opened in front of her. It was a woman dressed in the traditional Muslim Niqab, covering everything but her beautiful dark eyes. Rachel took a step back, but quickly caught herself and smiled.

"Bonjour"

Salma clasped her hands beneath her dark robe to stop the shaking.

"Bonjour Rachel."

Rachel tucked her hair behind her ear, and looked as nervous as Salma, but had no way of concealing it. She had not recognised the woman who had given her dinner only a few days before. The Niqab completely concealed her.

Rachel blurted out something to cover her own discomfort.

"Your son is a wonderful boy. I really enjoy our walks to school."

The noisy resident crashed out of his door across the landing, grunted at them both and brushed past.

Salma bent her head and paused until he was down the stairs. She levelled her dark eyes at Rachel and smiled.

"Thank-you. I had better go - Mamoun will be waiting."

Rachel watched as her neighbour glided off, and wondered if she had behaved correctly. She had no notion of the protocol when you spoke to a woman dressed like that.

Salma, in the meantime, was berating herself for her unfriendly behaviour, but it had taken her by surprise - you never expect to meet anyone here - in this building, people keep themselves to themselves. Apart from her Mamoun of course - he would talk to anyone. She loved that he was like that - not afraid, not conscious of the things that made him different to most people here, always ready to question bad behaviour when it was directed towards him, or somebody else. She clenched her teeth, remembering his account of Mme Tessier's comments about him needing to wash. It had taken all of her graciousness to hold back her anger and explain why the teacher had said that. It hurt, when things like that happened. She wondered if they thought different colour of skin meant insults just bounced off, or flew over your shoulder. Rachel was very pretty - and had the colouring that would make it easy for her to be accepted in life. Salma felt a tiny pang of envy, but it was followed by the familiar longing for her home country, where almost everyone looked like her, where she would feel normal. Ordinary. Safe from insult.

CHAPTER SEVEN

Civil unrest

It was overcast that morning as everyone at number 34 got ready for the day. Rachel checked her clock, remembered it was her day off and rolled over with a sigh of relief. Alberto buttoned his fading shirt, combed his hair and polished his shoes, ready for another day of understanding nothing and being misunderstood. Omar kissed his wife and son goodbye as they got things ready for school. Ann sipped tea in her sunny studio and contemplated her newest effort on the easel. Francois, as usual, was sleeping off his drinking session from the night before. Nobody felt any different in that building. None of them were ready.

The morning passed peacefully enough but if anyone looked up, they would have seen the dark clouds growing. Rachel ran out to get milk and wondered at how still and empty the street was. She looked up and down and saw no traffic. There were a few pedestrians walking briskly past, talking in low voices. As she paid the shopkeeper he said,

"It is lucky that you came now - I'm closing early today." He pointed to the pile of boards, hammer and nails beside the counter but Rachel was none the wiser.

She didn't ask about anything, just took her change and left. Maybe they had a funeral to go to, or a doctor's appointment. Maybe there was a strike on.

Salma had fixed her hair in a new way - she didn't care that nobody would see it under her hijab - she would know. She fixed the final pin and turned her head to admire her work. She smiled at the mirror - maybe Omar would notice later.

Mamoun jogged to school, oblivious to the random groups of people huddled together in side streets, passing round flags, looking at their watches. He didn't see the police coming in their jeeps, dressed in riot gear. All he noticed was the ice-cream van was still locked up. He arrived at school and was hurried in by one of the teachers. There were no children in the playground. It was only when he got to his classroom and Mme Tessier did not scowl at him that he knew something was wrong.

Omar realised a lot sooner than his son. He glanced at the newspapers outside some of the braver shops announcing 'European Summit' in bold black letters. He noticed that most of the local businesses had boarded up their doors and windows. He saw the protesters gathering and getting ready. He was more irritated than anything - all this fuss would put him out of business today. He couldn't afford to lose the money. With that thought, he headed for the train station - there was always Cannes.

"Tired of being marginalised? Sick of the wealthy white man? Join us and let your voice be heard!"

Someone was shouting at the crowds on the station platform. They spotted Omar and beckoned him over. He just put up his hand and shook his head.

"What's stopping you? This is your chance to speak up for yourself!"

Omar kept walking, the words ringing in his ears. Those fleeting battles, they didn't change anything. He'd seen them before. People don't change their minds about the likes of him. There was no point wasting your energy trying. He got on the train, planning to be away as long as possible. Salma and Mamoun would be fine without him.

In the afternoon Rachel flicked on her ancient TV and stood still as pictures of Nice filled the screen. The streets were filled with dark figures holding placards and flags, chanting. She recognised Avenue de la Republique and raced over to the skylight to look out. As usual, all she could see was blue sky but the sounds that burst through her window did not match it: the terrifying hiss of what she now knew were tear gas grenades, the roar of an angry mob, the shouts of police trying to get back control, screams as women and children got swallowed into the crowds, the beating of helicopter blades overhead. She looked back at the TV; it was all there and it was metres below her at the same time. She looked round the flat for a self-defence weapon as the noises got closer. She checked the locks, the phone line, her food supplies. There was no way she was going out into that. Remembering her neighbours, she started towards the door and opened it a crack. There was another bang then and she turned back. They would all be ok, no-one would leave the building today, surely?

Salma froze at the door, listening. Someone had come out. Her heart was pounding. The screams, shouts and bangs on the street below kept coming up through her window. Once she heard the person go back inside, she hurried over to the window and banged it shut. The terrifying noises were muffled now. She looked at the clock - where was Mamoun? Should she go and find him? But then, if he came back, she would not be here. She paced the faded Persian carpet, back and forth, back and forth, resolving to stay, then deciding to go look for him over and over again. She pulled her shoes on, checked her Hijab and marched to the door. She clattered down the stairs and burst out onto the street, already looking, searching for her son.

The noise on the street grew as she walked towards it, but the louder it got, the more desperate she was to find Mamoun. She didn't look at the faces level with her own, she just looked down for a child's head and shoulders. Any space on the pavement started to disappear as the crowds got more dense. She started to grip people's arms to get past them. Some protested, but most were too intent on their own mission to notice. Her breaths began to take the form of her son's name, as she began to call for him. Why had she let him walk home? How would he get through all these swarms of angry rioters? Would they let him past? Or would they ignore him as they were oblivious to her?

When Salma reached Place Garibaldi she realised she was on

a hopeless mission, and that she had simply put herself at an impossible distance from the child she had set out to rescue. She was still calling his name, but it was coming out like wails now, loud enough to draw attention to herself. Two police men spotted her - a woman in a hijab shouting was a concern for them. In fact, they saw her as a security threat. They approached her, lifted her up by both arms and carried her to the edge of the square.

"What is your name?"

Salma looked from one hostile face to another and shook her head. She didn't know what to do, all she knew was they had taken her even more out of sight of her son. She tried to shake off the grasping hands and run, but her struggle made them even angrier. One of them reached for his truncheon, and put his face close to hers. He shouted it this time,

"What is your name? What do you think you are doing?"

Salma began screaming for Mamoun again, over and over, until she was hit on the head. The square, the buildings, the people, the burning flags, the bursts of smoke blurred together. She sat down on the ground with a thump and buried her face in her hands. The police men shrugged their shoulders and hoisted her back to her feet. One stood on the look-out, partially shielding Salma from view while the other started patting her arms, her legs, her back, checking for weapons. He asked her repeatedly if she was carrying a bomb. She shook her head and started to cry for Mamoun again.

The police man stepped back, and Salma staggered forwards, thinking they were done with her. Then he stopped.

"Take off your scarf."

"What? No!"

"Take it off." He started to pull at the hijab. In Salma's struggle against him, it was ripped, revealing her face, her hair, her shoulders. His partner turned round, looked at her and told the officer to stop. Then they both walked away, leaving Salma exposed and crying on the side of the street.

She sensed a figure looking at her and quickly glanced up. It was the boy from their floor, looking at her with a frown on his face. Was it disapproval? Or concern? She turned away from him.

With shaking hands, she tried to cover herself up again, but the material was badly ripped, and sat in two split pieces on either side of her face. She tried to tuck it into the neck of her top, but it still exposed a slice of her face. There was no point looking for Mamoun now. He would be upset to see her in this state anyway. She sat for some time with her eyes shut and her head bowed. Eventually she got up and made her way across the square again. She wasn't calling for her son anymore - she was hiding from everyone, even from him.

School had finished early, as the teachers were worried about getting home. Most of them had hurried all the children out, not stopping to check they were all right getting home. Mme Tessier had ran out of the classroom before the bell went, abandoning all the children in the run to her battered old

Renault, and screeching out of the tiny car park to get away from the trouble. They had all rushed to the window to watch her wobbly run to the car. Her bag was not closed, and there were pens flying out as she ran. She must have heard them, but she didn't stop. Just before she got to her car, she slipped and ripped her tiny skirt, showing her red underwear. The children roared with laughter and whistled, safe in the knowledge they were out of hearing. After that sight, they turned and filed out of school, each one heading home in a different direction.

The streets of the Old Town looked the same as they always did, maybe a little busier that's all. Nothing that warned Mamoun, nothing out of the ordinary. It always looked dark at this point and the buildings were so close together it was impossible to see the smoke. When he reached the edge of Vieille Ville, Mamoun didn't notice the concerned, shared glances of the grown-up passers-by. He didn't see the two men running in the opposite direction with bricks in their hands, faces half-terrified, half-elated.

He heard the whistles before he saw them. He started coughing before he was aware of the growing smoke, clutching the roof-tops, reaching into and filling the narrow channels of the old streets behind him. He picked up his pace, and pulled his jumper up over his mouth to block the smoke. It was getting crowded now, but the little boy was able to dart past the groups. The only ones going in the opposite direction to him were running and crying. Most were moving, surging towards Place Garibaldi at the top of Mamoun's street. He was getting jostled, shoved and trod on now. It was hard to see anything beyond his feet, as the groups were pressing round him, blocking his view. He could hear blood-curdling shouts and the feeble whistles of the police. He had to move in the same direction as the crowds. They were unwittingly carrying him. He fell on one knee and put his hands out, grazing both. This didn't stop the people though, they just walked over him, pressing his face into the gravel, making his ear scream.

All of a sudden two hands lifted him up.

"You are safe now, Mamoun."

It was Alberto, his bristly face close, and his breath whistling in Mamoun's other ear. Mamoun hid his face in Alberto's arm and did not try to climb down again. Suddenly the sounds changed, The whistles got louder and there were bangs and hisses. The crowd stopped dead for a split second, and then everyone but Alberto turned. The forward movement splintered into individuals fleeing in the opposite direction. This gave Alberto a chance to see the way forward, and he started to run. Mamoun gripped his shoulders, and watched as one police-man close-by tossed a gas grenade. The force of the explosion knocked Alberto off his feet, hurling him to the ground. He did not let go of the little boy. He had only two more streets to pass until home. That's when the pain in his chest gripped him, and made a wide-eyed Mamoun slip to the ground. He looked up at Alberto bent double and clutching his chest, grabbed his big hand and pulled him along. Rue Smolett, Rue Beaumont, and they were there. He put his key in the lock and ran up the stairs, Alberto staggering up behind.

"Maman! Maman!"

Ann looked out and saw the crowds filling the street - spilling out from the pavements to cover the road. She watched as the police used their riot shields to block progress, and the rage of the rioters as they got stopped. They were throwing bricks, stones, bottles, anything they could find, and in return, the police hurled grenades, gas canisters and hit around themselves with batons. It was terrifying to watch, and somewhat annoying as she had no food in the house. She stepped back from the window and headed for her kettle. A cup of tea always helps in these situations. While the water heated, she selected a record and put it on, turning it up to drown out the shouts, bangs and screams from the street. She wondered how Alberto was, if he'd got to work or was house-bound.

As if on cue, her door-bell went. It was hard to say if it was the first time, as the music would have drowned it out, but when someone started banging on her door, she realised they had not had a reply. She set down her tea, and went to open the door. It was Alberto, covered in blood and gripping his chest. He stumbled in to the entrance hall and collapsed on the floor, his breaths coming out in shallow gasps.

Ann ran in to her kitchen, grabbed her phone, dialled the number for an ambulance and raided the medical cupboard, boxes and bottles flying all over the counter, as she looked for the aspirin. She knew this - it had happened to her father, When the call centre put her through to ambulance service, she told them what had happened and gave her address.

"Avenue de la République? Près du Sommet?"

The woman made a clicking noise in her throat.

"Please get here quickly, please!"

Ann put the phone down, grabbed an aspirin and a cushion and knelt beside Alberto. He was grey, but still conscious. She lifted him forward and put the cushion behind his back. She held out the pill.

"Alberto, help is coming, just chew this."

She watched as he shakily took the pill and put it in his mouth. He looked so vulnerable, Ann put her arms round him, and held on.

"Don't leave me, Alberto, please, not when we've only just met, not now."

They stayed like that for a long time, barely noticing that the record was finished and the needle was jumping in protest. Alberto drifted in and out of consciousness. Pictures of his home, the vineyards, the gentle hills, his daughters and his wife drifted past, interspersed with Ann's anxious face.

The buzzer rang. Ann raced to let the paramedics in. They moved swiftly, and had him on the stretcher in seconds. Ann threw a scribbled note on Rachel's doormat, grabbed her bag and went with them. The journey to the hospital was painfully slow, with crazed protesters banging the sides and trying to climb onto the ambulance. The driver swerved to throw them off and clear a path. His partner sat over Alberto and monitored his heart. Ann held onto her new friend's hand and prayed with all her might. He couldn't see her now. He didn't know she was there. But that didn't matter. All that mattered was that he came back.

✜

The way back was easier now, as the police had dispersed the crowds and the furore had petered out. The gas clouds had blown away, the burning flags were already just hot, glowing heaps of ash. Nobody was shouting; people were just going back to their hostels, apartments and bars, smoking and taking swigs of their beer. Salma kept her face turned away from the men who passed her and pressed on to her home. When she arrived back, she ran into the flat, expecting to see Mamoun. He wasn't there, but Rachel was.

"Salma! What happened?!"

"Is Mamoun here?"

"He's in my studio. He came back looking for you, but when he saw you weren't there, he came up to me."

Salma let out a wail, dropped to the settee and started to sob, keeping her hands over her face. Rachel got beside her and put one hand on her arm, unsure of what to do.

"Do you want to change, and then when you're ready, you can come and get Mamoun? He will be so very glad to see you. We were all worried."

Salma stood up,

"Yes, I will do that."

Rachel turned to leave.

"Thank-you Rachel."

"Oh, by the way, Alberto has been taken to hospital with a suspected heart attack. He is the one who brought Mamoun back through all those crowds. He was with Ann when it happened. She left me a note to tell me she'd gone with him."

It was too much to take in. Salma just nodded without speaking and moved towards her room, not even hearing Rachel's soft footsteps as she walked out of the apartment.

Salma stripped off her ripped hijab and went to splash water over her filthy, tear-stained face. She looked in the cracked, rusted mirror. A red-eyed, tight-lipped, haggard woman stared back at her. She lifted a fresh hijab, thankful for the coverage. She closed and opened her eyes slowly, trying to get rid of the redness. It was useless, she would just have to avoid looking at anyone. She turned and walked over to leave the apartment, not stopping to fix the chaos of her pacing panic before she'd gone to look for Mamoun; a chair was over-turned, the rug was worked into a corner, and there were tiny bits of note-paper which she had unconsciously ripped instead of using it to write a note for Mamoun, as a more level-headed person would have done. She stepped out into the hall, and jumped when she saw the boy standing at his door, looking over his shoulder at her. He shook his head and went inside. She paused on the concrete stairs and took a few shaky breaths, clearing her throat of the smoke residue that still lingered.

She had never been up to the top floor, despite having lived here for twelve years. The yellow door opened before she had reached it and Mamoun raced out.

"Maman, maman!"

He stretched out his short arms and flung them round her waist. Salma dropped to her knees to hug him, and kissed his face many times over. His hair was wet round the edges, so she knew he had washed the dirt off his face. He had bandages on his hands. She felt her throat clench, and her eyes filled all over again. They stayed there until Rachel made a noise behind them.

"Would you like to come in?"

Salma kissed Mamoun again, and shook her head.

"No thank you, we just want to go home now, don't we, Mamou?"

"Yes please, maman."

Rachel watched them going down the stairs hand in hand, let out a long sigh and turned to go back inside.

"Rachel! Rachel!"

Ann was coming up the stairs, gripping the banister with alternate hands as she went. Her colour was heightened in an unhealthy way and there were beads of sweat on her forehead. She reached the top, and fell into Rachel who supported her all the way to the futon.

Rachel got a glass of water, passed it to Ann then, seeing her shaking hands, set it beside her.

They said nothing for a while. Ann sipped her water and Rachel waited.

"He's going to be all right. They told me that and said to go home."

"Well that's great to hear, isn't it?"

Ann nodded. Her face crumpled and she started to sob. Rachel moved beside her and took hold of her hand.

"I thought he was going to die. It was horrible. He is such a nice, good man."

"He is. You saved his life, no doubt about it."

Ann let her breath out and waved the words away.

"Anyone would have done the same."

"Yes, but out of everyone he chose you Ann."

CHAPTER EIGHT

Back to normal, more or less.

The street sweepers had been going up and down the street below for over an hour now, sucking up the smashed glass bottles, cigarette butts, empty gas canisters, plastic bullets, torn pieces of a woman's hijab and the dust that always results from public unrest. By the time people were emerging from their homes the only hint that anything had ever happened the day before was the faint odour of gas. All the shops put up their shutters and carried their stalls outside onto the pavement. Passers-by briefly shook their heads at the recent memory of rioting, but kept on going about their business, on catch-up from the disruption yesterday. The sun was shining again -the clouds had flown away.

The politicians talked of a 'successful coming together'. Beneath the newspaper headlines were contradictory pictures of burning flags, people angrily brandishing placards, the immoveable line of riot police, faces hidden behind their shields. In the calm safety of the Acropolis, countries agreed to the treaty of Nice, after three days of late night discussions. Outside, however, the people violently demonstrated their anti-capitalist objection. A treaty in writing was never going to change their minds. Equally, the image of politicians shaking hands was never going to overturn the resentment towards the 'other' in their city exhibited by many Nicois.

Nothing had changed.

❖

Salma had only glossed over her experience at the hands of the police on the day of the Summit when Omar asked her about her change of hijab. She didn't want him to feel angry that he hadn't been there to defend her, or helpless because actually there was nothing either of them could have done. So nobody knew except Rachel, and somehow Salma knew she wouldn't say.

Going out had become terrifying again, but she had no choice - food had to be bought, her family had to eat, She started to leave the flat with Mamoun early in the morning, and bought everything in the closest supermarket. If her boys were tired of the same meals, they never complained.

Word came that Alberto was back home, and somehow with his return, the crazy day was put to bed. No-one had any reason to speak of it now it was done.

Only Salma struggled to forget. She lay awake at night remembering the policeman's gripping fingers on her arm, seeing his angry face as he shouted at her, hearing the rip of her hijab, feeling the slap of cold air as her face was exposed.

About two weeks after the incident, Salma made her way to Alberto's door, knocked and waited. She heard slow, shuffling footsteps before the door opened and a rather pale face peered round to see her.

"Hello."

Alberto nodded.

"I wanted to thank you for bringing my Mamoun home that day. You kept him safe, and I will never forget it."

Alberto frowned,

"Scusi. No French."

Salma looked at his puzzled frown, and took his hands in hers.

"Thank-you."

The light dawned, as Alberto shrugged his shoulders.

"It was nothing."

"No Alberto," Salma shook her head, still holding his hands,

"It was everything."

They both looked at each other, suddenly embarrassed. Salma was the first to turn away, and she went back up the stairs. Alberto stood and watched her, wondering when he was going to have a single conversation with a woman in this building without crying. He furiously wiped his eyes and closed his door again.

❖

"Allo? Rachel? I'm going up to Greolieres today with some friends. Would you like to come?"

Rachel held the phone and looked down at her pyjamas. She wasn't washed, she wasn't dressed.

"Well, when and where?"

"We'll meet at the train station in an hour. You going to come?"

Rachel was already taking off her pyjama bottoms with her free hand.

"Yes, I'll be there."

"That's super! See you then!"

Rachel threw the phone down and hurried to get ready. She knew Greolieres was in the mountains above Nice, but had no idea if they were hill walking, sightseeing round the medieval village, or something else. She put on her turquoise pumps, then took them off again. She considered her flip flops, but then settled for her sandals. They didn't look as pretty but they were the most sensible-looking ones she had. She pulled on some very short shorts and a tight corn-flour blue T-shirt. She grabbed a light cardigan, stuck her sunglasses on her head, flung her bag over her shoulder and raced out. Down one flight of stairs she crashed into somebody coming up.

"Sorry, I mean, excusez moi."

"That's fine, don't apologise for getting so close." She looked at the speaker, outraged. It was the new resident.

"Francois." He smiled awkwardly at her.

"Rachel."

She stepped around him, waved goodbye and continued down the stairs, wanting to put distance between her and the creepy boy. As she ran along Avenue de la Republique she stopped in at the bakery and bought a small baguette for lunch. She got an apple and a pack of Petit Beurre biscuits. Thankfully there was a bus waiting at Place Garibaldi that she jumped on, checking her watch. She'd be fifteen minutes late. Hopefully they'd wait.

They had. When Rachel got off the bus at the station, she saw Sebastian leaning against a car, looking out for her. She went over, sweating from her race to get there, and the stress of thinking she would have been too late. She greeted Sebastian and gabbled on about buses, and bad picnics. It was only when she stopped that she noticed another tall, striking girl, standing beside Sebastian, looking at her.

"Ah, Rachel. This is Elodie, my friend. She's coming with us. And here's Pierre and Luc."

Two tanned boys with baggy clothes and dishevelled hair about the same age as Sebastian nodded to her and leaned in to kiss her. Elodie was already getting in to the car beside Sebastian.

"Did you bring any other shoes?"

Pierre was looking down at her sandals, and up at Rachel, waiting for his answer.

"I don't have any others."

Rachel noticed that the rest of the group were wearing hiking boots. She stepped back,

"Maybe this was a bad idea, I'll just head home, and leave you all to it," cheeks burning, she adjusted her bag and made to leave.

"No, no, don't worry, we'll pick the easy paths for you."

Pierre patted her on the shoulder, Meanwhile, Sebastian and Elodie were giggling in the car, oblivious to the discussion.

"Ok, well, if you're sure?"

"Of course we're sure! You are the guest of honour today, Rachel!"

Pierre grinned at her, and led her to the car. When they got in, Sebastian turned round, winked at Rachel and started the engine. Elodie didn't say a thing. As the journey began and they mounted the hills beyond Nice, Rachel began to relax. Pierre and Luc asked her about Ireland, her family, her university, her interests. Unlike Sebastian, they didn't hold back on their own stories, and the conversation flowed. Meanwhile in the front of the car, Sebastian and Elodie were flirting. Sebastian met Rachel's eyes in the mirror once and made her heart flip, but then, as the boys kept talking to her, he looked away and let Elodie massage his shoulders.

The mountains were stunning - on every slope there were crags of white rocks surrounded by a surprising amount of green grass and trees, some still holding on to their leaves. Every now and then, little hamlets clung on to the steep mountain side, tricking you into thinking you had not just left a 21st century city, but were in fact carried into a medieval age. Other than the occasional car on the road, there were no signs of modernity. Even the occasional herd of animals standing precariously on the verge beside the road looked ancient.

Rachel checked her make-shift picnic lunch, and reached a hand down to tighten the straps on her sandals. When they slowed to let a solitary goat cross the road, Luc wound the window down and stuck his arm out. Rachel shivered as air colder than she had experienced in months rushed in to the car. Again, she felt underdressed for the occasion. Pierre saw her shaking with the cold and took off his thick woollen jumper to give it to her.

"But what about you?"

"I'm tough, I can manage don't worry."

Rachel pulled the jumper over her head, and as she fixed it round her, she caught Sebastian watching her before he jerked his head away.

They stopped and parked the car just after that. They were on the edge of a small courtyard on the outskirts of Greolieres. They all stretched and picked up their bags. Rachel wished she had a rucksack, not a shoulder bag that would need frequent re-adjusting. Then she saw Sebastian reaching out and grabbing it, fitting it into his more suitable back-pack.

"Thank-you."

Sebastian looked at her and shrugged his shoulders.

"It's nothing. I should have warned you, but maybe you haven't got anything with you that would be better?"

Rachel flushed.

"I didn't expect to be trekking across mountains on my year out. I feel stupid now though."

"You'll be fine, don't worry. Just stick close to me, and I'll look after you."

Sebastian and Rachel smiled at each other and, seeing the way Elodie was flirting with the other two, Rachel felt things were back to normal again.

In the end, the mountain path was dry and easy to pick over. They climbed for half an hour until they reached an open, level space, with trees around it. Elodie spread a rug out, and all of them emptied the contents of their bags onto it. Between them they had the makings of a varied lunch and Rachel's fears about her meagre contribution disappeared. When everyone was done, Elodie, Luc and Pierre stretched out for a siesta. Sebastian grabbed Rachel's hand and pulled her up. They walked a little further, then climbed onto a large, smooth rock. From there they could see a breath-taking panorama of mountains, villages, woods and fields, with the city beneath them settled alongside the blue Mediterranean.

"What do you think?"

Rachel just nodded, the words stuck in her throat.

"If you look hard enough, you can just about make out Corsica. See, right there on the horizon?"

She couldn't really see it, but she nodded again.

"Are you glad you came?"

"What, today?"

"Well yes, today, and all the days in Nice before that."

Sebastian was waiting for an answer, pretending to pout. Rachel laughed,

'Yes. It's growing on me now."

Sebastian mouthed a silent cheer, and swung her round, nearly knocking her off the rock.

"Mission accomplished?"

He was still holding onto her. She had no choice but to hold onto him, for fear of falling.

"Come on, you two! Time to get moving, before we all freeze."

Pierre, Luc and a frowning Elodie were standing below them,

ready to go. Elodie tossed her dark ponytail and started walking away. Sebastian jumped down and hurried after her, leaving Rachel to clamber and slip down the rock face herself. Pierre stepped over, and offered his rough hand.

"Sebastian never thinks, Rachel. The sooner you realise that, the better."

He half-mumbled the last words, making Rachel wonder whether he had actually said them. She took his hand and pasted a smile on her face, pretending she had not heard him, that she hadn't noticed Sebastian had deserted her to run after somebody else.

The descent was slow in her flimsy sandals, but Pierre kept pace with her, walking beside her, or stopping when he got too far ahead. She didn't really notice the other people with her, she was too busy stepping over small rocks and muddy patches, trying not to trip and fall. She didn't look too long at Sebastian holding hands with Elodie. She didn't let herself feel any entitlement to him. She felt alone. Again. And again, her thoughts turned to Charlie. He had never left her struggling, he had always been there, like Pierre today. She must write to him again, or phone. Maybe hearing his voice would clear up the muddle in her chest every time she thought about him.

✣

Rachel got out of the car at the station, slightly disappointed they weren't dropping her home and headed across the road to get a bus. As they had driven down into the city, it had got dark. With the darkness, came the cold. She could no longer feel her feet and her toes were tinged with purple. She pulled her jacket round her, noticed it didn't meet in the middle and realised she was still wearing Pierre's jumper. She ran back to the station, but the car was long gone. The street was badly lit. There were very few people about. Then she saw him. It was a North African man, walking towards her. She turned and walked in the other direction as quickly as she could manage with numb feet. She didn't look round. There was the sound of someone calling, but she didn't check if it was to her. She stepped out onto the black road, and a car horn blared at her. She raised her hand in an apology and kept going. The bus stop was further away than she had thought. She heard footsteps behind her and tensed her shoulders. Her bag felt heavy but it was because she was gripping it, pushing it into her arm. Her breath was roaring in her ears. She started to look in the faces of the few people who passed her, willing them to protect her.

"Madame?"

He was beside her now, his dark face inches from hers. She didn't answer but kept walking. He matched his pace to hers.

"Madame? Are you all right?"

He was touching her arm now, the one with her bag. She pulled away from him, saw the bus and jumped on. As it pulled away, she saw her follower look at her and lift his hands to show he meant no harm. She didn't care. She was safe from him now.

When she got back to her flat, she threw her bag down and collapsed on the futon. Her head was racing, her heart was still thumping. After sitting like that for a while, she got up and lifted the phone.

"Hello?"

"Hi Mrs McDonald, it's Rachel."

"Rachel! How are you? How's France?"

"It's all going well. Is Charlie in?"

"Oh, sorry, just hold on."

She called for Charlie, there was a pause and then a fumble.

"Hi, Rachel?"

"Hey."

Rachel felt an unstoppable grin spreading over her face.

"Well, hello. How's things, Rach?"

"All the better for hearing you. I've had some day today."

"Tell me."

So Rachel told Charlie about the mountain trip, leaving out the part about Sebastian.

"This Pierre, jumper boy, do you like him?"

She laughed, pleased.

"Oh, I've only just met him. He was nice to me, that's all."

"It all got a bit scary after that,"

"What did he do to you? If he hurt you, I'll come over right now and kill him."

"No, no, after they let me out at the station."

"They didn't drop you back home?"

"No, but then I didn't ask them to. The walk to the bus stop was a bit scary. This African guy was following me."

"Did he speak to you?"

"No, well just 'madame'."

"He got right beside me just before I got onto the bus. I thought he was going to steal my bag."

"Did he?"

"No, but he might have. He asked me if I was all right."

"And then what?"

"Nothing. I just got onto the bus and left him standing watching me. He kind of raised his hands as if to tell me he'd done nothing wrong, but I just don't know."

"Well, he hadn't, had he? He probably just saw you looking scared and wanted to help."

"Maybe. Well, he did scare me."

"Why?"

"Ach Charlie, you and your lack of sympathy. It's touching."

They changed the subject then and caught up on all their news. It was just like old times.

As they were saying their goodbyes, Charlie said,

"I've missed this, Rach."

There was a pause then. Charlie cleared his throat.

"You know I care about you, don't you?"

Rachel nodded. Then she remembered he couldn't see her.

"And I you, Charlie."

"Take care, and avoid those men with their jumpers, won't you?"

She laughed and hung up.

❖

Omar walked slowly back down Jean Medicin. The bus the foreign white girl had got on was his too, but she'd looked so scared he decided to stay off. The way she'd looked at him, like he was a monster, like he was going to rob her or worse still, hurt her. He'd just wanted to help - she was alone in a dark and dangerous part of the city, and she looked afraid. Or maybe she'd only looked like that when she saw him. He shook his head and sighed. It had been years now. He had been born here. He belonged here. And yet, no papers, no length of residency were going to change his race. His skin colour seemed to make others draw conclusions that belied the truth about who he really was.

He waited at the next stop and climbed on to the bus, not daring to look around him or try to speak to anyone - that didn't seem to be welcomed when different skin colour came into it. He spied a free seat beside a young man who looked like someone he once knew. When he turned to stare out the window he studied him. It was the profile that haunted him. Omar rubbed his hand over his face and told himself he was going mad. He needed to get home, he badly needed to sleep.

"I saw you trying to talk to her, you know."

Omar jumped and looked at the speaker.

"You shouldn't bother young girls who are far from home."

"I was only trying to help her."

"She was fine. I was looking out for her anyway, making sure she got on the bus safely."

Omar frowned at Sebastian.

"Were you following her?"

"No, no. Well, sort of. She'd been on a trip with me and my

friends today, and after we'd left her at the station I realised she needed me to accompany her home."

"Why didn't you get on the bus with her then?"

"I was making sure you didn't. Then I missed it too."

Omar shook his head at the feeble logic.

"Well, she will be home before you can get to her anyway, so why bother following her now?"

Sebastian laughed.

"I know. She'll be ok now."

He stood up, waved his hand to take his leave, and jumped off at the next stop.

Omar watched him walk past the window, and then it clicked. The boy had looked like Youssef, his brother. The spitting image. He chuckled to himself. Now that was impossible. Youssef had gone back to Morocco. How could he possibly have fathered a child here in Nice?

CHAPTER NINE

Christmas isn't for everyone

The wardrobe of Nice had suddenly changed, as the clear skies invited the cold of winter. The sun still shone, but its brightness was muted, its heat cooled. Even the sea changed from azur to smoky blue. T-shirts and dresses had been abandoned for thick coats and boots. In the lead up to Christmas, the city demonstrated it could do winter as well as summer; Place Massena was transformed into a winter wonderland with an ice-rink swirling with children and stalls serving hot spiced wine for watching parents. Flamboyant, sparkling lights made up for the shorter, darker days over the main city streets and the palm trees on Promenade des Anglais were transformed into Mediterranean Christmas trees. The old town pulled out all the stops with its window displays and Place Rosetti was gearing up for its annual animated animal Nativity scene.

At this time of year, the Christmas displays smiled on everybody, regardless of race or creed. The Muslim community carried on as usual and seemed to welcome the friendly change in their neighbours. As far as Rachel could make out, things were almost like they were back home.

"Well, Mamoun, I won't be here for the next two weeks. I'm going home for Christmas."

Mamoun stopped running down the stairs.

"Christmas? Oh, home for the holidays you mean?"

Rachel realised that Mamoun wouldn't celebrate Christmas. Why would he, he was a Muslim.

"Sorry, yes, home for the holidays."

"But you will come back, won't you?"

Mamoun turned his dark eyes to her.

"Of course."

"There are children in my class who talk about getting presents a long time before the holidays begin - toys and games and chocolates. My mother has warned me about that, and I do not join in. It is not the Muslim way you see."

Rachel looked at Mamoun and felt sad, but then wondered why - he was sticking to his beliefs, honouring his parents and not going along with his peers.

"I will miss our walks to school, Mamoun."

Mamoun nodded and glanced up at her.

"So will I, Madame Rachel."

After the last class of the term, Rachel made her way in the dusk through the Old Town and did her Christmas shopping - a woven purple basket for her mum, a silk scarf for her aunt, carved wooden bowls for her granny, jewellery for some of her friends. It was the best Christmas shopping experience she had ever had - the shops were all lit with colourful fairy lights, the smell of soaps and exotic spices wafted towards her, and all the gifts were carefully wrapped in silver tissue paper. The narrow streets were swarming, but she had got clever at dodging larger groups, and the busyness tonight just added to her Christmas feeling. It was cool outside, but not freezing -that was the only slightly odd feeling this time - no bite in the air, no sight of your breath when you stepped outside. She still needed her scarf and gloves, but the cold never got that sharp here.

She was just making to leave with her purchases when she stopped. Charlie. She had to get him something. She moved into a North African shop filled with wooden animals, exotic woven rugs and cushions. Then she saw a set of Moroccan tea glasses, and lifted them up - intricate gold detail on glass stained blue, red, green and yellow . As the shop assistant was wrapping them Rachel had a change of heart. This wasn't a present for Charlie - if she gave them to him, she would have to tell him about going to the cafe, and he would feel left out. It was a present for Sebastian. She'd save it for after Christmas now though as they'd already said their goodbyes in the cafe after school yesterday. She left the shop, and made her way to a skater shop to buy a hoodie for her childhood friend - that was more suitable. Rachel despaired of herself - buying presents for two boys, and only one of them had ever seen her as girlfriend material. Or had Sebastian ever thought of her like that either? Charlie was a good friend, but never anything more. Right?

✢

The flights home passed by uneventfully for Rachel. The nervousness of the trip out had left her, as she tried to re-set her thoughts, re-programme her spoken language, listen to conversations around her. She was in a daze - happy to be going back, but trying to rein in the excitement knowing she was going to have to leave again.

And there was mum, running towards her, flustered as usual.

"Rachel! You look different!"

Rachel took in her mum - same clothes, haircut, perfume. She took a deep breath and smiled. They hugged each other. Mum pulled back and winced,

"What's that in your pocket?"

Rachel looked down and made a face.

"It's the Yankee candle you gave me."

Mum groaned and laughed,

"Sorry about that - just a worrying mother."

She hugged Rachel again.

"It's good to have you home."

Getting back to the house felt odd, but comfortable. Rachel

dropped her bag on her bedroom floor and threw herself on the bed. She propped herself up and looked round. It was all the same, but it seemed smaller. She walked over to the window. Someone was building a new house in the field opposite, but other than that, nothing had changed. She peered over at Charlie's house. All the windows were dark. Were they away for Christmas? She walked down to the living room,

"Mum, is Charlie away?"

Mum looked up from her paper.

"Yes, they've gone skiing in France of all places for Christmas. I'm surprised you didn't know."

"He never said." Rachel forced herself to shrug and laughed a little. She ventured another care-free sounding question,

"So he'll be away until after I head back again?"

"Think so. You're not disappointed are you?"

"Oh no. No. No I'm not." Rachel left the room before mum could read her expression. Mum called after her, head still stuck in the paper,

"Phoebe and the others say they're having a party this weekend and they want you to come, so that will be nice, won't it?"

"Yeah, that sounds great."

What's a party without Charlie though, really?

The next morning mum surprised her with a plate of pain au chocolat. Rachel bit into one and missed the fresh baking in Nice. She waved away the teapot and hunted in the cupboard for an espresso maker, watched by her bewildered family.

That Saturday she donned her glad rags and walked down the road to Phoebe's house, smiling at how secure she felt on the unlit country roads compared to the terror of rats and North African men in Nice.

Phoebe threw open the door and shrieked, throwing her arms around her.

"Rachel! You look so tanned! And look at that gorgeous dress!"

She called over her shoulder,

"Hey guys, come see Rachel!"

Rachel blushed and smiled as her old school friends threw questions about Nice at her.

"Is it still hot?"

"Did you get any new clothes?"

"Are all the women really glamorous?"

"Can you swim at that beach?"

And then the one she knew was coming:

"Any men?"

"No, not really."

There were disappointed sounds, especially from Phoebe, which puzzled Rachel.

They all gradually moved away then, chatting about uni and mutual acquaintances. Rachel got a drink and leant against the living room arch. No-one had anything else to say to her, and she certainly wasn't going to bore them with details about the elusive Sebastian. She stood for a while, a smile pasted on her face.

"Can I ask you a question?" Rachel turned to face a boy she didn't recognise.

"I think so?"

He stuck out his hand,

"I'm David. And I know you're Rachel. I'm doing French at uni here and have my name down to go to Nice next year." He put his hands in his pockets and looked at the carpet,

"I just don't know if I'll be able to hack it for a year. No-one I know is going. Any advice?"

Rachel took in his worried face and knew exactly what he was feeling. She took a deep breath,

"The best thing I could tell you is be open. The people like you that you meet at first are not the only ones who may turn out to be your friends." She looked across the crowded room and thought how young they all looked,

"I had the chance to move into a studio flat and it's the best thing I could have done. The people there, well, they're the complete opposite to me, and to each other. Most don't even speak French fluently never mind English."

David's eyes widened.

"And did you speak to them?"

"Yes. The first was one of my pupils - a nine year old called Mamoun."

"Is he from Nice?"

"Yes, but his parents were originally from Morocco."

"So they're Beur?"

Rachel put her hand up,

"They are Moroccans trying to make a life for themselves in Nice. If you ever meet them, you'll never see them in the same light again."

"So is the dad a street seller?"

Rachel wished he was wrong.

"Yes that is one of his jobs."

"Oh right."

"Listen David, if you want a real Nicois experience, I'll hook you up with the details for the flat - it will be empty once I leave next summer."

David looked down as Rachel scribbled Margaret's number on a napkin. She held it out to him.

"Go on - it will make your year, I promise."

David took it and put it in his pocket. Rachel was not convinced he would ever do anything about it. She watched him walk away, and pictured him meeting Mamoun, Salma, Omar, Francois. She knew they would become his friends if he let them.

She made her way across the beige carpet to say goodbye to Phoebe who made a disappointed face, but quickly recovered when somebody else called her name.

As she walked home Rachel got to wondering why she had wanted to come home so desperately when it wasn't all that great really. She hoped David would take up her studio - it was good to think he might become part of her newfound friends' lives, the way they had become part of hers. She wondered what they were all doing back in 34 Avenue de la Republique. She reached into her bag, searching for her house keys. Her fingers closed round a card. She pulled it out and saw it was blank. As soon as she got in, she took the card and addressed it.

Dear Eloine, how are you? I have gone back to Ireland for Christmas. It is raining a lot here. I miss the sun! I hope you are having a nice holiday. Rachel xo

❖

Christmas. Ann sighed. A time for people who had people. A pain for those who were alone. She looked at the tiny pre-cooked, stuffed chicken and stood up, determined not to indulge her misery today. It had been just after Christmas when her parents had died and when he had decided to follow his dream - a dream that didn't include her. He had announced, just like that, that he couldn't wait any longer, and came to tell her, two days after she had buried her beloved father. Classy. She was so shell-shocked with grief that she didn't question his decision, didn't confess her love, didn't beg. She just stood there on the doorstep in her black dress and watched him walk away. Her everything, her reason for being, her life. She was on her own now, absolutely alone.

Stop it Ann. She found herself walking out her front door and over to Alberto's. He had got home from hospital after only one night of treatment, and seemed to have come out of the whole experience unscathed. Ann had been embarrassed by her melodrama that day and had been too afraid to knock on his door. But she was here this time, and knocking. He opened it wide, looking surprised.

"Are you by yourself there?"

"Si."

"Do you like chicken?"

"Si, of course."

"Come with me?"

It was such an awkward invitation it took Alberto a long minute to respond, but Ann was already back at her door, waiting for him. He reached up to get his coat, quickly snapped a flower off the pot outside his flat, and followed her in.

It was his eighth Christmas away from his homeland, and his family. The first one had been excruciating, the second infuriating, by the third he had given up. Missing home was just a part of him now and after all this time away, it seemed it would be a permanent state. Since falling ill the day of the summit, he had felt the need for getting back home turn into desperation. He held the photos of his girls and pressed his lips to them. His wife was there too, with her arms around them, looking happy, and oh so beautiful. Another wave of grief crashed over him, so sudden and violent he didn't have time to summon up tears. How he wished to be home again, away from this place where people didn't understand him, didn't expect anything spectacular of him. He was just a shadow now.

There was a rap on the door. He straightened his shirt, and went to answer it. It was Ann, looking a little frantic, smelling of garlic and chicken. She was inviting him to dinner. He guessed but wasn't sure until she went back to her door, and turned to wait for him. He thought about his measly dinner, waiting to be cooked. He considered his state of mind. He would be mad not to go.

When he presented Ann with the geranium, she thanked him as if he'd just given her a dozen roses. She went through to the egg-shell blue kitchen to find a vase and check on the chicken heating up in the oven. She skilfully chopped some basil and scattered it over a painted china bowl of roasted cherry tomatoes, glistening with olive oil. She drained the Charlotte potatoes, and checked the sauce. Alberto stood watching her, thinking how pleasant it was to have a woman cooking for him again, after years of Spartan meals for one. The Mediterranean smells floated round the room, making his mouth water. Ann grabbed a bottle of Chianti. She passed it to him,

"It is Christmas, after all" she said, with a quick smile. Alberto took the wine from her, and realised that this was the first wine he had drunk in nearly eight years. His eyes filled with tears, but he bent his head and busied himself with the corkscrew. Ann had seen his sadness, but pretended she hadn't. Neither spoke of the heart attack incident - Alberto because he had only a faint recollection of that day and wasn't even certain Ann had been with him, Ann because she was too embarrassed about her behaviour then.

Alberto set the table, carried the dinner over and placed the flower in the jam jar come vase in the middle of the thick wooden table in between them.

After they sat down and busied themselves with their dinner, they looked up at each other.

Ann lifted her glass,

"Buon Natale, Alberto."

Alberto clinked his glass against hers,

"Happy Christmas, Ann."

They smiled at each other and started to eat.

"Your family?"

"My wife is dead, my two daughters are in Italy. My work - it's here. My home is there."

Somehow those four statements were enough to reveal Alberto's pain.

"And you?"

Ann stood up all of a sudden.

"Music." She hurried over to the wooden bureau and opened the sloped door, revealing an antique gramophone with a pile of vinyls propped up against it. She lifted one and showed it to Alberto.

"The Beatles?"

He looked puzzled. Ann selected another one.

"Miles Davis?"

No luck there either. She lifted out another, smiling.

"Puccini?"

Alberto clapped his hands, "Ovviamente!"

Ann took the record out, wiped it with her sleeve, positioned it beneath the needle and turned it on. Rich, evocative music rose and fell into the room, filling in the gaps of language and understanding with its expression of universal, human experience. Alberto closed his eyes, his fork still piled up with his dinner. Ann stole glances at him, and felt as though she had known him forever. At last, she thought, he has really come back.

"Maman?"

Salma was scrubbing the kitchen floor, but she stopped and straightened up.

"Yes, Mamou?"

Mamoun kept tossing his ball up in the air and catching it.

"Why does everyone else here celebrate Christmas, go on holiday and buy presents? It all sounds like fun, to me."

Salma paused before answering.

"Well, they are not Muslim like us, so they have different things to celebrate."

"Like what?"

Salma sighed,

"Well, they believe that Christmas is when God came to earth, in His Son."

"But why all the presents, and food?"

"It's just their way of celebrating, Mamou."

"Well, I think it's all bete, and Rachel shouldn't have gone away just because of some party."

Mamou threw his ball into the bucket of water beside Salma, splashing her, and then stormed off in a rage.

Salma picked the ball out, shook her head and started back on the floor. What do you do with a nine-come-fourteen year old? Patience. More than her parents showed to her when she was young. And a lot more than they had when she told them she was leaving with Omar, especially her mother. Had it been the right decision? She had certainly thought so at the time, because she was in the throes of new love. Now, as Mamoun's questions increased and she became more uncomfortable dressing to cover up her face and body, when most were in strappy tops and mini-skirts, she couldn't help but question her decision. Being part of a minority was isolating. But then, Omar was here, and she had her precious Mamou. That should be enough, shouldn't it.

He was fed up. Raging. Mamoun stormed out into the hallway, then realised he had nowhere to go. He stood there feeling a bit stupid. The front door across the gloomy hall burst open, and a man stepped out, carrying a case. His long hair needed washed, his clothes were full of holes. He noticed Mamoun standing there staring. He grunted at him and started to move towards the stairs. Mamoun hurried towards him, smelling strongly of onions and garlic.

"Who are you? My name is Mamoun."

Francois growled at him and kept walking.

Mamoun skipped down a few steps in front of him and grinned. He pointed to the case.

"What's in there?" His voice dropped to a stage whisper, "Is it a gun?"

Francois rolled his eyes and sighed. He muttered,

"My name is Francois and this," he held up the case, "is a clarinet."

Mamoun clapped his hands.

"Will you play it for me?"

"No." Francois kept going down the stairs.

"Please?" Mamoun called after him.

Francois did not reply, but continued down the stairs. Mamoun was quicker. He was at the main door, blocking Francois' way out.

"Step aside, pest."

"Not until you promise to play your clarinet for me soon."

Francois groaned.

"All right. I will. Sometime. Possibly."

Mamoun punched the air and then put out his hand. Francois stared at it for a minute, then took it for a split second before making his escape. The door slammed shut on a grinning, triumphant Mamoun.

"I will not forget your promise, Monsieur!" he shouted.

Francois walked away from the flats and shook his head at Mamoun's childish threat. Still, it was the first time in a long while that anyone beyond the band had shown an interest in his music. His parents resented it as it had taken him away from politics. He loved it for that very reason. When he played, he was in control. No-one could make him do anything else.

He wondered who Mamoun's parents were. He guessed they lived in the flat opposite but other than mouth-watering cooking smells there had been no sign of them. It was strange; a North African family living here and not in the banlieue where people like his father had banished them to. The boy was the first dark-skinned child Francois had ever really met. Sure, he'd seen them, but his private schooling had kept them beyond his reach. Personally, he didn't think he had a problem with Maghrebs being in Nice. Everyone had to make a living one way or another, didn't they?

He glanced across the road and saw a dark-skinned family of four laden with shopping bags. Why was it that his father had such a problem with people of a different race? He hadn't fought in any wars, he wasn't suffering from a bad experience that Francois knew of. He snorted. It was just an ill-informed opinion, based on an unwillingness to share anything; be it housing, jobs, resources, or even breathing space. Who did they think they were, thinking they could decide who deserved to be here? A wave of irritation rushed over Francois as he pictured his 'perfect' parents. He'd show them. He'd let Mamoun into his life, and his family too. And if anyone had a problem with that, well...

CHAPTER TEN

Back again

Rachel sat in the yellow bath, wishing it was avocado. The tiles were small and black, pressed narrowly against each other, closing in on her. There was no window, just a noisy fan and hurtful electric light. She couldn't hear anything beyond that fan, and the slosh of water. Not even the echo of foreign voices in the stairwell.

At home, she thought, there would be other sounds. Birds singing in the garden below. Mum busily banging pots for dinner. Dad cutting the grass, or opening the garage door on his arrival back from the shops, car filled with bags of unsurprising, familiar foods.

At home, she would not be 'broadening her horizons' in a tiny black bathroom with a yellow bath, but she would definitely be able to hear more. Here, she had no people to shape her routines, nothing to listen out for that was familiar and safe. She stared at the taps and realised what it really felt like to be cut off.

She laid back, put her ears under the water and closed her eyes. The dark and silence were suffocating. She opened her eyes, sat up, pushed all her melancholy off an imaginary shelf and forced herself to get out, leaving the bathroom with a towel wrapped round her.

There was someone at the door. She wondered how long they'd been knocking. She tightened her towel, and opened the door a crack.

It was Mamoun. His eyes and mouth opened very wide when he saw her.

"Madame Rachel! You're back!"

Rachel could feel the drips of water running down her legs, drying into her shoulders.

"Hello Mamoun. Have you had a good holiday?"

Mamoun took a step back, looking very uncomfortable.

"Yes, the opposite of Christmas was ok, Madame." Mamoun looked serious and on the point of saying something else when Rachel opened the door a little wider. He took one look at her, turned and ran back down the stairs.

Rachel laughed to herself - that will teach him for visiting unannounced. She was closing the door again when Laura and Francesca piled in, faces bright with their latest plan.

"We're going to Italy next week! For the half-term break!"

"Oh. That's nice."

"No, you silly, we mean you too!"

"But how did you pay for the tickets?"

"With money of course."

Rachel shook her head,

"I'll need to pay my share. Was it a lot?"

"Nothing that last month's salary and a wee splash of Visa can't cover."

"I don't know, it's so soon and unexpected."

"Ach Rachel, would you just let yourself live a little!"

Rachel turned away to hide her face.

Laura softened,

"Sorry, it's just that you keep saying no to things - like the party in Cannes, or the overnight in Grasse. You've got to come with us this time Rachel. You know you do."

"It'll be fun - all those designer shops, the glamour."

"Well, that wouldn't sell it to me Francesca, but I suppose there's nothing stopping me from going so - "

The other two squealed and started dancing round Rachel, grabbing her hands and pulling her round.

Rachel tried to smile, her heart heavy with misgiving.

Getting back into the swing of things at school was not hard, but Rachel was running out of lesson ideas, especially considering the unsupportive silence of the teachers. She had brought two children's books from home and was using them to teach a few basic words. *Things that go Bump in the Night* by Dr Seuss with prepositions was probably too advanced, but the rhyme of 'over the bridge', 'up the tree', 'out the window' was fun, and with actions, they'd get it. *The Very Hungry Caterpillar* had nice pictures and what odds if they never needed the words 'watermelon' or 'cocoon'? She knew that English would be taught properly when they were older, but for now, it had to be enjoyed. When she brought out Dr Seuss, Madame Tessier got very animated and snatched it off her to photocopy. That was a surprising turn of events. Rachel looked at her for a longer moment, and saw that, with green make-up, she could pass for the Grinch. Just about.

The next day was Sebastian's school. Rachel took extra care as she got ready. She swept on gold eye shadow, brushed bronzer over her shoulder bones and spritzed Tommy Hilfiger over her head. She was excited to see him, but going home had changed how she felt a bit. She remembered the kiss, the way he'd swung her round on the rock, and felt her heart flip. Maybe it was just time for a bit of fun, just like teaching Dr Seuss to the kids in school. No real purpose, no end goal, a 'just for the sake of it' kind of a thing. She grabbed the tea glasses she'd bought for him, and left the flat.

After her lesson, she opened the classroom door, expecting to see him coming towards her, but he wasn't there. Maybe he was late, maybe he was sick, maybe he was avoiding her. She half-ran, half-walked down the echoing corridor, past all the art pinned to the notice boards and the windowed classrooms packed with fidgety children to the school office.

She knocked on the clouded glass divider, and waited. When it was opened, the smell of garlic wafted out.

"Excuse me, but I was wondering if Sebastian was coming in today?"

The secretary peered over her glasses at Rachel.

"Who?"

"The teaching student."

She swivelled around on the office chair and lifted a folder from her desk, running her manicured finger nail down a list.

"Ah, yes. He has moved to another school."

Rachel gripped the edges of the shelf between her and the office.

She managed to whisper "Why?"

"He has finished here. He must go somewhere else."

With that, the secretary shut the glass, turned back to her keyboard and started typing again. Rachel left, feeling her heart sinking. Why hadn't he told her? She didn't have his number, he just had hers. There was no way of finding him. Maybe that's what he wanted - to disappear. Her heart thudded with the thought. She had genuinely thought there was something there. She got to the door and stopped. She had to do something. She re-traced her steps and knocked again on the partition. The secretary slid it open, then frowned when she saw it was Rachel again.

"Yes?"

"Do you have any contact details for Sebastian, such as his phone number, or his address?"

There was a long pause. The secretary pursed her lips.

"I cannot give that to you, it is confidential."

Tears sprang to Rachel's eyes.

"I need to contact him, and I have nothing."

The secretary lifted her hands up helplessly.

"I cannot give out this boy's details."

Rachel made one last attempt.

"Could you tell me the name of his new school at least?"

She waited as the secretary moved over to the papers again. Then she stopped flicking and turned back.

"He is taking some time out before the next placement."

"Why? Where is he?"

"He has gone to Morocco for two months."

"Why? Why would he go without telling me?"

Rachel was close to tears, but the hardness of the woman's face held them back.

She looked round her office to check she was alone. She spoke quietly,

"Ok. I will tell you his address. But you must not let on how you got it. Have you got paper and pen?"

Rachel's hands were shaking as she wrote down the apartment block name, and the number of Sebastian's flat.

"Thank-you, a thousand thank-yous!"

The partition was slid closed again, and Rachel was left standing there, holding her only hope tightly in her hands.

Mamoun put his bony shoulders back, patted his frizzy hair down and knocked on Francois' battered door. Seconds passed. He knocked again. The door opened a crack, still on the snub. One bleary eye looked at him.

"What is it?"

Mamoun put his face close to the crack.

"I want you to play your clarinet."

There was a loud sigh and a whispered curse.

"I will sometime, just not right now."

"In ten minutes?"

"No." The door started to close.

Mamoun stuck his fingers into the gap.

"Please, Monsieur."

Francois looked at the tiny fingers, and relented.

"All right. One piece, OK? |

He opened the door and Mamoun raced in before he could change his mind. He looked round at the shabby decor, the meagre furniture and whistled.

"This place is old."

Francois shrugged his shoulders and picked up his clarinet. He played a couple of bum notes and stopped, looking down at Mamoun.

"Is that it?"

The real music started then - moody, soulful, laid-back jazz. Mamoun dropped to the ground and crossed his legs, mesmerised. When it stopped, Francois smiled at him for the first time.

"Happy now?"

"Monsieur, your music is nearly as good as ice-cream."

Francois laughed.

"Now will you leave me alone?"

"Just wait until I tell Maman, and Madame Rachel!"

Francois grabbed his skinny arm,

"Listen you, I do not play for just anybody, so don't go blabbing."

Mamoun grinned,

"But you played for me."

He was shoved out the door then, still smiling. Francois walked back into his lounge, shaking his head. What had he started? He was going soft in the head, and for a Beur kid too.

Christmas was over, thankfully. Alberto had worked right through, as much as he could - blocking out memories, thoughts of his daughters, of his beautiful Mia, of Italy, scraping together more money to add to his measly savings. He could hear faint jazz music playing somewhere in the building. He looked down at the table and the small piles of money on it and sighed. He would never be able to save enough for the ticket and to cancel his business debts. He could never show his face there again if he hadn't paid what he owed. Unless he stopped eating. "You must eat, cara mio." He started and looked round, expecting to see her, but there was no-one there. Her voice had sounded so real. He put his head in his hands and wept. There was a knock on the door. He thought about ignoring it, but the person kept knocking, so he rubbed his face with a tea towel and moved to answer it.

It was Mamoun.

"Bonjour, Monsieur."

"Bonjour."

Mamoun was jumping from one foot to the other, bursting with news.

"I am going to Morocco. With Papa. Tomorrow."

Alberto frowned, not understanding. Mamoun repeated it, more slowly, with actions this time. The light dawned.

"Morocco is home?"

Mamoun laughed.

"No Monsieur, here is home for me. But Morocco is home for Papa."

Alberto felt his tears rising again, but cleared his throat and managed to smile at his little neighbour.

"Good news, no?"

Mamoun clapped his hands and skipped back down the stairs. Alberto turned back inside, feeling even more miserable. He was barely in the kitchen when the door went again.

It was Ann this time. He felt surprisingly happy to see her face.

"Please don't tell me you are going home as well," he muttered in Italian.

"Sorry, did you say something?"

He shook his head and waved the words away with his hand.

"I was just wondering if you would like to come with me to Antibes next Sunday?"

Ann put a leaflet into his hand, so he would understand.

"Sunday?"

"Not tomorrow, but next week. Do you understand?"

Alberto paused for a dangerous moment, but then started to smile.

"Good."

Ann caught herself grinning back like a school-girl.

"Ok, I'll come and get you at ten."

"Ten, ok."

She backed out of the room, and nearly tripped over the door.

Alberto caught her arm and steadied her. He held on a little longer, long enough for them to look at each other, slightly embarrassed. Ann coughed, and pulled away.

"See you next Sunday, Alberto."

"Yes. Sunday. Not tomorrow, next week." He raised his finger and made it jump in the air to show he'd understood. He stepped back and started to close the door behind her.

"Goodbye Ann."

As she went over to her door, Rachel and two other girls hurried past, chatting about their 'trip to Italy'. Ann glanced over, but thankfully Alberto's door was closed again, and he wouldn't have heard. He didn't need to know that some people could go to Italy whenever they felt like it.

CHAPTER ELEVEN

Stuck

The February day was crisp, making the sea icy blue, the pebbles like hoards of snowballs. School had been unsatisfactory; the children had been restless, reluctant to learn.

Rachel skipped her usual glace and hurried down to the beach. She pulled her fluffy collared coat round her, and shoved her hands deeper in her pockets. It would be too cold to sit today, but she could lean against the railing and just look out. She contemplated the sea and realised that the reason she loved coming here was because it reminded her she was connected to home - with the planes and the sea it felt possible to get there. That was comforting. People had asked what she liked most about Nice, and she'd said the sea. They always nodded, but didn't understand that it wasn't because of its brilliant colour or the millionaires' yachts sailing across it, but because it was the closest thing to home she'd found here. A young couple walked behind her, laughing and holding onto each other. She thought of Charlie, and shook her head. He was a friend, nothing more. She looked down at the bracelet he'd given her, and remembered what he'd said, *think of me sometimes.* She was. Nearly all the time, as it turned out.

She took one last look at the horizon and headed for home. There was a letter waiting for her in the flat pigeon hole. She took it out, assuming it was one of mum's weekly updates, but then stopped. That wasn't mum's writing, it was Charlie's. She ran up to the apartment, calling hello to Ann as she passed her. Ann took in the delighted face, the letter clutched in Rachel's hand and smiled to herself.

Hey Rachel!

How's things in la France? I'm an ass - I should have been writing to you before now. Letters aren't really my thing, as you know.

Life's all same-old here. I've finished my exams, and now it's just the dreaded dissertation to do. It's hard to get down to it every day, but Phoebe has been here to nag me so it'll get done, thanks to her.

Phoebe? What's she doing with Charlie?

I hope you are having a great time. Just enjoy it Rach, it'll be over before you know it.

I'm sorry I missed seeing you at Christmas. I would have given up my stupid skiing holiday if it meant seeing you.

Anyhow, must head on and pretend to study,

Look after yourself,

Charlie

Look after yourself?! Was that it? Rachel crumpled the letter up and hurled it to the opposite corner of the room. She'd show him. She lifted her bag to dig out Sebastian's address and her map of Nice.

Soon. She would go find out about him after Italy. She couldn't just accept he was gone with no explanation. He probably would have told her, if she'd asked. This was her only chance to keep the links that they'd started to make last term. Stuff Charlie and his 'study buddy' Phoebe. She'd show them both. What did they know about living abroad? Nothing. What new experiences were they having? Hopefully none. Her heart twisted painfully but she just shook her head, and got busy looking round for things to scrub. Cleaning: the cure for any heartache. She tried to focus on the white hob, the yellow bath, the ceramic tiles, tried to sing U2 so loudly she couldn't hear his name, or the cold words he'd written.

You've got to get yourself together/ You've got stuck in a moment and now you can't get out of it

Rachel lifted the jar of chutney she'd bought in Marks and Spencer's and tried to unscrew it. Damn. It wouldn't open. She started towards the door to get help and at that moment there was a knock on the other side.

"Alberto?! Hello."

Alberto took his cap off and started to wring it in his hands.

Rachel opened the door wider and motioned for him to come

in. He stayed standing in the doorway.

"You teach me English?"

His face flushed.

"Of course, Alberto."

There was a pause. Alberto pulled a brochure out of his pocket.

"Ann go " he pointed to the front picture of Antibes and then himself.

Rachel took the brochure and walked up the stairs to her living space, hoping he would follow.

"Right. Have a seat and let's begin."

An hour later, Alberto was able to introduce himself, count to twenty and name some foods. He stood to leave,

"Grazie, Rachel."

Rachel shook her head slightly and waited.

"Thank-you Rachel."

She clapped her hands,

"We should meet again soon, to learn more?"

Alberto kissed her on both cheeks,

"Yes?"

"Of course."

He paused, his hand on the door handle,

"How do you say, 'ti amo'?

Rachel stopped herself from asking why and told him,

"It's 'I love you'."

Alberto repeated the words slowly and nodded. Rachel wondered if he was going to say them again soon, but said nothing.

He ran down the stairs and out the door, whistling.

Rachel locked the door behind him and walked back up to her unopened chutney jar. Some things were better than dinner. She looked at Charlie's letter, still lying in the corner of the room. She put her shoulders back and picked up the jar again. This time she would try Salma's door. She had a vague recollection of Mamoun telling her he was going away with his dad, but he had never said his mum was going too. What if she'd been there by herself and Rachel had never checked to see if she was ok? She hurried down the stairs.

✤

It had been four nights, five days since Mamoun and Omar had left for Morocco. Salma had not left the flat that whole time. She had got Omar to buy enough food so that she wouldn't have to go out, but now she felt she was going mad staying in. She had cleaned every cupboard, washed all the curtains, painted the kitchen, re-arranged the sitting area seats and knitted two jumpers.

There had been no point in her going with them - her parents were both dead and she had not spoken to her sisters in years. She would just have been in the way. She sighed. Where was her home now anyway? Not there. Not here.

The door rattled with a quiet knock. Salma froze. Then she heard a voice,

"Salma? It's Rachel. Just wanted to see if you were ok?"

Salma did not move. She could not move.

She waited for the steps on the stairs and then hid her head in her hands. What was she becoming?

Florence looked up at the kitchen clock and did the calculations. It would be evening in Morocco now. Sebastian had not phoned for two days, and she was going mad with worry. Why had she let him go? What did she think was going to happen - a miraculous family re-union? Not likely. She walked around the immaculate apartment, running her finger-tips over the surfaces, hoping for some dust to wipe off. There was none.

It had been a hard twenty years, living here with no friends, no family. Apart from her son. The only home she had was with him. She looked down at the green space and the roads round it below her window. Why had she agreed to live here, all those years before? She thought of the mothers and children begging on Jean Medicin and knew why.

She stood up, grabbed her bag, willed the phone to ring one last time and then left for work at the gallery in Ville France sur Mer. As it turned out, the languages she had studied at university before she had had to leave prematurely had given her a job. There was very little human interaction there, but she was used to that. L'usure quotidienne would always drag her through the lonely days. Metro-boulot-dodo, as the French say.

CHAPTER TWELVE

Away

Alberto and Ann stood awkwardly beside each other scanning the board for train times. Alberto only had a small shopping bag for his money and lunch but he was still looking about himself for potential pocket pickers. He scanned the groups of people and stopped at three girls, one looking distressed. It was Rachel. He turned to Ann to see if she had spotted them too, but Ann was looking in her bag, and hadn't noticed. He stepped forward, wanting to help and then moved back; what was the point - he had nothing to offer. As usual.

Ann felt in her bag for her newly purchased Italian phrase book, hoping it would be enough to revive her rusty O level Italian. She craved a proper conversation, but this was a start. She looked again at the arrivals board.

"Our train's come up! Let's go!"

Alberto glanced over towards Rachel and her friends again, but turned away to keep up with Ann.

Ann started moving in the direction of the platforms, Alberto checked his cap and hurried to catch up, cursing his lack of English. He puffed beside Ann. She looked at him and frowned,

"Are you ok? Sorry, I always walk fast."

"You see Rachel?"

"No, is that them away?"

"Where?"

"Oh, I don't know, they never said."

Alberto shrugged his shoulders and gestured to the nearest carriage. All the English words he had practised with Rachel had deserted him already.

They got on to the train, and sat in silence the whole way to Antibes. Ann had been several times before, but always by herself. It made sense of her move to Nice - the very fact of Picasso having been there, the picturesque buildings, the rugged earth-coloured rocks, the bright choppy sea. She stared out the window, and watched as they passed Cagnes-sur-Mer and snaked round the coast to Antibes. Alberto was looking out the opposite side, until Ann pointed to the sea. He cleared his throat and leant over her to see out. Ann looked down at her phrase book and used it to name the landmarks as they passed them. Alberto clapped his hands when he heard his native tongue, and made a show of listening attentively to her.

When they got out there was a moment of indecision before

Ann announced they would go to the Picasso museum first. It didn't take long to see that Alberto was not a fan of modern art but he did his best to look interested.

"Let's have our lunch beside the sea, I know it's cold but it will be worth it." They both walked from the museum to the road by the edge of the sea. Ann started clambering over the rocks to find a better site, slowly followed by Alberto. They settled themselves and got out their picnics. Alberto looked down at his dry baguette and then Ann's tupperware container of Nicois salad.

"I brought two forks." Ann waved her cutlery at a red-faced Alberto, who broke his bread in two, gave half to her and took a fork.

"See, we're all set now."

"Bon appetit!"

They smiled at each other and tried not to cross forks as they tucked into Ann's salad. Ann gripped her sides to try and hide her shivering. Alberto noticed and put his coat around her. The clouds had separated, revealing a clear, February blue. There was a slight wind, making the waves break rhythmically against the rocks and sand of the nearby beach. Ann dug out a flask of coffee and they shared a mug. Alberto produced two pains au chocolat, quietly relieved he had at least brought something.

When they had finished Ann bent down to take off her slip-ons. She edged down to the icy water, lifted her long cream skirt and dipped her toes in. She gasped as the cold water grabbed her feet. Alberto watched her.

"You going to join me?"

He shook his head and held up his hands.

"I look," he smiled and tipped his hat.

Anyone who was walking by would have thought they were a long married, middle-aged couple out for their usual day by the sea, not an English spinster and an Italian widower who had only a handful of words to say to each other.

The funny thing was, each felt as though they had known the other for years.

"Have you got the tickets?"

"Bien sur, m'amie!"

Rachel, Laura and Francesca were standing at the entrance to the train station, their bags at their feet, Francesca's at least twice as big as the others, belying the fact they were only going to Florence for a few days. It was a cloudy day in February, but still she had her massive Ray Ban sunglasses on. Standing in her shadow, Rachel felt frumpy in her ripped jeans and Converse sneakers. Laura was unashamedly mismatched, with her knee-length floral gypsy skirt over khaki trousers, a red bandana round her head and massive hoop ear-rings. She handed out the tickets, dancing from foot to foot with excitement.

"Bonjour, mesdames. Des lunettes?"

He had snuck up on them unawares. Francesca shooed him away with her hand, Laura shook her head and started to move away. Rachel stood there, forcing herself to not run. She looked at the dark-skinned, poorly clothed man straight in the face - his eyes were darting around; he looked desperate. The one pair of glasses he was holding out to her didn't look too bad. She reached for her wallet, and before she could open it, his hand shot out and grabbed it before he ran off.

She called out eventually, but she was too late - he was long gone. Her heart was pounding, and her breaths were coming out in shallow gasps.

"Rachel! What happened?!"

Laura was standing beside her now, looking concerned.

"He took my wallet."

"Ah, le con!"

Rachel dropped down on her bag, and gripped her knees.

"Don't worry, there's bound to be a police officer nearby. We'll report it." Rachel stared at the tiled floor, and let people walk around her. After a few moments she looked up in a panic.

"My bank cards - I need to cancel them."

"Right. You find a phone box and I'll find the station guard.

Will you be ok? You look as white as a ghost."

Rachel nodded, and rummaged through her bag to find that bit of paper she had with all the vital phone numbers on it. She found it and ran over to the phone beside the ticket desk.

"Our train is in ten minutes! Hurry!"

Laura glared at Francesca and kept scanning the crowds until she saw two police men. She turned to Francesca.

"I am going over, you mind the bags." She shoved them at her and rushed over.

Rachel came back after five minutes, looked at Francesca's angry face and burst into tears. Laura arrived then, alone.

She put her arm round Rachel.

"Did you get them cancelled?"

"Yes, though it wasn't easy - you'd think getting a card would be tricky, not telling them one had been stolen. I think when they heard how upset I was, they sped it up." Her head was crying for her dad to be there, to sort everything out.

"We have to hurry now. You can talk in the train." Francesca pushed her sunglasses up onto her head, and flicked her hair back.

"You're a piece of work, Francesca. Look at her, she's traumatised!"

Francesca started lifting all the bags and didn't say a word.

Picking up on her urgency, the other two hurried after her. They got to the train just as its engine revved up and the doors beeped to signal closing. Francesca stuck her hand out, and held the door open for them to get in.

Rachel stopped once they were inside.

"What am I doing? I've no money for this. The card dad gave me for emergencies is in the flat."

Now that they were safely on the train, Francesca softened.

"Don't worry about that, I'll lend you money."

They found an empty side-carriage and started putting their bags up on the shelf above them, apart from Rachel who kept hers on her knee.

"I'm not risking losing this as well."

Laura patted her knee.

"So did you report it?"

"Well, I tried, but the police just shooed me away, saying it happened all the time, and there was no point thinking you'd get it back. They just said, 'that's Beurs for you' and walked off."

Rachel sighed. Francesca leant over,

"Now do you see what they're really like Rachel?"

Rachel didn't reply. She just stared out at the Cote d'Azur, racing past, blurring into a sparkling kaleidoscope of forest greens, shining whites and deep blues.

Once they had passed through Monte Carlo, they reached Ventimiglia and the train started to fill up with Italians. There were three spare seats in the girls' carriage, and it didn't take long before three very jolly middle-aged men shuffled in. They smiled at them and started to speak in French with thick Italian accents. When Laura told them they were from England, Brazil and Ireland, the men raised their hands and cheered. The people in Nice had never been like this - warm, cheerful, interested. The girls had a fantastic time, talking with the Italians for two hours until they got off at their stop.

"Well. Maybe we chose the wrong language and country? Italians are so much more friendly, aren't they?"

Francesca raised her eyebrows at Laura,

"You wouldn't have met your Jean then."

"Oh, I'll trade him in for an Italian lover any day." Laura gave a dirty laugh which made the other two giggle.

"Italians are definitely better than the Nicois."

"Have you met all Italians? Or everyone in Nice?"

"Oh Rachel, you and your diplomacy!"

After another three hours of travelling, they arrived in Florence. The sun was out, and the hills glowed with a unique, Tuscan light as the train approached the station. Francesca had put another layer of make-up on her already immaculate face, applied bright red stain to her lips, dabbed on what seemed like half a bottle of Dior perfume and brushed her jet black hair, tying it up in a severe high ponytail. Laura and Rachel just sprayed vaporised water over their faces and stuck some minty chewing gum in their mouths.

They left the train and stood to one side, deliberating.

"Where's your Lonely Planet? We need to find somewhere to sleep tonight."

Laura pulled out a dog-eared copy and flicked through until she found where she'd bookmarked Florence.

"There's a hostel ten minutes walk away."

"Ten minutes? I can't walk that far with this bag."

"Can I help, Señorita? I have a place - very close - I carry bag for you?"

There he was - another North African man, pushing his way into their little group, trying to take Francesca's bag from her.

Francesca snatched her luggage back and looked over to the others.

"Is your hostel in here?"

Laura pointed to her book.

"It is good. I show you. Come!"

The three looked at each other. It was getting dark, and a long walk through the city seemed as risky as going with this man. Laura was still looking through Lonely Planet in desperation. They started to walk after the man, sticking close together, crossing busy roads, passing a dubious, poorly lit park, and stepping over a pot-holed cycle path. He stopped outside a battered door and made a flamboyant gesture to tell them they had arrived. They hesitated at the door but he pointed up to the window on the first floor which had a cardboard sign saying 'hostel' in black pen on it. Exchanging worried glances, the girls climbed the flight of stairs and entered into what looked like student accommodation. He led them through the kitchen, where two women and another man were sitting. Rachel stared at the violin case propped up in the corner. Somehow it comforted her. At the other side of the kitchen there was a curtain. He pushed it back, and the ribbon one behind it to reveal a very make-shift shower. All the girls resolved to stay unwashed that night. Back through the kitchen, he showed them their room - two sets of bunk-beds covered with fairly clean-looking quilts. Bowing, he left them to it.

They stayed standing for a few minutes, uncertain.

"So. This is a bit crazy isn't it?" Laura whispered.

"I need the toilet. Can one of you come with me?" Francesca whispered too.

They all went - one stood outside the door, one inside while the other used the toilet. There was no lock, and the door did not click shut. They quietly got back to their room, jammed a chair against it and got ready for bed.

"I am not going to sleep this night."

"Good. You can keep watch then Francesca." Laura yawned, and shifted on the lumpy mattress to get comfortable.

Rachel pulled the covers over her head, as if that would keep her safe.

"We are finding that hostel in the morning, you two. I am not staying here for another night." Francesca was sitting cross-legged on her bed, with her torch pointed at the door.

They all whispered their agreement.

After their now well-practised toilet routine, the girls handed over the tiny amount of lire the hostel owner had asked for, gathered up their bags and headed out into the streets of Florence. He had been friendly and harmless to the end and they all felt partly ashamed of their mistrust of him but mostly, they were relieved.

"I can't believe we went with a total stranger to a place not even on the Lonely Planet, and stayed there overnight!"

Even laid-back Laura was in shock after the ordeal.

"Definitely not something I will be telling my father - he'd totally freak out."

"Oh well, just look at it as the first of many crazy things you've got up to this year, Francesca."

The girls all laughed and set off in search of breakfast. They passed through the bus station again, grabbing a bus-timetable on their way through. Soon, a croissant in their hand, they climbed on to the bus heading up the hill to the Piazzale Michel Angelo. It was another clear, sunny winter day, and the views from the top were astounding. After pausing for the obligatory photos with Michel and the views of the city and the famous Ponte Vecchio, they headed along the path to the Basilica San Miniato al Monte, an ancient church set higher still above Florence. While Laura and Francesca took more photographs, Rachel stepped out of the sunlight and into the darkness of the church. It took her a few moments to make anything out, but as her eyes adapted, she saw a group of monks clothed in white, filing into the front of the church. She stopped when they did, and found herself sitting down as wonderful choral sounds started to echo around her, surrounding her with a blanket of calm. She had never heard a Gregorian chant before, and would spend the rest of her life longing to hear it again. The monks held their notes in perfect harmony, and seemed oblivious to their earthly surroundings as they reached up to the heavens.

"Rachel - there you are! Are you crying?"

Rachel snapped out of her blissful state, and shushed Laura, pointing at the monks. Francesca arrived, and the other two put their fingers to their lips before she started speaking. Once they were finished, the monks silently filed out again, keeping their heads down, their hands held together in pious meditation.

When they had broken out into the sunshine Francesca and Laura started chatting straightaway, but Rachel didn't join in, still stunned by what she had just experienced. How could they talk, how could they not feel the need to stay in that church, savouring its silence?

"Well. Next stop: lunch, then Galleria Uffizi?"

"Let's do it!"

Once they had polished off their panini, they walked past the many statues and fountains in the square beside the museum. By the time the girls had reached the end of the queue outside the museum, they had had their fill of sculptures. It was a long wait to get in, and as usual Francesca was paying the price for her impractical footwear. The people in front of them were speaking an unfamiliar language, as were the people behind. Situated in a long corridor of stone arches and cloisters, the area created astonishing echoes of multi-national voices, bouncing off the ground and the walls, flying up into the space above them all.

"Well, well, if it isn't the three girls from Nice!"

Laura groaned, Francesca rolled her eyes and Rachel smiled.

"Nick! Are you following us?"

Nick lit his roll-up and muttered through it,

"Or are you following me?"

"Are you on your own?"

"Always, Rachel. That's how I roll."

"Do you want to come round with us?"

"Nah, I'll do it in a while. See y'all."

As Nick sauntered off, Rachel felt envy at his independence, his self-sufficiency. She wondered if she would ever be like that.

Once they got in, the gallery was overwhelming but clearly a must-see in Florence. This time, it was Francesca who lingered, forcing Laura and Rachel to sit down on the long benches and contemplate massive Botticelli paintings. Rachel remembered laughing over Matisse's nudes with Sebastian, and wondered how he was, where he was, what he would have said or done if he had been sitting there with her. Charlie wouldn't have sat, that's for sure.

Francesca lifted one mustard, navy and red patterned curtain and looked out.

"Maybe we should skip dinner - it looks like it's going to rain."

"No way, it's our last night. We are going out, whatever the weather."

All three girls had ironed their only dresses with the travel iron they'd found in the wardrobe, pulled out smarter shoes and made up their faces. Laura had used Rachel's wooden beads to tie her blond hair back for her, after slapping Francesca's comb and hair gel away. They all looked at each other, nodding approval. Francesca was striking in a dark red shoulderless satin two-piece, Laura was wearing a navy full-length floaty wrap dress with a chunky necklace and Rachel was in a white linen tunic, a deep sky-blue shawl round her upper arms. They had booked into a low-budget hotel for the last two nights, with the permission of Francesca's dad, and they had been able to relax after the stress of the first hostel.

As they stepped out and looked up at the heavy sky, they shrugged their shoulders and carried on. Francesca had put plastic bags over her precious Manolo Blaniks, much to the amusement of her companions.

"Well, I'll be the one laughing when you two are walking back with soaking feet."

They followed Laura's guide to Florence, running past brightly lit haut couture boutiques, 5 star hotels and Michelin starred restaurants. The cobbled streets were dark apart from the lights of the shops that ran alongside them but the girls were not bothered.

After a few minutes of rushing through the side-streets, shrieking at the rat who suddenly dashed across their path, Rachel stopped dead, causing the others to crash into her.

"Listen!"

It was the sound of a violinist playing a beautiful, haunting piece of music.

"Where is it coming from? Can you see who's playing?"

They followed the sound for a few minutes, but couldn't locate its source. Laura linked her arms through Francesca's and Rachel's.

"Come on - it's like a rainbow - we'll never find its end. And I'm starving."

As she spoke, the raindrops started to fall - slowly at first, and then in a clattering downpour.

The Moroccan violinist stepped further into the shadows as they went by, his music forgotten.

They all started to run, screaming and laughing with Laura leading the way to their restaurant, trying to keep her guide dry underneath one of her arms. So much for the careful make-up, the crease-free outfits, the smooth hair. But they didn't care, they just ran through the streets of Florence with abandon, and pure delight.

CHAPTER THIRTEEN

Revelations

"So where exactly are you living now?"

Cutlery scraped against gold-edged china. Francois motioned to show his mouth was full. Both his parents stopped, sat straighter in their plush chairs and waited for his answer.

"It's an apartment on Avenue de la Republique, near Place Garibaldi."

"Which letting agency are you with?"

"No-one, it's a mate's. Well, it was his grandad's but he's dead now."

His father sighed, and his mother tutted.

"Have I not told you before to always act responsibly? How do you even know this friend?"

Nobody was eating now.

Francois looked down at his salad, then started picking out the olives with his fingers.

"He's in the band," he answered with an olive shoved in the side of his mouth.

"Francois. We told you to stop that. What about your studies?"

He could hear his mum's voice creeping up to her trademark shrill bark. He looked at her - her blond hair rigid in its pony tail, her face tight with anger and frustration. There had never been any affection from this cold woman. Only a frantic need to keep up appearances. He rolled his eyes.

"My studies are fine - they can wait. It's the band that makes me money, not books."

His dad slammed his fist down on the white table cloth, making the plates and glasses rattle.

"We are paying for your education, you ungrateful boy. And you are squandering it."

He slowly folded his napkin and placed it beside his dish. Then he tucked his shirt around his bulging stomach and stood up.

"If you are not going to appreciate the education we are paying for, then we will stop."

He ran his hand over his balding head. This reflected badly on him as a prominent member of Le Front Nationale, the education secretary no less.

"Sit down, Henri. Let's finish our meal civilly at least. So tell me Francois, have you met any of your neighbours?"

Henri sat down with a grunt.

"I've only spoken to one so far. He's a Maghreb kid."

His mum sucked in her breath.

"Why did you speak to him? Why are they even there?"

She looked at her husband who shrugged.

"He's a good kid, mum. He wanted me to play my clarinet for him. I think he's a bit of a loner actually."

"Of course he is - he's Beur in a Nicois apartment. What's his name?"

"He *is* Nicois, mother. He's called Mahmoud, or Mohammed, or something like that."

"Mamoun. It's Mamoun isn't it?"

"Yes! That's him! Is he one of your students?"

She exchanged a tight-lipped glance with her husband.

"Unfortunately he is. A little dark child muddying the waters of my pure French class."

His dad grunted in agreement. Francois looked from one to

the other and felt his stomach turn over.

"He has every right to be there. You, on the other hand, have no right to decide anything!"

He pushed his chair back, feeling the heat rise around his face.

"Thank you for the dinner. I'm not staying here to share in your bigoted, hateful notions for another second."

He bowed to his open-mouthed parents.

"Good night."

As he walked out of the suffocating dining room, Francois heard his father commanding him to come back, and his mother expressing her self-righteous indignation. There was no turning back now, financed education or not. As he stepped out into the fresh air, he smiled to himself. So this is what independence feels like. He headed back to his new home with a spring in his step.

Rachel did her two lessons that day on auto-pilot, her mind racing with thoughts and fears over what she would find out about the mysterious Sebastian. Who did he live with? Why had he gone to Morocco, of all places? What secrets was he keeping from her, that made him go silent every time they were together? She knew there had only been three times, and Italy had kept her mind off him but still, she was dying to know more about this boy who had befriended her so readily, and then disappeared. Now that Charlie had chosen Phoebe, she had to make it work with her people here. She pulled her sleeve over the bracelet, and pushed it up her jumper as far as it would go.

She grabbed a quick espresso from La Dolce Vita, with the owner commenting on her newfound liking for the coffee she had covered with three sachets of sugar the first time she tried it. Holding the address and the map in her hand, she started off up the hill. She had decided to walk, as she might miss the street if she bussed it. As she climbed the hill, she noticed that the majority of the people she passed were dark-skinned. This must be close to the banlieue ghettos second generation North Africans were pushed into, away from the hostile eyes of the white Nicois.

She looked down at the scribbled address and checked the map. She crossed the wide street and took the next street on the left. There were two high-rise apartment blocks at the end and it seemed the address was leading her to them. She stuffed the map and address back into her bag as she passed a group of black adolescents sitting on the kerb smoking, listening to an angry rapper shouting from their ghetto-blaster. One of them looked up at her as she walked by, trying to pretend she knew where she was going. She heard a whistle and a lewd comment, but kept walking, praying she wouldn't be followed. The music began to fade as she walked away from the group. She knew the number, and the building name, so she hurried towards it, trying to keep herself from breaking into a sprint. The main door was locked. Beside it there was a board with about forty metal buzzers labelled with the apartment number on white stickers beside them. At this point, she could have turned around and given up. What on earth was she going to say, anyway? But the group on the street had seen her going over, and she had to hide her indecision. This was it. She looked up at the steady blue sky, steeled herself and pressed the button. Silence. She pushed it again, harder this time, and heard the harsh sound echoing. Nothing happened then, and she started to turn away.

"Allo?"

The intercom startled her. It was a woman's voice. She said something else, but Rachel couldn't make it out. Then the door clicked as the buzzer sounded. She was being let in. She stepped in to the foyer, located the flat number, saw it was on the fourth floor, and headed for the stairs. There was no way she was taking the lift - the building was too worn down for it to be safe, and there was no way she wanted to share it with someone. How do you conduct yourself in a lift in France? Do you speak? Do you smile? Yes, the stairs were safer.

By the time she had reached the fourth floor, Rachel's courage had all but left her. She knocked on the door and waited, shifting her bag up onto her shoulder, running her hand through her hair, straightening her blouse.

The door opened with the chain still on. One half of a woman's face looked out,

"Oui?"

Rachel took a deep breath,

"Bonjour, my name is Rachel. I'm from Northern Ireland and on my year out here in Nice. I met your son Sebastian a few months ago - we both taught at the same school. I was away but when I got back I found out that he'd gone away."

The chain was slid off, and the door opened wide. A light haired lady dressed in a faded rose skirt and twin-set stood aside to let Rachel in, smiling and talking too fast for her to understand. Then she stopped,

"Would you like something to drink? Lemonade? Coffee?"

Rachel hesitated.

"I'm really just here to see if he's all right. If he's coming back."

It sounded so ridiculous. She stood there, not knowing what to do next.

"Please - sit down and I will bring you something."

Rachel sat on the edge of the worn tweed sofa, and set down her bag, thinking what a fool she'd been to come there. The lady disappeared and came back with a jug of lemon water and some crisps in a bowl.

"I'm sorry for coming here. It's just - well - Sebastian was nice to me, and I didn't know he was going away and I don't have his number. The school secretary gave me this address. Sorry."

She started to stand up, when the lady put her hand up and started to speak English, clearly aware now of Rachel's lack of fluency in French.

"No, no. You are most welcome here. My name is Florence by the way. I'm glad Sebastian was nice to you. He's a good boy."

She reached over to pour the lemonade.

"It's been hard for him, growing up without a father, and just me to talk to."

"Oh, I'm sorry, I didn't know your husband had died."

Florence laughed.

"Oh, Youssef's not dead. And he isn't my husband."

Rachel stuttered an apology.

Sebastian's mother smoothed her skirt and, eyes down, told her story. It turned out she and Youssef had met at college, and had fallen in love. When she was nineteen, Sebastian was born. Shamed by his immoral deed, Youssef had run away, and was sent back by his family to his homeland in Tangiers, Morocco. He never came back. He did send some money from time to time, and enclosed his address.

Once she was finished, Sebastian's mother lifted her eyes expecting a frown, but Rachel's were full of sympathy.

"I'm so sorry. Thank-you for telling me." She gripped her knees,

"Can I ask you something?"

The lady raised her eyebrows.

"If he has never met his father, why has Sebastian gone to Morocco?"

Florence paused and sighed.

"Because he wanted to know who he was, where he belonged."

"Is he going to find his father?"

"Perhaps - that depends on Youssef. We wrote to him two months ago, and didn't get a reply so we just don't know."

"Wow, that's brave."

Florence shrugged her shoulders.

"Brave or foolish, we will see."

Rachel finished her water and started to stand up. As Florence stood too, she asked her,

"Why did you choose to live here?"

"It was Youssef's when he was a student here, and he gave it to me when he left. He posted a letter with the key through my door the night before he returned to Africa. I had nowhere to go - my parents were horrified by what I had done, and didn't want me to live with them any longer. Once I was here and Sebastian was born, it was the only place we could afford. The people here have always accepted me, and they've never given me any bother for being different. We have been happy here, Sebastian and I."

Florence and Rachel faced each other. They moved to kiss cheeks,

"He will be back when he has found the answers to his questions, or when his money runs out. I'm sorry, I can't give you a date."

"I understand. I hope he finds what he's looking for. I hope I'll see him before I go back home too."

"Well, I will tell him you were here, and you know where I am now, so all is not lost, my dear."

Rachel started for the door then. She stopped suddenly, and reached into her bag. She pulled out the tea glasses she'd got Sebastian for Christmas. She handed them to Florence,

"I got these for Sebastian at Christmas, but never had a chance to give them to him. Could you keep them for him?"

"Of course." Florence lifted them up to the light and smiled,

"What a lovely gift."

Rachel nodded and turned back to leave, hiding her sadness. When the door clicked shut behind her, she let the tears fall, crying for poor Florence, worrying about Sebastian, wishing someone was there to give her a hug. She ran back down the hill, searching for a phone box.

The money dropped down into the phone, and it started to ring.

"Hello?"

"Is that you Charlie?"

"Hello? Hello? Is there someone there? The line is bad. Hello?"

Click and then a dead ring tone.

Rachel put the phone receiver back on its hook and stood there, staring at it. Someone banged on the glass of the phone box, startling her out of her reverie. She stepped out and the man rushed in. She walked over to the bus stop and waited. Her heart thudded with loneliness.

By the time she arrived back at the apartment building, Rachel had summoned up the plan of eating chocolate, soaking in a deep bath, and looking at her photos of home. She did not want to see anybody, talk to anybody, or hear anybody. If she got into her studio, she could almost pretend she was no longer in France, hadn't heard Florence's heartbreaking story, and just had her own small problems to deal with.

"Madame Rachel! Madame! Je suis revenue!"

It was a very excited Mamoun, jumping up and down in her path.

"Papa and I were in Morocco, seeing my uncle and his family. We had so much fun, playing, eating, going to the beach."

Rachel froze.

"I didn't know you were in Morocco?!"

"Oui, bien sur!"

"Did you see anyone you recognised?"

Mamoun shook his head.

"I have never been to Morocco before, Madame, so how could I recognise anyone?"

Rachel laughed at herself - it was a long shot, and a ridiculous one at that.

"Well, you must tell me all about it on our next walk. It sounds like you had a great time there."

Mamoun cocked his head to one side, considering.

"I did have fun, Madame Rachel, but I am also very happy to be here again. Home is best, isn't it?"

"Oh yes, Mamoun. For most people home is best. Sometimes -"

She stopped herself, remembering she was talking to a child, not a world-weary grown-up.

Mamoun took her hand, and looked up, serious all of a sudden.

"I hope you see this as your home, Madame Rachel. Even if only for a little while?"

Rachel looked at Mamoun's kind face, and made herself smile.

"I will try to Mamoun, I will try for you."

Mamoun did a happy skip, and clattered down the stairs. Another door opened, and Rachel heard a man's voice speaking to Mamoun. She moved over to the top of the stairs to see who it was.

"Madame Rachel! Come and meet my new friend!"

Rachel heard a deeper voice telling Mamoun to be quiet. Her curiosity got the better of her and she went down to see for herself. A more unlikely pairing she had never seen - a small nine year old Maghreb boy standing next to a scruffy, long-haired, dour faced teenager. She looked from one to the other and raised her eyebrows.

"Je vous présente: Francois!"

Francois gave a nod and made a move to go back inside.

"Nice to meet you Francois. Have you only just moved in?"

He nodded again.

"He can play clarinet!"

Rachel lips formed an O but she couldn't think what to say to that. She looked again, and was sure he was the one who had been playing at the hostel below her balcony that first day,

"I think I already knew that."

She smiled, and felt Francois' eyes on her.

"You are not French?"

"No, I'm Irish. Just here as an English language assistant for a year, working in primary schools."

"Oh right."

Mamoun was looking from one to the other, mouth open with concentration.

"Well, I must head back in- things to do and all." He scratched his greasy head, looked awkward and headed back inside, swatting away an over-eager Mamoun from his heels.

Rachel let herself in to the studio, and turned the TV on, pushing all thoughts of home to the back of her mind. She had to turn away from that. No more browsing over photos, no more moping after planes. She only had three months left in Nice, and she had to make the most of them. She had to really *be* in this beautiful sun-drenched city. She had to shut out the calls of home and just enjoy being here.

The next day was bright, tempting Rachel out of the studio and towards the bus stop. She took the shuttle bus up the hill towards the fort. When it stopped at the top she got out and

walked the last stretch along the sandy, gravelled path through the dappled shade of deep green conifers. Soon the trees fell away to reveal an astonishing panorama of sprawling city and sparkling Mediterranean. Looking down she could see the small town of Ville Franche, the boats moored at another port, the unassuming houses lining short stretches of narrow roads. Towards the horizon she could spy a hint of land that she guessed was the island of Corsica.

She reached the fort and noticed a smattering of couples and small groups pointing their cameras at the view. Everyone else had companions but it didn't sting Rachel this time. She took a deep breath in and put her shoulders back feeling a newfound sense of independence settling upon her. She took a few photos, stood a while with her hands on her hips and then followed the uneven route down the other side of the hill to Ville Franche sur Mer.

She stopped at the roadside and searched her Lonely Planet guide for things to see in the small town. She wandered past the cannons above the harbour then headed in to the chapel of Sainte Elisabeth to look at some art. When she got inside and her eyes had adjusted after the bright sunlight, she spotted Ann and Alberto. They were staring at one of the paintings. Alberto was looking from it to Ann, confusion written all over his face. Ann was shaking her head in disbelief.

✢

"Are you alright, Ann?"

Ann didn't answer, she just pointed to the artist's signature on the bottom right hand corner of the painting. Rachel and Alberto both leant in to read it, but the name meant nothing to either.

They looked at Ann and waited for an explanation but at that moment her legs seemed to buckle and Alberto had to reach out to catch her. They both helped her out to the seats outside, and Rachel went over to the coffee stand to get some water.

They all sat there as Ann sipped her drink. Eventually she started to speak, slowly and deliberately, staring down at the cup,

"The painting was by my once fiance, Richard. He left for Spain many years ago, and has never been in touch. He could have been dead, for all I knew."

She gave a brittle laugh. Alberto was sitting with a puzzled look on his face, as the explanation passed him by. All he could understand was that Ann had a past, and it had come back to upset her. He remained silent, eyes down, body slightly turned away.

"We were insanely happy for a time, planning our wedding, imagining having children, going to see houses on the market and talking about making them into our home."

She wiped her eyes, then shook her head.

"But it wasn't to be - Richard didn't want to wait for my parents to die; he had the urge to travel, to paint, and when I made it clear I couldn't go, he just left."

She shrugged her shoulders.

"Wasn't worth it in the end."

Rachel watched Ann shutting her face down again, and knew she was done explaining. Ann reached over to Alberto,

"I'm sorry, Alberto."

He looked up, searching her face and then lifted his rough hand to hers. They stayed like that, unable to communicate further.

Rachel moved slowly away and set out for the train station, thinking about the transience of the label 'soul-mate'. Was there always only one?

CHAPTER FOURTEEN

The difficulty of belonging

Rachel was in a hurry. She'd slept in after staying up too late trying to get her head round what Ann had told her yesterday. She tossed and turned thinking about her neighbour and her lost chances, her plans all thrown away in the blink of a eye. She forgot about Alberto, and the hope he offered. Alberto.

He was standing outside his door, not moving, holding his key in the lock and staring at it blankly.

"Alberto! Are you ok?"

He jumped shocked out of his daze. He took the key out and turned to face Rachel.

"Sorry. Yes. Hello Rachel, how are you?"

He looked worn, wide-eyed and decidedly unwell. His thick, wiry grey hair, normally neatly combed back, was dishevelled. His face was haggard. He was more stooped than usual.

Rachel put her hand on the arm of his faded blazer.

"What's wrong. Alberto?"

He shook his head and lifted his hands in a sign of helplessness.

"It's Ann. I haven't seen her."

He rubbed his hand across his face.

"She's probably busy. I wouldn't worry."

"Yes. She needs time."

Rachel gave him a brief hug, and then took her leave. Instead of going down with her, he stayed standing at his door seemingly unable to make himself move. He looked over at Ann's flat, paused and then almost ran to knock on it. There was no answer. He tried again. Still nothing. He called to her,

"Ann, it is me, Alberto. I hope you are ok. I'm here. I'm here."

He sighed and left, cursing the re-surfacing of her old lover, cursing the cruelty of the past, and the way it had a terrible knack of ruining the present.

He was off today, and he knew exactly what he had to do.

He had to go back and see that painting again. If Ann's past would not leave her, then he would confront it himself,

213

whether that meant losing her or not.

The exhibition was still running that day. Alberto made a bee-line for the painting, took out a piece of paper and pen to write the artist's name down. Then he walked over to the fair-haired woman sitting on a chair in the corner of the room.

"Scusi?"

She looked up, and to his delight, answered in Italian.

"This name - do you have an address for him?"

She frowned at it, then went over to the desk on the other edge of the room and started flicking through a folder stuffed with papers, business cards and brochures. Alberto walked over and watched her. She lifted her finger,

"Aha!"

She took out a card, and showed it to him.

"He lives in Spain, but is visiting here during the exhibition. He will be here later today, with his students."

This was more than Alberto had expected. Much more. He hadn't wanted to meet the man, just make contact with him for Ann's sake. He thanked the lady and then stepped back, thinking. After minutes, he took his leave and went out onto the cobbled lane. He ducked into the darkness of Rue Obscure, the irony eluding him. He wandered up and down the winding streets. He leant on the railing eating the sandwich he had bought in the nearby street cafe. He looked out over the port. The waves were gently rocking the boats, and the horizon was an unsteady line. The sun sparkled on the masts, the water, the stone of the pier, his wedding ring. He thought about his wife Mia, and wondered what she would tell him to do. He lifted his hand to his mouth, and put his lips to the ring.

He knew what he had to do.

He wiped the crumbs from his mouth and cleaned his hands on the napkin then made his way back to the Chapelle Saint Elisabeth. When he entered, the Italian-speaking guide went over to him.

"He has been delayed. They will be here later this afternoon."

Alberto nodded, and looked undecided. Then he turned and made his way to the nearest seat.

He would wait.

It had been two hours sitting there. The plastic chair was curving in the wrong way, pressing into his back. His legs were getting clammy and hot, his beige trousers crumpled. He wished he had kept the bottle of water from lunch; his mouth was dry and his chest was tight. He mopped his brow with his handkerchief, and laughed a little. Wouldn't it be typical if he collapsed again, just before the wretched man arrived. The woman kept glancing over, perhaps he was wrecking the clean lines of the exhibition, maybe she too worried he would faint. There were visitors coming in and out in dribs and drabs. During the next quiet spell, she walked over to him, carrying a cup of water.

"Thank-you. It is very hot. Do you think he will be here soon?"

She shrugged.

"You know these artists, they take strange notions, and time-keeping is definitely not one of them."

They both laughed. The double doors swung open and a group charged in. Florence hurried over saying,

"Welcome. Is one of you Monsieur Richard Peterson?"

To Alberto's surprise, a teenage girl stepped forward.

"I am Mademoiselle Peterson, Madame."

The guide spluttered, trying to conceal her shock. Alberto leant forward.

"The painting displayed here is my late father's. I am here to represent him, with his former students."

"I'm sorry, I wasn't informed, I just assumed..."

"It is all right. He died a year ago, of cancer, and I promised him I would make sure his final work was displayed here, in Nice. He was very clear about that, said there might be someone here who would know him."

With that, the guide looked at Alberto and beckoned him

over. He stood up, stiff, and walked slowly over. She then told him everything that the girl had said. Alberto then asked her to tell the girl about his father's first love, that she was here in Nice, that she had seen the painting.

The daughter nodded, and showed no surprise. She embraced Alberto and thanked him.

"Tell your friend that this painting was displayed for her, that my father spoke of her often before he died, that he never forgot."

Alberto did not ask any questions about the girl's mother, or why his father had never returned to find Ann. What he had just been told was enough. It was not his place to push for anything more, and he wasn't sure his own heart would bear it anyway. He nodded his thanks and turned away. The guide caught up with him,

"Did you get what you needed?"

"Yes, thank-you, em..?" He raised his thick eyebrows.

"Florence."

"You helped me more than I had ever expected." He cleared his throat,

"It is hard, you know, not knowing much of the language everyone else is speaking." He looked into her eyes,

"Lonely."

Florence felt as though he was not just talking about himself when he said that.   Her eyes filled and she hurried away. Alberto watched her and shook his head sadly.

What a story he had accidentally come upon, what a difficult thing to share with Ann.   But he couldn't keep it from her now, he had to tell her.   He headed to the station, got on the train and made his way back.

She had been painting in a frenzy all night.   There were crumpled pages all over the floor, and her most recent canvas where she had included the child was now covered in angry, jagged orange and red brush-strokes.   The original golden and turquoise beach scene had been swallowed up by furious flames.   You could just about make out the little figure beneath, but he looked as though he might disappear any minute.

How dare Richard come back into her world?   Why had he not waited for her?   Why had he gone away without her?

She looked down at her paint-covered hands and put them to her face, an orange and red version of Edvard Munch's screaming man.

She sat like that for some time, closing her eyes to the carnage of her usually cheerful studio.   She heard Alberto calling to her but she didn't respond.   She didn't want to see his confused, hurt eyes today.   She stood up suddenly, grabbed her sketching kit and walked away without looking back. She started to tidy herself up.   She scrubbed at her face until it was red raw, changed out of her paint-covered clothes and left.

The sea had always healed her before; it was the only place she could think of running to. There was nowhere else anyway.

It was still early in the morning when she got to the beach. One rollerskating girl was gliding gracefully on the promenade, lost in the music of her walkman. She moved like a ballerina, fluid and rhythmical. Ann stopped and watched her, her artist's eye already awake to beauty again. The girl did one final arabesque then pirouetted to a stop, pulled her headphones off sleek, long black hair and smiled at Ann, showing a perfect row of white teeth and sparkling brown eyes. Ann considered asking permission to paint her, but she was already heading away from the beach. It didn't matter, she could sketch the image from memory. It was joyful, beautiful, different to all her other pieces. And it was of someone that was here, not another re-creation of memory and imagination.

She picked her way over the pebbles, taking care not to scrape her easel on the way. She stopped a few yards from the promenade, and set the easel so it was facing the land, not the sea. This was a new perspective. Ann smiled to herself, feeling the freedom of breaking from the norm. She mixed browns, blacks, and the coral shade of the girl's loose T-shirt. She hunted for the correct combination for the promenade and the roller boots. She stopped looking. She wasn't going to paint what she had seen just then. She was going to express how it had made her *feel*.

After half-an-hour, Ann had filled most of the paper. She didn't know whether it was good, but she was happy. She stepped back and looked around her. The beach was steadily filling with people. Then, only ten steps away from her, she saw them.

The days were getting longer, and the bite of the cold weather had been softened by a strengthening sun. Salma looked out her window and up at the blue. It was time to stop hiding and step out into the city again. Mamoun would meet her there. She didn't let herself think about what had happened the day of the riots, she just grabbed her bag, checked her hijab and went out. She ran down the steps to the front door, not stopping to consider that she was doing. It was early afternoon and the street was gently busy with delivery vans, a smattering of shoppers and the odd tourist. Nobody looked at her, or if they did, she didn't notice. Her dark clothes hid her like a shadow as she moved down Avenue de la Republique, across the square and along the street on the edge of Vielle Ville. She loved this part of Nice - the narrow streets sheltering her from the stares of others, the shops selling food she knew, people with the same colour of skin as her. Reaching the other side, she noticed an ice-cream kiosk and thought of Mamoun. A refreshing boule of passion fruit ice-cream was appealing, but she couldn't eat it in public, dressed like this.

By the time Salma reached the Promenade des Anglais, she was able to hold her head high, and look about her. The sea was calling to her - its deep Azur inviting her to sit close, watching the gentle, foaming waves breaking on the pebbles, making them glisten in the sun. She lifted her skirts and went down the steps to the beach. She picked her way over the stones, put her bag down and sat on it. She lifted her face to be kissed by the sun, and then turned her eyes to the sea. She knew not to look at her fellow sun-bathers, so was oblivious to them taking furtive glances at her. She was alone, but felt no fear. She looked at the sweeping beach, the airport on one side, the castle hidden in a mix of deciduous trees on the hill at the other. A strong feeling of fondness rose up in her chest. Why would she not feel as though she belonged here? Why would she doubt her right to it? Omar had brought her to this bright place, and right at this moment, she was glad of it.

"Maman!" A little finger tapped her on the shoulder. It was her son. She reached up and pulled him into her arms.

"I didn't see you coming, Mamou!"

She kissed his head and let him go so he could sit next to her.

"How was school?"

"She was all right today."

Salma smiled to herself -school and the enjoyment of it depended entirely on the unpredictable moods of Madame Tessier. On a good day, she was too pre-occupied to notice her pupils, or too happy about some personal success to bother herself telling anyone off, On a bad day, well...

"I saw your ice-cream shop on my way here."

"Did you get one?"

Salma shook her head.

"Well, which one would you pick?"

"Oh, that's easy. The passion fruit flavour."

Mamoun shook his head,

"No no no. It has to be chocolate! Every time!"

Salma grabbed him again, and tickled him. He giggled and squealed.

People were staring now, but the pair were oblivious. Once they had calmed down, they sat side by side, hand in hand and looked out at the sea.

"Nice is a good place for us, isn't it Maman?"

"Yes, I think it might be Mamou."

"Excuse me, Madame."

A tall dark figure stood between Salma and the sun. She froze, recognising the uniform. Not again, please. She got to her feet, unsteady on the stones and aware now of other people looking at her, of Mamoun's frightened, puzzled face.

"Yes, officer."

"You must take off your niqab."

"But I - "

Salma felt the sweat start to trickle down between her

shoulder blades and prickle her face. Mamoun's eyes were wide. People weren't staring any more, they had all looked away. The waves were still breaking, the sea and sky were still blue, but Salma was far from the scene now - looking at it as though from a great distance.

"Please, Monsieur, I must wear this. It is important in my faith."

The officer spat on the pebbles beside her.

"You and your religion do not belong here. Take the scarf off."

Salma lifted her shaking fingers to find the edge the head covering. She was fighting the tears that were rising from her throat, looking at her little boy all the time, willing herself to be strong for him. She had just started to reveal her face when somebody else came over.

"What is all this? Salma, are you OK?"

It was Ann, her easel under her arm, a paintbrush pointed at the police man. She had an angry, determined look about her.

"I have just asked that this woman take off her niqab as it is not tolerated here. It is putting the other beach-goers off, making them uneasy."

Ann bristled.

"I am an English lady, a white woman, and I certainly do not feel remotely uneasy by a woman adhering to the customs of her faith. You show no respect, Officer. You should be

223

ashamed of yourself."

The officer started to take a step back, stared down by a furious Ann. He held his hands up, turned on his heel and stumbled away.

Ann went over to Mamoun and patted him on the head. Salma fixed her scarf and cleared the shakiness out of her voice.

"Thank-you, Ann."

Ann nodded and waved the thanks away with her paintbrush.

"Are you heading home now?" She looked from one to the other.

They looked at each other, and said together,

"Definitely."

Ann nodded decisively, picked up her things and led the way. Salma's eyes were back down, her head was bowed again. Only Mamoun saw the sympathy in the faces of those they passed. Not one face was hostile. He would tell Maman that later, when she felt better. It is never everyone. He would tell her.

Rachel reached her front door, and lifted her hand to unlock it.

"Madame Rachel!"

Oh no. People. She didn't want to speak to anyone, she just wanted to go up to her bed and hide for a while.

Mamoun caught up with her and stopped to catch his breath. She saw Salma and Ann, an unlikely pairing, walking slowly after him. Curiosity piqued, Rachel waited for them.

"There was a police man. On the beach. He was asking Maman to take off her hijab, and she didn't want to and then Ann came and she didn't have to any more and we came home. We didn't get ice cream."

Rachel glanced at Salma, and saw the same face she had seen on the day of the riots. Not again, surely? Ann looked as if she had just come from a battle-field - her once dark now greying hair was hanging in straggles over her flushed cheeks, her eyes were angry slits, her red lips were in a tight line and her easel was slipping under her arm. She had a paint-brush in one of her hands, angled like a dagger, poised for the deadly plunge. It was a sight to behold; a colourful, Boadicea-esque white woman standing bodyguard to a timid North African lady dressed completely in black.

Rachel crouched down and got level with Mamoun.

"Are you ok?"

Mamoun nodded, holding his two fists to his eyes for a moment. Rachel stood up again and looked over to the two women.

"Do you want me to take Mamoun for a little while?"

Salma's eyes teared up again and she couldn't speak. They all stood on the pavement outside the grubby apartment block, waiting for a decision. People were stepping around them, looking irritated at the obstruction. The shadows on the street were lengthening. Horns blared in the perpetual traffic jams as drivers tried to get home after their day's work. Life was carrying relentlessly on, oblivious.

It was Ann who broke the awkward silence.

"I think that is a great idea, Rachel. Just so you can freshen up, Salma? Mamoun will go with Rachel, I will take my easel in and try to salvage the splodges. Unless you two want to come in and see my house?"

Ann winked at Mamoun.

"I may have chocolates, and a blank canvas just waiting for a nine year old to cover it in colours."

Mamoun looked from one woman to another, but mostly at Salma.

"Maman?"

"You can go, Mamoun. Just be back for dinner, OK?" Salma's voice came out higher than usual.

Ann passed her easel over to Mamoun who took it with a surprised smile. All of a sudden the tension and bad memories had abated, brushed away by her simple act of kindness. As they all climbed up the steps inside, the clatter of their feet and Mamoun's excited chatter echoed happily around them. Only Salma was silent, her clothes concealing her tear-stained face, her shaking body. She went in to her apartment without a word, closely watched by Ann and Rachel. They frowned at each other over Mamoun's head, but knew better than to say anything.

"So! Here's my home, Mamoun!"

Ann flung open the door and Mamoun stood on the threshold, his dark, wide eyes moving around the space, taking it all in - the rag rugs scattered over the wooden floor boards, the photo-less mantelpiece, the half-open doors to her cluttered, sun-lit studio tempting you in with numerous blue paintings propped up against the walls.

He spotted her gramophone and slowly walked over to it, looking over his shoulder to check it was OK with Ann. She gestured with her hand,

"Go on, have a look."

"What is it?"

Ann got beside him and showed him how it worked. After a short moment, Mozart filled the apartment. Mamoun clapped his hands. He pointed to the studio,

"Can I see?"

Ann hesitated.

"Why not? Just don't touch anything."

She caught her voice going shrill, and cleared her throat, following him in. Rachel sat down on the sofa, leaving them to it. She listened as Mamoun exclaimed over the paintings, asking questions about each one.

"Who is that, Madame?"

Rachel leant forward to listen. There was a long pause, and the sound of Ann moving things around.

"Is he your husband?"

Ann laughed,

"No, no. He's an old friend, that's all."

"An important friend I think. He's in nearly every picture - although he is very small in this one, is that him too? When he was little like me?"

There was a pause before Ann said in a falsely cheery voice,

"Why don't I show you your canvas, and you can have a go at painting?"

"Ok, Madame. I hope I meet your little friend sometime."

Ann took a shaky breath,

"Oh, you can't."

"Why not?"

"Because."

"Does he live here? Is he in England? Maybe he is big now?"

There was silence, then the sound of Ann moving around, clattering brushes. Mamoun was waiting. Ann cleared her throat, dropping to a whisper.

"The thing is, Mamoun, he never actually was a real person."

Rachel realised she was standing up, craning to hear. Suddenly Ann walked out and caught her. Both of them had tears in their eyes - Ann because she knew, Rachel because she remembered their conversation in Ville Franche sur Mer. Ann shook her head, unwilling to talk about it.

"Tea?"

Mamoun's little voice called out from the studio,

"And chocolates?"

Rachel and Ann laughed, grateful for the deflection.

A key was turned in the door. Salma leapt up and rushed into the kitchen, grabbing a spoon to stir the curry.

"Hello my love, you're back early." She hoped he wouldn't look at her, or notice how her voice sounded hoarse from tears.

Omar pulled out a chair and sat down, his faded shirt

slipping off one shoulder, his face craggy with too much sun.

" I've sold more than enough glasses this afternoon so I decided to call it a day."

Salma forced a smile and nodded. Omar frowned, getting up and moving towards her,

"What has happened? Where is Mamou?"

"He is with Ann and Rachel."

"Why?"

"They asked him."

"And not you?"

"They wanted to give me a chance to rest after," she caught herself and turned back to the saucepan.

"After what? What happened to you?"

His voice was getting louder, and he was gripping her arm too tightly.

"Oh, they wanted me to take off my hijab again. But Ann was there and she stopped him."

Omar's face darkened.

"Again? Who is them?"

Salma stopped stirring and led Omar back to the chairs. They both sat down and Omar listened, trying not to interrupt as Salma told him in a level voice about the beach that day, and the riots in December. When she was finished Omar slammed his hand down on the table and stood up, his chair clattering behind him.

"How long do we have to bear this? How much are they going to hurl at us just because of our race, our religion, our culture? You have the right to cover your face, you have done nothing wrong, you are not a criminal!"

"Please stop. Please." The tears came again, and Omar took her in his arms.

"I'm so scared, Omi. I can't go outside again. And Mamou saw it this time. That's why he's gone to our neighbours. What will we do? Things are getting worse, not better."

Omar held her more tightly and looked over her head, thinking.

Eventually he broke the silence.

"We don't have the money to go back home. I suppose we could save somehow, but that would take years. I can't ask Youssef again - his paying for me and Mamoun to come visit was too much to begin with."

"No, we have to make the most of life here. I will stop wearing my hijab. That might make it easier."

Omar hit the table again as he shouted "No!"

Salma stepped back, trying not to cry again.

"I'm just trying to fit in. For our son's sake."

"Has Mamoun ever complained about you dressing as Muslim women are commanded to do?"

Salma shook her head.

"Well then, you continue to wear it, and if anyone gives you trouble again, I will take a complaint straight to the Chief of Police."

His eyes glittered with anger as he spoke.

Salma lifted his hands in hers.

"There are good things here too - good people and Mamoun is happy. Maybe by the time he is an adult, everything will have got better."

Omar set his mouth in a tight line, biting back the accounts of worsening racism in the city. Maybe she was right. He hoped she was.

He had bought an English/Italian dictionary with his money for food that day. He sat up late into the night writing down the key words, deliberating over how to tell her - with a note? A conversation? Taking her to the multi-lingual lady at the gallery? He looked down at his handwriting and made a face. Checking all the words for the hundredth time, he folded the paper in two, combed his hair and walked over the landing. This time, Ann opened the door after the first knock. She looked much better than the last time he'd seen her, and had multi-coloured paint smudges all over her face, her hands and her smock. Her hair was falling down over her shoulders. Her eyes were bright and her cheeks were flushed.

"Alberto, good morning!"

Alberto nodded then raised his eyebrows towards the inside of Ann's flat.

"Yes, yes, come in!"

He walked to the kitchen table, pulled out a chair and waited for Ann to sit down with him. Once she had come back from shutting the door on a very cluttered studio, she came over to sit opposite him. Still saying nothing, Alberto pushed the folded note over to her. She frowned at him,

"Read it. Please?"

Ann opened the page and started to read. Alberto leant towards her, watching her face. She was silent right to the end of the letter, then looked up at him.

"You met his daughter?"

Alberto nodded.

"He died?" Ann's voice shook, and as Alberto inclined his head, she began to cry. He reached across and held onto her arms, not saying a word.

The tears continued for a brief moment, until Ann wiped her face, and started to speak.

"You went yesterday and found all this out? How did you understand it all?"

He pointed to his words 'Italian speaker'.

"Was she nice, his daughter?"

"I think yes."

"So he met someone, and they had a child."

She let out a shaky sigh.

"Of course, he was terrible at being alone. One of the reasons why I couldn't quite believe that he would have the gumption to leave me. He had the life I thought we would have together. A family. A home."

Alberto sat and let Ann talk it through with herself. He didn't have the words to answer back. Eventually, she remembered he was there. At that point, he stood up to go. He was at the door when he heard her behind him,

"You did all this for me." Alberto froze, his hand on the door handle and answered her without turning round.

"Ovviamente mia cara."

✣

CHAPTER FIFTEEN

A discovery

Rachel had asked Ann, and then Salma, if they would like to come to the beach with her but they had both made their excuses - Ann because she was in the painting zone, Salma because, well, she hadn't actually had a reason but had looked terrified at the thought. It was probably too soon after the last time. As she was about to walk away from Salma's door, a man's voice called to her,

"I am going to the beach now. I can walk with you."

Salma froze, seeing Rachel's surprise. A dark-haired man came up beside her. He opened the folded bag he was carrying and showed Rachel a cluttered display of sunglasses. She automatically stepped back and shook her head. The man recognised the response and quickly put the display behind his back.

"Rachel, this is my husband Omar. He sells sunglasses most of the day, and works as a cleaner in school the rest of the time."

Rachel flushed,

"Oh right. I'm sorry. Nice to meet you, Omar."

She put her hand out, then put it in her pocket again.

They all stood looking at the floor, until Salma spoke,

"Omar, you need to go. Rachel, you don't need to walk with him, if you'd rather not."

"No, no, that's fine, if we're both heading the same direction then of course…"

Omar flashed a smile, stepped out beside Rachel and let her lead the way down the stairs.

As they walked along Avenue de la Republique Rachel noticed that at least four different people had crossed the road before they got to them. Omar did not pass comment so she tried to pretend she hadn't seen it. The silence between them was pressing in. She knew it was now or never. She opened her mouth and dove straight in.

"So, you are from Morocco?"

Omar kept striding forwards.

"Yes, that's right."

"And your brother lives there?"

Omar turned his puzzled face to her.

"He does."

Rachel's next words came out in a high-pitched rush,

"This is a silly question, but is his name Youssef?"

Omar stopped, making the woman walking towards him jump sideways.

"Why do you ask that?"

Rachel stopped too and gave a nervous laugh.

"I'm sure it's just coincidence, but I may know his son."

Omar looked puzzled,

"His son is in Morocco. How could you know him?"

Rachel shook her head,

"His other son." The words hung there. Omar shook his head in near disbelief, but Rachel saw his face considering it, as though this was not the first time he had wondered. He laughed.

"Are you saying that my brother has a child here, in Nice?"

What had she done? This was too huge for a pavement conversation.

"Will we go get an espresso? I'll buy a pair of your sunglasses to make it worth your while."

Omar stood still, thinking, then he headed across to the nearest cafe. Rachel followed him even though he hadn't turned back to invite her.

Omar sat down and waited for Rachel to order. They held onto their tiny coffee cups and Rachel started to talk about Sebastian. At the beginning Omar was looking away unconvinced but the longer she talked, the more still and attentive he became.

"So, do you think he might be your brother's child?"

Omar didn't answer. Rachel held out Sebastian's mum's number and address. He stared at it, then snatched it and put it in his pocket.

"I must work now."

His face was closed as he stood up. Rachel remained seated, unsure what to do, cursing herself for saying anything at all. He bowed to her, reminding her of Mamoun, and then walked away, hitching his satchel over his shoulder, seemingly oblivious to all the people rolling their eyes and turning their backs to him.

Rachel opened a sugar sachet and poured it straight into her mouth. What had she done?

✢

Francois threw the tennis ball against the wall behind his bed for the tenth time. He looked up at the ceiling and chose a character for the biggest mould patterns, like they were clouds in the sky.

He sat up. This was getting beyond acceptable: he was bored, he was broke, he had nowhere to be other than the jazz club in the evenings, and now he was naming damp patches. He pushed himself up from the bed and decided to go outside. At least there, there would be people, sunshine and conversation, even if it wasn't with him. He pulled on his battered Converse, tucked his hair behind his ears and opened the front door. He quickly shut it again. The Italian man was knocking on one of the doors and there was Rachel coming down the stairs. He heard muffled voices as they spoke to each other, and then the sound of retreating footsteps. He was avoiding her now he guessed she had met his mother. He was curious as to what she thought of her, but he was already expecting the worst. Although, the fact that Rachel was white would probably work in her favour, even if she wasn't French. It was hard to tell.

Anyway, he needed to go to the beach, so he'd wait until the coast was clear and then sneak out. He opened the door again, peered through the crack, and made his way out to the street. He dug into his pockets and found some Francs from the gig the night before. He side-stepped into the boulangerie and bought breakfast. Then he took the next left turn and headed in the direction of the port. No point going straight to the beach when he had hours to kill.

He was on the pebbles in half an hour. Somehow it's hard to saunter when you're walking alone. He sat down and regretted not bringing anything with him. How long could he look like he was busy when he'd nothing to read, or listen to? He took off his jumper, rolled it up and laid his head on it. He put his arm over his eyes to shield them from the sun and fell asleep.

He awoke when someone stepped over him. He sat up to protest. It was a Maghreb, selling sunglasses. He swore at him then watched as he walked away as quickly as you could on loose stones. Wait, was that the guy who lived in his building, Mamoun's dad? He squinted after him, but couldn't tell. He chuckled to himself - they were hard enough to distinguish from the front, never mind the back. And now he sounded like his mother. He sighed. When had she become like that - so bigoted and cruel? Was it dad's fault? He'd certainly not helped. If he was speaking to her right now, he'd ask her. But they hadn't contacted each other since he'd stormed out. The sudden lack of funds arriving in his bank balance was the only sign that they were aware of his existence.

It was a hot, slow day pushing his wares, getting rebuffed a thousand times more than making a sale. As he trudged along the beach, nodding to the odd like-minded sales person, he considered what Rachel had told him. Youssef had made a sudden U-turn just before he left. It had always been the plan that he would join the family business and stay in Nice but when he told Omar at dinner one night, his parents had not questioned it, not shown any surprise. Why hadn't they? Had they known his reasons? Surely they would make him stay and pay for his wrongdoing, not send him away? Youssef had said nothing this time when they were together. But perhaps he hadn't had the chance. No, he could have said, and he'd had a hundred chances before then to tell him. Omar kicked the stones. A middle-aged woman sitting close by gasped. He lifted his hand and smiled in apology.

He laughed to himself. It was all a big mistake, there's no way Youssef would have made a girl pregnant and then fled. He had always been awkward, gawkish, not popular with girls of his own race never mind the French ones. Omar shifted his bag, stepped over a vaguely familiar teenager sleeping on the stones and started his age-old sales pitch to a group of over-weight tourists. It was the perfect target - three middle-aged American ladies, husbands not nearby to tell them not to be taken in by the fake labels. They exclaimed over the glasses, and the low price. Omar walked away with three less sunglasses, thirty more francs.

He looked out to the sparkling sea and thought of Morocco, of his supposed philanderer of a brother. Ha! It was an impossible story. Life never shifted to that extent. It couldn't.

Later on that day, when his feet were weary, he decided to take a bus home. As he took his seat, a memory of the last time he was on a bus hit him with force.

It was the boy, following the girl who turned out to be Rachel, and looking so very like someone.

Like his brother.

✛

Rachel took a swig of water and swirled it round her mouth to wash off the sugar sticking to her teeth. She watched Omar walking away, people side-stepping and keeping their eyes straight ahead, to avoid all contact with him. She thought about Madame Tessier telling Mamoun to wash his beautiful brown skin away, the police man telling Salma to take off her hijab, the begging woman with her child on the pavement. She thought about her instant fear when she had seen the Maghreb man at the airport, when Omar had offered to walk with her to the beach. There had been one incident where her fears had been confirmed, when her wallet was stolen. But every other time, nothing had happened. It was terror of the other. But, this year, that was her too - a white-skinned, English speaking student who would rather have a bowl of Shreddies than a croissant, a cup of tea than an expresso, a bag of chips than a plate of oysters.

She packed up, deciding to just head back to the flat rather than risk an awkward encounter with Omar on the beach. It was clouding over anyway and she was getting goose-bumps sitting there out of the sun. She scraped her chair back, making the pigeons scatter. She would go to Place Massena and watch the fountains for a while.

It didn't take long to get there. There was a smattering of tourists climbing onto the grey stone edges of the fountain, posing for photographs, their hands over their eyes as they squinted into the bright sky. A few Maghreb's loitered with nothing better to do. Rachel fished her music from her bag and headed for the nearest empty bench. Just as she neared it, somebody else got there first. She glanced at them, looked for another place to sit then glanced back. Was that Sebastian? He was looking straight at her but not waving. She hesitated, unsure. Then she found herself walking over to him.

He was more tanned, his hair needed cut, his clothes needed

ironed.

"Hi Sebastian."

He smiled then, for an instant. Rachel stayed standing, waiting. After an awkward moment he stood up and kissed her on each cheek, scraping his stubble against her face. They stepped back from each other.

"How are you?"

Sebastian shrugged, looking shifty.

"I'm good. You?"

Rachel burst out,

"You didn't tell me you were going away. I looked for you, even went to see your mum. I had no idea your dad was from Morocco, Sebastian. Why didn't you tell me? Why didn't you tell me any of it? I told you about my family."

Rachel's voice sounded shaky. She felt her face getting hot, her eyes getting wet.

Sebastian looked at the ground between their feet.

"That's exactly why I didn't tell you. Rachel, your family is straightforward, normal. Mine...well, it's complicated."

He motioned for her to sit down.

"I went to Morocco because I have never met him. I wanted to see him, look at him, ask him why he left my mum on her own."

His dark eyebrows came together.

Rachel held her breath, waiting for the end of the story.

"He was never in, or, he never answered the door or the phone."

He let his breath out slowly.

"He must have seen me, or heard my messages. But he didn't want to see me."

Rachel said nothing, just reached out to touch Sebastian's knee.

"So that was that. The trip was a waste of time. I will never know that part of who I am. I will never belong there, or here."

He put his hand over Rachel's.

"Watching you smile when you talked about home, seeing how much you missed it, I just wanted to find out where *my* home really was. Now the decision has been made for me, by my father. I will never quite fit in anywhere, knowing that I am part Nicois, part Beur."

"But you will always be Sebastian." She checked to see how that had gone down, and saw him look down to hide his eyes. Then, heart pounding in her ears, she took a breath and said it,

"I think I might have found some of your family. Here."

Sebastian frowned, and Rachel blundered on.

"They are a Moroccan family living below my studio- there's Mamoun, he's nine, Salma his mum and Omar, his dad. And possibly your uncle."

Sebastian turned to face her, scowling.

"Do you think that all North Africans are related? That we're just one big family? What you're telling me is impossible Rachel."

"Omar has a brother who went back to Morocco shortly before you were born. His name is Youssef."

There was the second dumbfounded, echoing silence of Rachel's day then. She inwardly congratulated herself on single-handedly upending the lives of two men in the space of an hour.

A teenage boy trundled past on his skateboard. Two American girls walked by, eating panini, talking loudly. Two planes flew slowly overhead, one nearing the airport, one leaving. A group of teachers were sounding klaxons and chanting their protest slogans one street behind them. Sebastian said nothing. He stood up and walked away without saying goodbye, his hands clenched into fists at his sides, his shoulders rigid.

Rachel stayed sitting on the edge of her seat, disappointment beating its heavy drum in her chest. This was not the way she had imagined it going. Actually, she had not expected to see Sebastian again, let alone tell him things that would turn his whole world upside down. She should have just left well alone. Possibly…

Rachel turned her music up, leant against the back of the bench and watched the clouds growing, swallowing up the blue.

Who's to say where the wind will take you/ Who's to know what it is will break you/ I don't know which way the wind will blow/ Who's to know when the time has come around/ Don't wanna see you cry/ I know that this is not good bye

Omar nodded to Alberto as he passed him on the stairs. The Italian was hovering outside the flat opposite, but Omar had heard him knock a minute previously, and the door had not been opened. As far as he knew, that door belonged to the English lady, but he had never spoken to her, or seen her close-up. Maybe she was avoiding him, and now the Italian too.

Salma was in the kitchen, helping Mamoun with his homework, or possibly Mamoun was helping her. They both looked up and Mamoun ran across to hug him.

"You're early today."

Salma raised her eyebrows at him.

"Yes. I had sold enough."

"How was the walk with Rachel? Did you speak to her?"

Omar busied himself clearing up Mammon's abandoned pencil case.

"What did you talk about?"

"Nothing interesting, just this and that."

Salma groaned,

"Men! You never remember anything!"

Omar shrugged, then turned to read Mamoun's homework.

"Were you nice to her, Omar? She's a long way from home."

Omar lifted up the page of Mamoun's French nouns.

"What does this one mean, Mamou?"

Mamoun laughed, then saw his father was serious.

"That word is 'lapin', meaning rabbit." Mamoun said the word in Arabic and looked up to see the light dawning on Omar's face.

"But tell me, when would you have the occasion to use that word in normal conversation?"

Mamoun wrinkled his face, thinking hard.

"Well. If I saw a child younger than me getting excited and jumping up and down I would say, 'Look at that rabbit.'"

Salma and Omar laughed.

"You are never going to use that word, my son."

"But I might. You never know. Maybe when I grow up I will look after rabbits as my job."

Mamoun marched out of the kitchen towards his room.

"He is going to get farther than me, that's certain. His French is close to fluent. And he is ambitious. We are doing something right there."

Salma put her hand on Omar's arm to note her agreement.

"So Rachel told you nothing?"

Omar got up from his seat and peered into the tagine.

"That dinner smells delicious, my love."

Salma rolled her eyes and sighed. He was never going to tell her anything.

CHAPTER SIXTEEN

New bonds, old ties

As he had done every day since telling her what he had found out in Ville Franche, Alberto knocked on Ann's door and waited. She had not let him in yet. He had raged at himself for interfering, for not letting things take their own course, for telling her such painful news. He wondered why he had took it upon himself to go back that day. Was it curiosity? Wanting to win Ann's attention for some masculine pride reason? Was it the act of a friend? Or was it love? Alberto touched his ring, and felt his heart ache. His head was down, and he started to turn to go back inside. There was the sound of Ann's lock opening, and then there she was. She stood, her arms by her sides. Alberto grabbed them, and lifted her hands up, searching her pale face. She had been crying and there were purple circles beneath her eyes. Her skin looked as though it hadn't seen the sun or fresh air for days.

"La plage?"

Alberto raised his eyebrows in question. The sea was the answer today, the beach would help, he was sure of it. Ann considered the proposal for a moment, then nodded. Alberto let his breath out, and she laughed.

"Just give me a minute." She ran inside to get ready, and Alberto remained on the other side of the door. He took out his comb and smoothed his bristly hair, tucking his blue shirt into grey linen trousers. When Ann came back, dark glasses covered her sad eyes, and a straw hat with a orange scarf tied around it lifted her worn out face. She was wearing the shoes she had on the day they went to Antibes. Alberto crooked his arm and offered it to her. She slipped her hand onto it, and they climbed down the stairs. They heard Rachel's door opening and then saw her leaning over the banister, giving them a cheery wave, but waiting there, giving them their time together. Mamoun and Salma came hurrying up past them. Mamoun stopped and opened his mouth to talk, but Salma just smiled at the pair and grabbed his arm to pull him past. Alberto and Ann shared a look, bewildered, but happy not to have to talk to anyone other than each other.

They walked side by side in companionable silence, letting the other groups walking towards them step aside for them. Ann nearly tripped over an uneven paving stone. Alberto reached out and took her arm. He didn't let go for the rest of the way. She didn't ask him to. They climbed down the steps to the pebbled shore, found a less crowded space, and sat down. Ann let out an audible sigh and lifted her face to the bright sky.

"Ok?"

Alberto asked the one question he knew they both understood.

Ann nodded and attempted a smile. Alberto put his hand to his chest and looked into her eyes.

"Mi spiace. I am sorry."

He knew his eyes were watering and his voice was weak, but he had to say it. He'd been waiting for days to get the chance to.

Ann looked at him, considering her next move. Suddenly he felt her arms around him, her lips on his cheek, his forehead, his mouth. She started to move away, apologising, but Alberto lifted his arms and pulled her back. People were walking past them - children with ice-creams, tourists with bum bags and cameras, Maghrebs searching for a sale, couples half-walking, half-kissing, teenage boys loping over the stones towards Promenade des Anglais with skateboards in their hands, young girls in short skirts whispering and giggling, elderly women stepping at their own slow pace - but the couple did not care. This was their story, their unremarkable, wonderful beginning.

❖

"Hello Salma. How are you?"

Salma jumped at Rachel's voice behind her. She was standing fishing out her keys, a bag of groceries slung over her arm. Rachel looked at her lustrous black hair, her open face. Salma flushed at the attention - she had hoped to not see anyone looking like this, particularly her husband.

"You look nice. I had no idea…"

Rachel stopped when she noticed her neighbour's discomfort.

"Thank you. I must be getting on - dinner to cook."

She turned back to her front door, and shakily selected the right key. Rachel tried to edge past, then when the keys clattered to the ground, she stopped to pick them up. As her and Salma's hands met, they glanced at each other, and Salma spoke,

"Would you like to come in?"

"I don't want to put you to any trouble. I have a free morning, so I'm just going out to get some bread for my lunch."

Salma's eyes lit up.

"I have bread. Please come eat with me."

She opened the door and hurried in. Rachel followed her and watched as she dumped the groceries on the table and grabbed a scarf to expertly cover her hair. As soon as her head was hidden again, Salma seemed more at ease. She looked more like herself now, Rachel realised. She sat down on a kitchen chair as Salma sliced the crusty baguette and spread apricot jam on top. The espresso maker was already hissing on the gas hob, and two plates were set out on the table. Rachel hadn't even noticed that happening. Salma took a seat and smiled at her.

"So. Omar told me you spoke of nothing the other day."

She turned to reach the espresso cups and get the coffee. Rachel hesitated to speak.

"Was he nice to you?"

"Oh yes. Especially when I - "

Rachel stopped herself. Salma raised her dark eyebrows.

"What is it?"

"It's nothing. It would be better if you heard it from Omar, not me."

Salma laughed,

"Omar will not tell me anything, Rachel. What is it?"

Rachel stood up, knocking her chair back onto the floor.

"I've just remembered I need something," she paused to think, "from the supermarket. I'm sorry, I have to go."

Salma stood up too, "But you haven't eaten any bread, or drunk any coffee. Please stay, Rachel."

Rachel hurried to the door, biting the words back.

"I'm sorry. I really must run."

Salma moved to the door to see Rachel out. They both saw the unlikely middle-aged woman knocking at Francois' door. Rachel moved towards her but Salma stepped away, sensing hostility.

She went back inside and stared at the untouched bread, the still full coffee cups.

She cleared the table, lips pressed together. Omar had some explaining to do, that's for sure.

She had a scarf tied under her chin, and huge sunglasses covering her eyes. She did not want anybody to speak to her, or, worst of all, recognise her. She waited behind the pillar until someone else was buzzed in, and she caught the door before it closed. She knew he was on the first floor, but unsure of the number. She started up the stairs, noticed the echoing clack of her heels and tiptoed the rest of the way. It was a stale, stuffy place, and she held her scarf over her nose as she climbed, taking care to avoid touching the banister. When she reached the first floor, a door opened. She froze, hand still holding her scarf over her face.

"Mme Tessier?"

Damn. It was that wretched Irish girl, with a Beur standing in the doorway behind her. She nodded and quickly turned to knock on the other door. There was no answer. She tried again, louder this time. She could feel the eyes of the two women on her, but she was not going to turn round. She heard them taking their leave of each other, Rachel's footsteps going up, and the door closing behind.

Eventually, Francois opened the door looking dishevelled and half-dressed. He looked blankly at his mother.

"What's with the Audrey Hepburn, mother?"

"Just let me in, would you. I can't breathe in this place."

She pushed past Francois and strode into his hall. He heard her swear in disgust and suppressed a weary sigh.

He shuffled over to the espresso maker and got busy making coffees for them both until he remembered he only had one cup. He turned the gas off and leant against the counter, watching her get steadily more disgusted as she opened cupboards, ran her finger over surfaces and unstuck her foot from the floor in front of the fridge. She faced him and folded her arms.

"Why do you live in this bordel?"

She moved closer and touched his arm, pleading,

"You could just apologise to your father and come home."

Francois gave a snort of laughter.

"So this is why you came, is it - to try and recover a besmirched public image? Oh that the son of eminent Front Nationale politician would deign to live in a hovel, and with foreigners next door no less!"

Mme Tessier pursed her lips and tightened the knot in her scarf.

"Well, it's true. You are bringing disgrace on us. And there is really no need. At least move somewhere that has more suitable neighbours. French people."

Francois put his fists on the table and spoke with a dangerously quiet voice,

"They are French. They have every right to be here."

"And the Irish girl, what about her?"

"She'll be gone soon enough."

Francois elected not to mention the Italian gentleman and the English woman living downstairs.

"As will you, mother." He opened the door and stood waiting.

She hissed at him, "What will you do for money? You need us."

Francois laughed unhappily.

"I will think of something. Perhaps I will sell sunglasses like Omar across the hall."

His mother made a horrified sound and clattered out of the apartment.

"Always a pleasure maman," Francois murmured as he let the door slam shut behind her.

There was a quiet knock at the door. Salma went over to it, checking her scarf, expecting Mamoun, or Rachel coming back with an apology. She flung it open with a pleased smile on her face, but took a step back when she saw the dishevelled young man standing there, hands by his sides, already half-turned away, prepared to run back down the stairs. She pushed the door closed, put the chain on then opened it a crack.

"Yes?"

The man turned to directly face her, and she was reminded of someone she once knew. The woman in the Hermes scarf and sunglasses came out of the apartment opposite and rushed down the stairs, looking furious. The boy raised his eyebrows and then looked at Salma again.

"Are you Salma, Omar's wife?"

"Yes."

He ran his hand through his curly dark hair and let his breath out in a whistle.

"Is your husband there?"

Salma's heart was thumping as she shook her head. The boy looked beaten. She took a risk,

"My son will be back very soon. If you could wait for him?"

There were footsteps running up the stairs

"Sebastian! You came!"

It was a red-faced Rachel. She reached the pair and took in his turned away posture, the chain on the door, Salma's confused, terrified eyes.

"It's ok Salma, he's my friend."

The chain was slid off, the door opened wide, and Salma stepped back to let them in.

The three stood avoiding each other's eyes. Rachel was the first to break the silence,

"Salma. This is my friend Sebastian."

Salma nodded to him and waited. The question burst out of him in a rush.

"Is your brother-in-law called Youssef?"

Salma nodded. She studied his face, and the mention of the name made her realise who he reminded her of.

"Do you know Youssef?"

Sebastian and Rachel exchanged glances. She jerked her head, encouraging him to answer. He shook his and laughed with embarrassment. He sighed.

"I don't know him, but I think he could be my father."

Salma thudded down on the chair behind her.

Sebastian went on,

"My mother and Youssef were in a relationship when they were at university and she got pregnant. With me."

Sebastian put his hands up apologetically.

Salma's mouth was still open.

Rachel jumped in and picked up the story. She had just got to the bit where Youssef went back to Morocco when Mamoun crashed in. When he saw everyone, he stopped and scratched his head, looking from one to the other. No-one was talking.

"Maman? Who is that man?" He pointed a grubby finger at Sebastian, who gave a nervous cough.

Salma glanced from Mamoun, to Rachel, to Sebastian. She beckoned Mamoun over and put an arm round him.

"This is Sebastian, he's here to talk to me about Morocco."

"Why?"

Rachel spoke up.

"He's my friend, and he may have family there."

"Your boyfriend?" Mamoun frowned, Sebastian looked at the floor and Rachel blushed.

"No no, he's just my friend." She studiously avoided Sebastian's face.

"Oh. That's ok." Mamoun held up his hand to high five Sebastian. Then he stopped, folded his arms and squinted up at him.

"You look like my uncle."

Salma tutted.

"That's enough of your silliness, Mamou. Let's get you something to eat."

Sebastian cleared his throat,

"I should get going."

Rachel turned to him,

"Do you want to get a drink in my flat before you go?"

"No." He coughed again and ran his hands through his hair.

"I'm meeting Elodie in half an hour, so have to push on. Thanks anyway."

Rachel swallowed and tried to look like she hadn't just been given the brush-off. Mamoun frowned at Sebastian and opened his mouth to speak. Salma steered him away to the kitchen table.

"Ok. Well. I'll leave you all to it." Rachel turned to the door and headed up the stairs, her heart sinking.

Rachel heard footsteps behind her but she kept going.

"Rachel!" Sebastian was right behind her, out of breath.

"I just want to see if Elodie and me, you know…"

Rachel didn't help him finish.

"The thing is, well, you're not going to be here for much longer, so…"

Again, Rachel waited.

"I've got to look around me, to the people I have here, now that I know there's no life for me anywhere else. You know?"

Rachel nodded, unable to speak.

He grabbed her arms and kissed her on both cheeks.

"Thank-you."

He turned to go back down.

"Wait,"

Rachel wiped her face with the end of her sleeve.

"Sebastian. I'm glad things are getting clearer for you. I hope it all works out with Elodie."

He rubbed her tears away with his thumb.

"Maybe in another life, we would have…"

"Maybe, but you're headed for your real life now so…"

Sebastian hugged her, and mumbled into her hair,

"Don't leave without saying goodbye."

Rachel nodded, and they parted. She heard his footsteps retreating, and stood until they stopped. She went in to her sun-lit studio, sat on the edge of the futon and cried.

Waiting here for you/ Waiting here for you/ Wanting to tell you/ How I get my ends and beginnings mixed up too/ Just the way you do/ Thought if I told you/ You might want to stay for just another day or two.

CHAPTER SEVENTEEN

Past secrets uncovered

When Omar got home, he was not expecting to see Salma sitting at the table, hands clasped, lips pursed, face frowning. There were no saucepans on the hob, no places set at the table. She hadn't touched the coffee in front of her or closed the windows clattering in an April storm. Her scarf had slipped off, and her hair was blowing in every direction with the gusts howling across the room. There was no sight nor sound of Mamoun.

"What has happened?" Omar moved over and pulled the window shut. He placed his hands on the table, and bent down to Salma.

"I have just met your nephew."

Omar froze.

"He came looking for you, and then Rachel came and as he is her friend, I asked them both in."

She fixed her scarf.

"Turns out, his father is Youssef."

She laughed a little.

"You don't look surprised Omar."

She tilted her head and said in a sing-song voice,

"Could it be that you have been told this already, say by Rachel, that time when you talked about nothing."

She was close to tears, but holding them back.

"Why did you keep it from me? How long have you known?"

Omar sat down and put his head in his hands.

"Only since Rachel told me, or maybe a bit before when I saw him and wondered if it could be true." He sighed.

"I didn't tell you because I'm finding it hard to believe. I mean, you've met Youssef - did he look like he would be capable of this?"

The window rattled in its frame as Salma thought.

"If he was in love with her, then it is very possible."

Omar slammed his hand down and shouted,

"Has he not read the Qur'an?!"

Salma got up and took a step back,

"It's too late for anger now, Omar. There is a child, a young man, who is looking for his father. He told me he went to Morocco to meet him, and was not allowed in. That is not right. That is not in keeping with the teaching of Muhammed."

Omar waved the argument away.

"You are mistaken if you think that. Anyway, if Youssef does not want to see the boy, we shouldn't either."

Salma started to shake her head.

"You know in your heart that we have to, Omar."

At that moment Mamoun got back.

"Have to what?"

Omar looked at Salma and nodded, shrugging his shoulders.

"We have to meet your cousin."

"Are they here? Over from Morocco?"

"No, Mamou, a new cousin." Salma reached over and pulled him close to her.

"A baby?"

She shook her head.

"You know the boy Sebastian who you met here?"

Mamoun's eyes widened, then he jumped away from her and punched the air.

"I knew it! Didn't I say he looked like uncle Youssef? Didn't I say?!"

He jumped in a tight circle, clapping his hands.

Omar's mouth was tight with disapproval. Salma chose not to notice, and smiled at Mamoun's excitement.

"So will he come here for dinner? Will we meet him at the beach? Will we go to his house?"

"Maybe. I could ask Rachel for his number."

"No!" The pair froze as Omar stood, fists by his sides, eyes narrowed.

"Why not, Omar? Is it not our duty to show him a family welcome?"

"That boy is not our family."

Salma gasped and Mamoun pouted.

"He is. He should be."

"You don't know for certain if his story is true. His mother may have made it up."

"Shame on you Omar! You only have to look at him to know

it's true."

Omar folded his arms.

"Everyone is getting over-excited. We need to pause."

"No, you need to. We don't."

Omar glared at his wife and walked out of the room.

Mamoun and Salma looked at each other.

"I've got a new cousin! Here in Nice!"

She hugged him, and hoped that Omar would come round.

⁂

Omar stormed past Ann and Alberto on the stairs, not looking at either of them.

"What's the matter with him?" Ann whispered, not really expecting an answer.

Omar stopped a few steps from the door, realising he hadn't brought his sunglasses with him. He hesitated, then kept walking. He'd work double time tomorrow. He did not want to listen to any more of Salma's insubordinate nonsense. They didn't know for certain and anyway, Youssef had not wanted to meet him. Maybe he had his reasons. Maybe they were enough. Maybe .

He stopped at the end of the street. It wasn't working. The

arguments he had in his head were not stopping the rising crisis of conscience happening in his gut right now. He reached in to his trouser pocket and pulled out the address Rachel had given him. He headed to the bus stop on the square and jumped on to the next bus, heart racing, mouth dry. He could just not get off. He could not press the buzzer on the flats. He didn't have to do anything.

Maybe next time, he said to himself over and over. It doesn't have to happen today.

He got down. He walked up the hill to the apartment blocks. He went round each one until he found the right number. He ran his finger down the list of names, saw F. Martin and buzzed.

"Oui?"

Omar looked at the intercom with alarm, turned and started walking away. He only covered a few metres when he bumped into someone heading the other direction.

"Sorry." He looked at the figure who had collided with him. They both stepped back in surprise.

"It's you."

Sebastian nodded.

"Why are you here?"

Omar shrugged and started to turn away.

Sebastian put out his hand to stop him.

"Did you come here looking for me?"

"I don't know why I'm here. It was a stupid idea and I'm going back now."

Omar put the piece of paper back in his pocket and zipped his faded jacket up. He didn't move. He just kept frowning at Sebastian.

"Would you like to come meet my mother?"

"Oh no no. Not today."

"But surely that's why you came?"

Omar sighed,

"I have no idea why I came."

Sebastian ran over to the door, unlocked it and held it open, waiting for Omar. It was a stand-off. The pair did not budge or say a word for a long minute. Busta Flex rap sounded out in the grass area between the flats and teenagers started to gather. The clouds were growing to cover the blue, sending a warning of thunder.

Eventually, Omar spoke.

"Are you completely certain that my brother is your father?"

Sebastian nodded.

"And you're not after money from me, because I don't have

much."

"I don't need your money. I just want a family."

His voice was quiet. Omar groaned and lifted his hands,

"All right all right, I give up. I will come in."

Florence put back the receiver and shook her head. She was forever letting random people in, and, apart from Sebastian, it was never to see her. Her parents had more or less disowned her when she told them she was expecting, and a half-Beur child at that. Her memories of that time were still like shards of broken glass: the terror when the test was positive, the anger of her dad and worst of all, the realisation that Youssef would not stand by her. She had thought he would at least be there through the pregnancy and the birth, she didn't ever expect him to marry her, although sometimes, at the beginning, that had been a wild hope.

It had been a cruel ride through rejection, abandonment, fear. Loneliness. That one had never left her. The women in her building had been civil, but very uncertain of her. She was the only white mother there. The only unmarried one. Sebastian had filled her days when he was younger, but now, well, he had his own life to live, and his need of her was rapidly diminishing. Letting him go to Morocco had been the hardest thing she'd ever done. Of course, he would never know that.

She walked over to the window. There were youths listening

to rap music on the only green space there was, tossing their bottles and cigarette butts on it, not caring. Everything was grey here, relentlessly the same. Even the sky was grey today. Florence looked in the mirror above the electric fire and frowned. Her skin was sallow, her face lined, her mouth in a permanent downward curve. She noted the tears building in her eyes and rubbed them away. Sebastian would be home any minute, and the last thing he needed was a miserable mother. He was the only thing that kept her from despair. There was nobody else.

A key turned in the lock, and she lifted her head to greet him.

He was not alone. A familiar looking Maghreb man was behind him.

"Maman. This is Omar, Youssef's brother. My uncle."

Florence put her shaking hand to her mouth and took a step back.

"What?"

Omar moved closer and nodded his head.

"Why are you here? In my home?"

Sebastian gave a nervous laugh.

"He has only just found out about us, maman, and came across the city to see you."

Florence shook her head.

"You have been here, all this time? And he never told you?"

She let out a sob and grabbed onto the table beside her.

Omar didn't move. Sebastian's face flushed.

"But he's here now, maman."

There was a crash as Florence hit the table.

"Too late. He's too late."

She turned to Omar.

"What need have I of you now? None." She lifted her chin.
"Please leave."

She stood still and gestured to the door. Omar started to
speak and then stopped. He nodded to Sebastian, who
followed him out.

Florence dropped to a chair and gripped her arms, holding
them close to her chest. She tried to stop herself shaking,
tried to slow down her breathing.

Sebastian returned and stood in front of her. His face was set.
He shook his head.

"That was my best chance, maman. My only shot at having a
family. Of knowing who I am."

"I am your family, Sebastian. I will always be." She was
crying again.

Sebastian sighed and stuck his hands into the pockets of his khaki shorts.

"You knew how important this was to me. You knew it. And you sent him away." His voice rose in frustration. Florence reached out to him, but he shook her hand off and marched out of the flat, slamming the door behind him.

❖

Omar had told her about his unsuccessful meeting with Florence, about Sebastian's obvious disappointment. For Omar, it was over. He had tried and failed, and that was that. As he recounted the tale, Salma was already planning her remedy. If there was another child, grown-up or not, he had to be made a part of their lives. Maybe, she thought, this was the missing piece, the reason she always felt something was lacking.

She kissed Mamoun goodbye, watched Omar leave to make up for his zero sale of yesterday, sat down on a kitchen chair and waited. The sun was already heating up the city, pushing blue sky between the roof tops, stretching like bright cellophane over everything. The flat was silent apart from the occasional crack of wood responding to the heat, and the steady drip of a tap crying out for a new washer. She could hear steps and voices on the stairs, but those quickly retreated leaving her to her racing thoughts. She looked at her watch. Fifteen minutes had passed. She stood up, checked herself in the hall mirror, grabbed her sequinned bag and stepped out into the stairwell.

"Salma! Hi."

Rachel paused on her way down the stairs and waited for the North African woman to join her. Salma quickly recovered her disappointment at being caught on the run, and pasted a smile on her unveiled face.

"Hello Rachel. You on your way to school?" There was always a hope.

"No no. Wednesdays are my quiet days. I'm just going out for a wander - haven't decided where yet. What about you?"

There was a pause as Salma re-calibrated her plans.

"You would never believe me if I told you."

Rachel stopped on the stairs and turned to face her.

Salma tucked her hair behind her ear and gave a little laugh.

"I am going to visit Sebastian's mother."

She grabbed Rachel's arm.

"I haven't told anyone yet. I just wanted to go see for myself, you know?"

Rachel's eyes were wide.

"Please don't say anything Rachel."

"No. Of course not. "

Salma started walking again, bi-passing Rachel.

"I'm coming with you."

Rachel passed Salma and headed for the door, not looking back.

They didn't speak to each other at the beginning, as Salma tried to think of a way to stop Rachel coming, and then as it became clear she had no say in the matter, a way to thank her.

On the bus, two heavily veiled women stared at Salma's uncovered head, and muttered to each other. Salma kept her head down, her flushed face hidden beneath her long dark hair. Rachel saw her agitation, and started chatting about inconsequential things as they rode along. When it came to their stop, she nudged her companion and led her off.

Out in the fresh air, Salma lifted her head and breathed with relief.

"Are you ok, Salma?"

She squinted back at Rachel and pointed to her face.

"I should have worn my hijab. I just thought it would help for her to see my face."

"You look beautiful. I think that was very brave of you?"

Rachel raised her voice in question at the end, having no clue about the protocol of hijab wearing.

Salma gave a slight smile and checked the directions she'd taken from the table where Omar had discarded them. Her hands were shaking.   Rachel put hers over them and squeezed,

"I know the way, I came once before, looking for Sebastian."

They walked to the door and pressed the now popular buzzer.

"I hope I am doing the right thing?" Salma looked over at Rachel, her dark eyes wide.

"I think you are."

The intercom crackled and both women stepped back.

"Oui?"

Rachel raised her eyebrows in question to Salma, who nodded.

"It's Rachel. We met the other day. About Sebastian?"

They were buzzed in. The stairwell smelt of bleach over urine and the walls were covered with graffiti - some offensive, most showing teenage malaise. Salma kept her eyes down, and did not speak. Just before Rachel knocked on the unstained door, she found her arm grabbed. Salma dug in her bag and pulled out a spare scarf of burgundy chiffon, arranging it over her head, draped across the bottom half of her face. She sighed.

"You can knock now. I'm ready."

Florence opened the door a small amount, and took in the two figures standing on the other side. She did a good job of concealing her surprise at Rachel's dark-skinned, scarf-wearing companion and stepped back to let them in.

"Nice to see you again, Florence. This is Salma, Omar's wife."

Florence's face closed.

"Sebastian is not here."

She hadn't sat down, and didn't motion to them to sit either.

"I didn't come to see Sebastian. I came to see you."

Salma pushed back her head-covering to show how earnest she was.

"Why?"

Florence had not budged, other than to fold her arms across her chest. The scarf removal didn't seem to have moved her.

Salma got closer.

"Because I am a mother of one child, just like you. Because you are family now."

Florence cleared her tightening throat.

"Florence, I am sorry I never knew about you or Sebastian until now. I am sorry for all the times you have needed us, and we were not there. I too know what it is like to be lonely."

Florence was crying then, but Salma carried on.

"Perhaps now, we could be friends? I hope it is not too late?"

Rachel edged away, leaving the other two to cry together. She looked at all the photographs on the shelf - Sebastian as a baby, sitting on the grassy square in between the apartment blocks, a small toy car in each hand, his first day at school, his first gappy smile, his first bicycle and then all grown up, graduating from lycée. She headed for the door.

"Wait! You must stay for a cafe at least?"

"And one day soon, you must come to my home Florence." Salma looked over at Rachel, who gave her covert thumbs up.

Florence moved over to put the espresso maker on the gas hob, and the other two sat down. Rachel watched as the two women sat down together. It would only take one cup of coffee to seal a new friendship, of that she was almost certain.

"Visitors, maman?"

Florence looked up from washing the cups and smiled at her son, hoping his anger with her had dissipated. She grabbed a tea towel and dried her hands, thinking about what to say.

"Sit down, Sebastian."

He slung his bag onto the table and pulled out a chair.

"What is it?"

Florence felt her heart thumping. She looked at the table.

"Rachel was here."

"Oh, did you tell her where I was?"

"No, it was me she wanted to visit." He did a double take.

She took a deep breath.

"Salma was with her."

Sebastian started to stand up. Florence put out her hand,

"No it's ok. We talked. She apologised."

"And what did you say to her?"

Sebastian's voice was sharp. Defensive.

"I just said I understood, don't worry. She seemed very nice and quite shy too."

"She is nice. So is her husband."

Florence caught herself frowning and fiddled with Sebastian's bag in front of her.

Sebastian leant over and grabbed her hand.

"Do you see now that they are family, that we could get to know them, belong to somebody other than eachother?"

"I'm trying, Sebastian. It's just all so sudden - to go from two to four in the space of a day."

"Five. They have a son. My cousin."

Sebastian smiled as he said that, and Florence's heart softened.

"I don't think it would be long before we get an invitation to their home. Would you like that?"

"Would you?"

"I don't know, but I'd go if that was what you wanted."

Sebastian put his arm round his mum and squeezed.

"I can't believe that I travelled the whole way to Morocco when there was family right here, in this city."

"I'm sorry your father wouldn't see you though."

Sebastian sighed.

"I'll have to let that one go I think."

Florence registered the pain in her son's face and felt the familiar wave of anger breaking over her. Her face flushed, and her eyes filled.

"There are always loose ends in life, son. No perfect endings for any of us."

Sebastian nodded.

"Sure, that's what makes it interesting." He shrugged and lifted his hands with a smile.

CHAPTER EIGHTEEN

Home is where the heart is.

"Close your eyes, my love." Alberto frowned at Ann, but humoured her. They were in her apartment, and had just had their Sunday morning coffee together. Ann had been distracted since she had let him in earlier, barely touching her coffee, and not responding to the things he said to her, in his halting English/Italian lingo. Faithful as ever, the sun pushed through the windows, catching the curves of their china, bouncing off the pots hanging above the hob, drawing out the flecks of silver in Ann's hair. She had put on the skirt she wore the day they went to Antibes, and earrings glittered in her ears. Alberto watched her every move, a half-smile on his face. When her back was turned, he hastily ran a pocket comb through his hair and straightened his shirt.

"Close them and hold out your hand."

He could feel the whisper of her warm breath on his face as she put something in his hands.

"Now. Look."

There, in his rough hands, was a ticket. He looked up at her, his eyes a question.

"It's a ticket, Alberto. To Italy. For you to go home and see your family."

Alberto stayed looking at the piece of card for minutes without saying a word. Then all of a sudden, a moan escaped his lips and then another.

"I managed to collect enough money from my paintings." Ann laughed. "It has taken me all the months since we first met." She started gabbling about seats, paintings, buyers and exchange rates until Alberto's sob stopped her. He had his hands over his face, his shoulders were shaking.

"Oh Alberto, was it wrong of me?"

Ann moved behind him to put her hands on his shoulders. He let out a long, shaky breath, then reached up and squeezed her hands.

"I'm going home!" He stood up, lifted Ann and swung her round. She gave him an overly bright smile.

He stopped and picked up the ticket, examining it.

"This is a return, yes?"

Ann laughed unhappily.

"It can be, if you want it to be."

Alberto looked at her, a question in his eyes. He reverted to his mother tongue, not knowing if she would understand or not.

"This is so kind of you." He returned her half-hearted smile then sighed again, shaking his head.

"I can't quite take it in." He touched his head, and then his chest.

"Forgive me, but I have to be alone."

With that, he kissed her apologetically, slowly made his way across the creaking floorboards and left, leaving the ticket on the table in front of Ann.

✙

Ann picked up the ticket, and went after Alberto. His door was already shut. She stood with her fist hovering over it, hesitating to knock. There was a sudden sound of people coming in from the street below. She dropped her hand and moved quietly back to her flat, shutting the door with a gentle click behind her. She looked at the half-finished coffee and croissants, the seats still out from the table. She lifted up the ticket and sighed. What had she been thinking? That this was Alberto's one wish, and he would love her forever for giving it to him? And that he would come running back to her again, his home-sickness dealt with once and for all? She was a naive fool. She should never have asked Rachel in that day, or Alberto so soon after.

Her life before had been fine - just the way she had wanted it - no complications, no relationships; just simple, straightforward solitude. She dropped the ticket on the counter and headed for her studio. Now this was where she was meant to be.

The blank canvas mocked her determined stance before it, brush and palette of colours poised. Nothing came. She touched the bristles to the paper and tried one short stroke, then another, then another, then another...

If someone had asked her what she was intending, what she was thinking, she couldn't have told them, not at first. But then, she took a step back and looked. The first few strokes had provided a back-drop for the main feature. It was a man. He had a shock of grey/white hair, a grey crumpled shirt, and a rugged face. His eyes were looking at her from behind creased eye lids. She started to laugh. She was dreadful at portraits. Landscapes were her forte. She knew it was Alberto, but she doubted anyone else would.

She picked up her brush, intending to paint in an Italian village in the distance behind him but she couldn't do it. She couldn't paint the one thing that might take him away from her for good. She set her painting things down and moved over to look out the window. The best of the light was almost gone without her noticing it. She moved into the kitchen and opened the fridge. She looked at the single egg, the handful of lettuce, the two tomatoes and began to cry. She didn't want this anymore. Not now that people had come into her life. Not now that she had found someone to love, after all these years of nothing. She picked an apricot out of the fruit bowl and dropped to the couch to eat. Sitting down at the table tonight would be a mockery.

It was morning, but Alberto had not slept. He had spent the night sitting at the kitchen table. A chance to go back, after all this time; it felt like a strange dream. Of course he had spoken to his daughters on the payphone down the street at least once a week, but that was it. For the first six months they had begged him to come back, but he hadn't. Financially he was ruined. Emotionally he was emptied. The possibility of going home became increasingly remote.

As time went on his absence became the norm and they accepted it. They were both busy with their own families, always rushing to get back to a dinner that was boiling over, or a child who needed changing. He still called every Saturday at five o'clock sharp. They started to sound falsely pleased to hear from him. Or maybe that was his loneliness making it feel like that. His three grand-children had never seen him. He was just another stranger.

Unless he went back. Would they still seem slightly bothered by him, or would actually being there make it right again? Would the bank still come banging on his door demanding more payments even though he'd settled them already? He wouldn't tell anyone there until it was definite. He twisted his wedding band with shaking fingers. He spoke into the empty room, "What should I do, Mia? What should I do?"

He pushed himself up to standing. He had to go. He was a father and a grandfather. His family had done without him for too long. He would take the ticket. He would go and get it tomorrow from Ann.

Ann. He let out a heavy sigh and pressed the flat of his palm against the wall. That was the anchor keeping him here. Or was it that she had made him want to stay more than leave? He thought back over all the precious times he had spent with her these last few months: the time she paddled at Antibes, the meal they had shared at Christmas, the faint memory of her face the day he had fallen ill, the vulnerability as she read what he had found out about her past lover. After all those years of loneliness, Ann had come into his world and now he could not for the life of him imagine being happy without her.

✣

"Well, Mamoun, how are you this week?"

Rachel and Mamoun were walking to school. They had missed a few days the week before, as Rachel was sleeping in a lot - a sign of the approaching end of term. She stopped and put her hand over her eyes to see his sunlit face. He was half-smiling, but his eyes were cast down. She bent over and got close to his face.

"What's wrong?"

He shrugged.

"Papa is angry with Maman."

"Oh."

Rachel stood up and started walking again, not wanting to involve herself, knowing the story already. Mamoun hurried after her.

"She went to see Sebastian's mother, and now she wants to have her for a meal. Papa is angry."

He shook his head slowly, looking like a grown-up.

"I'm sure it will all work out, Mamoun. It's just, this is a huge thing, finding out about your cousin."

Mamoun kicked an empty juice carton along the pavement and didn't answer.

She couldn't help herself.

"Aren't you excited though - to have a big cousin?"

Mamoun picked the carton up and threw it onto the middle of the street, not answering.

Rachel shifted her shoulder bag and changed the subject.

"You know I'll be heading home soon?" Mamoun stopped dead, and then broke into a run.

Rachel called after him, and then started running herself. He was fast, and skilled at dodging people. She kept her eyes on his little brown head, determined not to lose him. Eventually, she ran out of puff, and leant against the ice-cream van, panting.

"Please don't leave, Madame Rachel."

Mamoun was standing in front of her, his arms straight by his sides, his shoulders drooping.

"You can't leave." His dark eyes filled with tears.

Rachel laughed softly,

"And yet I must. Soon this teaching job will be over, and I will have no money coming in."

"But you have been my friend."

Rachel dropped down and held onto Mamoun's shoulder, meeting his eyes,

"And you mine, Mamoun. My first here."

Rachel took in his dark-skinned face, his too-short T-shirt over a scrawny body, his earnest eyes, and realised she was going to miss him.

"I'm not gone yet, though, so…"

His face brightened.

"An ice-cream?"

"You know I don't approve of eating ice-cream at this hour of the day,"

She wagged her finger at him and he made a disappointed 'Awww'.

"But today, for our friendship, I will get you ice-cream. Just this once."

They had ten minutes before school, and so they sat on the edge of the sun-sparkling fountain in the square, licking two boules of strawberry ice-cream in companionable silent

Mamoun went over to a bin and threw his napkin out. He walked back and stopped in front of her, "Madame Rachel?"

"What is it Mamoun?"

"Will you come back after the summer?"

Rachel closed her eyes and thought for a moment.

"I have to finish my degree, Mamoun. But maybe after that…"

Mamoun scratched his head,

"What else?"

"What do you mean?"

He stood looking at her.

"Apart from your degree."

Rachel gave a nervous laugh,

"Not really anything else, except for my parents."

"Then, you must come back."

He put his shoulders back and puffed out his chest,

"When I am sixteen, I will ask you to marry me."

Rachel smiled and patted him on the head. He stepped back out of the shade of the ice-cream kiosk, the sunlight catching the red lights in his curls.

"I will, just you wait and see."

She put her hand out,

"All right. Let's wait and see. You know I'll be 23 then?"

Mamoun shrugged his shoulders,

"That is nothing. Not when you're in love."

Rachel fought back a smile and stood to go. If only decisions in life were really that simple.

CHAPTER NINETEEN

Altered perspectives

He'd sat with his back to the front door for an hour now, jumping up and peering through the peep hole every time somebody walked past. He had tried to talk himself out of it, this crazy, impossible notion that had got its hooks into him, but he was still watching and waiting. He'd been cleaning the floor in between times, for the first time since he moved in. The water in the bucket was black, the mop beyond repair. The floor was actually a white marble, not the grey granite he'd thought. Footsteps on the stairs. He leapt over and peered out. It was him! He opened the door and cleared his throat.

Omar stopped looking for his keys and turned round.

"Salut, Omar? That's your name isn't it? I've met your son. I'm Francois, your neighbour."

He stuck his hand out and smiled, hopeful.

Omar nodded and took his hand.

"So. I was wondering. You sell sunglasses, right?"

An acknowledgement.

"Could I tag along, next time you go, learn the trade so to speak?"

Omar stared at him, and then laughed out loud, for an uncomfortably long time. When he had calmed down, he wiped his eyes.

"Why?"

Francois flushed. "I need the money."

"That is a good reason. All right, I'm leaving tomorrow morning at 8"

Francois whistled, clocked Omar's frown and stood up straighter.

"That sounds good. I will be ready."

"If you're not, I will go without you."

Francois gave a salute, and the pair went in to their opposite doors, Omar scratching his head, Francois laughing at himself - who'd have thought it? Pursuing a career commonly done by Maghrebs. But why not? Everyone needs a way to make a living, don't they.

Francois woke to the sound of someone rapping on his door. He cursed, remembering. He rolled off his mattress, stumbled to the toilet, pulled some clothes on, grabbed his clarinet and opened the door to Omar, who was just turning away.

"Sorry! I don't really do mornings."

Omar just shrugged and headed downstairs leaving his young apprentice to scramble down after him, still tucking in his t-shirt.

They got out into the sunlight. Omar pointed to Francois' hair, who frowned and opened his mouth to object, then thought twice and smoothed the spikes down with both hands.

"So where are we going first?"

Omar didn't reply; he just kept walking down the street, heading towards the city centre. Francois was two steps behind, and watched as people side-stepped the Moroccan, frowning, rolling their eyes, shaking their heads, or just looking straight past him. At the fountains on Place Massena he looked round, selected a corner and started to lay out his wares.

"Do you choose this corner every time?"

Omar shook his head.

"You think it's the best spot?"

Omar shrugged.

Francois walked over to the opposite corner and beckoned Omar over. The salesman mouthed 'no' and Francois called over, "why not?" He walked back over, a question on his face.

"Someone else uses that space."

"Well, there's nobody there now so…"

"No." As Omar spoke, a man on a motorbike with a trailer roared up. He was clearly a Nicois, if there was such a person - white with a dark ponytail and a pencil-line moustache. He jumped off his bike and went to open up his trailer which turned out to be a self-contained CD stall. He lifted out a stereo and put some pumping music on.

"That's louder than I play mine!" Francois shouted in Omar's ear. His companion just crouched down and adjusted his sunglasses. When he stood up he passed two pairs to Francois and gestured to him to go to work. Francois straightened his shoulders, lifted his head and swaggered over to two unsuspecting teenage tourists. He showed the girls the glasses, put one pair on himself, one on the giggling red-head opposite him. When her friend pouted at being left out, he gave her his pair. He gave them a price, and they bought them, smiling the whole time. He walked back over to Omar, who applauded him.

"That was pretty easy. Your turn now?"

Omar picked another few, and turned to find some customers. There was a group of middle-aged women wandering across the square, looking a bit lost. He made a bee-line for them. When he got near, they saw him and backed away, their hands flapping. He came back over to Francois shrugging his shoulders.

"What did they say? They seemed pretty rude."

Omar busied himself with the glasses and didn't reply.

"Do you get that a lot?"

More silence. When Omar finally stood up he faced Francois and said,

"No-one trusts Maghrebs."

Francois couldn't think of anything to say. He knew Omar was right. He looked at the despondent man, and clapped his hands once.

"They'll trust you when they see I do."

"Pass me those glasses."

Omar gave them to Francois, who made a show of giving him a twenty franc note. A few people glanced over as he exclaimed loudly and put the glasses on. He moon-walked away from Omar, spun round and bowed to the small crowd now gathered round the pair. Francois ambled over to the music guy and made a deal with him. The music stopped and Francois started to play his clarinet.

People started to look at the sunglasses and offer money for them. Omar couldn't collect the notes quick enough, and it wasn't long before they were all sold. When they were just finishing up - two hours earlier than Omar could ever manage, they spotted Rachel sitting down on the next bench down from them. She hadn't seen them. Omar went over and stood in front of her, Francois followed behind.

It was at roll-call that Rachel cracked. She was sitting on her child-sized chair waiting for all the morning preliminaries to end, glad that this was the last time she had to be in the presence of the terrible Madame Tessier. It was because of this one horrible woman that Rachel had struggled to find anything enjoyable about working as an English assistant. She looked at all the white faces, and wondered how they would all turn out. She hoped that Eloine's kindness would take her far from there, that her health would improve. She really must not forget to write to her when she was back. And then there was Mamoun - the only North African child in the class, the only one with dark skin, the only Muslim. The only one to take her under his wing.

Admittedly, Mamoun was showing off and fidgeting, probably for her benefit, but no-one expected Madame Tessier to react like she did.

"Espece d'imbecile!" She lunged at his desk, pushing it against his stomach, causing him to yelp with pain. The whole class froze, faces terrified, eyes down. Mamoun looked up at the cruel face close to his and said in a small voice,

"Desolee, Madame Tessier. Sorry."

She gave the desk one last shove.

Rachel stood up, her face red, her voice shaking.

"Please leave him alone."

Madame Tessier slowly turned towards her.

"Pardon?"

Rachel looked at Mamoun, then back at the teacher.

"You treat him unfairly. He was not doing anything worse than anyone else here."

"Il ne fait rien," the teacher parroted back, mimicking Rachel's accent.

"He should not be here, in my class, in this school. He should go back to Africa. With the rest of them."

"Excuse me, but his home is here."

Madame Tessier threw her head back and guffawed. She pointed her finger at Rachel,

"You have no right to talk to me about my city when you don't belong here either!"

Rachel glanced over at Mamoun, who was still looking at the floor. She stood taller, eyes glittering, face hot.

"Nice is a city full of people from other religions, other races, other cultures. You cannot tell us all we don't belong."

Madame Tessier just threw her hands up in the air, no answer ready. Rachel said goodbye to the class and left the room. It was done.

✣

She had intended to go straight home after her show-down with Mme Tessier, horrified and pleased with herself in equal measure. She had been wanting to put that witch in her place the whole time she'd known her. Maybe there was an explanation for her attitude, but there was no excuse for her behaviour. She looked at the faces walking past her - black, brown, sallow eastern European, almond Asian. This was not a city exclusively for Caucasians. It was for everyone. She saw two Japanese couples holding onto each other, not caring where they were. She watched an old homeless black man shuffling casually from bin to bin. She stepped off the pavement to avoid a group of Maghreb teenagers swaggering past.

If she were to ask any of them where home was, most would have said somewhere other than Nice. And yet, here they all were looking like they belonged. She sat down on a bench in Place Massena, and asked herself, 'where do I belong?', 'who do I belong to?'. For the first few months here, she would have said Ireland. Then for a short time she had thought maybe her future was with Sebastian, but that was a silly dream with no legs. She shaded her eyes with her hand and watched the fountain jumping up and cascading down, water caught in sunlight.

"Rachel." It was Omar, sweating in his heavy jacket, head

covered with an old bandana. Francois was standing behind him, looking embarrassed. Rachel stared in surprise at him then turned her attention back,

"Oh hi Omar. How are you?"

Rachel shifted over on the bench to let Omar sit, but he stayed where he was, face frowning as he searched for the words he needed.

"I say thank-you. For Sebastian."

Francois looked from one to the other, baffled.

Rachel's eyes filled.

"That's ok. I am sorry if I interfered too much."

Omar shook his head, guessing at her meaning. An aeroplane flew overhead, and he lifted his head to watch it, then turned back to her, pointing to the sky,

"Home?"

"In two weeks."

Then Omar did a peculiar thing; he put his hand over his chest, and patted,

"Home."

He nodded to her, and headed back to the flat. Francois ambled after him. As Rachel watched him slowly saunter off, she wondered at his meaning. Was he talking about himself?

Was that how he coped with being here, not in Morocco? Being at ease with himself, finding his own identity in his heart, with the people he loved? She put her forearms on her knees and leant over, holding her head in her hands.

Or did he mean her? Where was home really? When she's back with her family will everything fall into place again, or has too much changed? She watched people walking, skating, cycling past the fountain, and realised something - she hadn't felt the homesick pang for months now - she'd been too preoccupied with Sebastian and his new-found family to dwell on anything else. But now that was reaching its conclusion, what would she do? Who would she focus on now?

"Rachel!" It was Ann, her easel under her arm, paintbrush behind her ear.

Rachel sat up straight and squinted at the dark figure standing in front of her.

"Hello Ann."

Ann dropped to the seat beside her and sighed heavily.

"What's wrong?"

The artist propped her easel against her legs.

"It's Alberto."

"A-hah." Rachel started putting her hair in a ponytail, waiting.

"I got him a ticket to his home town in Italy, and gave it to him yesterday."

"And?"

"He left it in my apartment, and I haven't seen him since."

"Did he forget it?"

"No. He just asked me if there was a return and I didn't really answer him properly. It was as if it was too much for him, and he was upset."

She pulled out a cloth rag and blew her nose.

"I did not see it going like that - I thought he would grab the ticket and go off to pack."

She sighed again.

"Give him time Ann - it's been years of wanting this and he's probably needing to process it."

Ann looked over at the fountain, not acknowledging Rachel's advice.

"It's just that, well, I care about him and I thought this was a way to show that."

"And it will have. He'll come back, just wait and see."

"I was trying to imagine how I would react if someone gave me a ticket back to England, but then I remembered it's different: I have no-one wanting me there, and no desire to go back. Alberto has his family."

"Who have never bothered to come here and see him."

Ann reached up and adjusted her straw hat.

"I'd never thought of that. Maybe they don't want to?"

Rachel shrugged.

"Maybe he's happy where he is. Maybe there's something, somebody, keeping him here."

They sat in silence as the minutes ticked by, the fountain rose and fell.

"Is there somebody keeping you here, Rachel?"

"Not any more."

Ann patted her back.

"And is there somebody calling you back? It certainly seemed that way several months ago."

It was Rachel's turn to sigh then.

"I don't think so. Things have changed a lot this year. For both of us. And I have no idea what I want anyway."

Ann stood up and lifted her easel.

"Seems like you need to wait and see. Just like me."

Rachel watched Ann walk away and did not feel the need to join her. They both preferred to be alone with their thoughts. Especially today.

"Rachel!" It was Laura running towards her, her unzipped bag slipping down her arm. She collapsed down beside Rachel and groaned,

"So that's it; classes done, kids' presents distributed, teachers thanked. My year as an English assistant is fini! Thank God."

"Hold on, you gave out presents? And thanked the teachers?! For what, exactly?"

Laura raised her eyebrows,

"Unlike your experience Rachel, the teachers and students in my school were fantastique!"

She patted Rachel on the back,

"Sorry. You were just unlucky."

"Where's Francesca?"

Laura laughed.

"She's with her boyfriend."

"What?!"

"Oh yes, our glamorous Brazilian friend has given her heart away to an older French man. With a car."

"Is he safe?"

"He is surprisingly lovely. It was all kept hush hush until she'd finished at their school."

Rachel gasped.

"A teacher?"

"A widower. I've barely seen her this past month, and it looks like she'll be extending her stay too."

"Who'd have thought it? Francesca has settled in more than we ever did."

Rachel leant back and thought over all the good things that had happened to her and was surprised to find she did not feel sorry she had been placed where she had.

"Did you have a good year anyway?"

Rachel looked Laura in the eye,

"I did. You?"

"Absolument."

"Tell me this Laura - if you'd been on a year out in Italy, say, would you have mixed Italian words into your English too?"

"Ovviamente! It's my secret trick to feel like I always belong, see?"

"Did it work?"

"Sort of. I'll just need to remember to drop it when I'm back in England."

"It's going to be weird, leaving."

They fell silent and stared at the people milling about the square.

"You looked at your photos much, since I told you off that first day?"

"Actually no, I haven't really."

"Well done Rachel. I know it was harder for you than for me."

Rachel flushed with recognition. Laura flung her bangled arms round her,

"I'll miss you, my homesick buddy."

CHAPTER TWENTY

Neighbours

Francois kept glancing over at Omar as they walked back to Avenue de la Republique, wondering what all that with Rachel was about, and who on earth was Sebastian? He knew better than to ask this stern man anything personal so bit his tongue on all the questions flying round his head. He tried a safer tack.

"Rachel's settled in well hasn't she? Despite having to face my mother four days a week."

Omar stopped dead.

"Your mother?"

"Putain, you didn't know. I am the cast-off son of the inimitable Madame Tessier, colleague of Rachel, teacher of Mamoun."

Omar stared at Francois, his mouth open, his head moving from side to side.

"But you, I'm sorry," he scratched his head, "but you wanted to work with me?!"

"We don't all think the same way as our parents."

"Is this why you are living in the apartment?"

"Sort of, that and a need to make my own way, you know?"

"We all have to do that, I think."

It was now or never.

"Omar, is Sebastian your son?"

Omar laughed and shook his head,

"No no."

Francois opened his mouth to apologise but was stopped short.

"He's my brother's."

Another torrent of questions were bit back from Francois. They had reached the front door, and the end of their revelations that day.

❖

Salma put the phone down and looked at Mamoun.

"She said yes, and Sebastian did too."

Mamoun clapped his hands and lifted two spoons to bang a rhythm on the table. Then he stopped, spoons in mid-air.

"Does papa know?"

Salma started wiping the counter. She blew a stray hair away from her eyes.

"Maman?"

"I'll tell him later."

"Does papa not like them?"

"Who?"

"Florence and Sebastian."

The tap was dripping and Salma reached over to tighten it. She turned back to Mamoun.

"He does like them. It's just, well, it was a surprise and he needs time to get used to it."

"Get used to what?"

Omar was standing just inside the door, looking at them both with a frown on his face. Mamoun waved to him and backed out of the room. Salma was wringing the dishcloth in her hands. She took a breath,

"Florence and Sebastian are coming for curry this Thursday."

Omar lifted his eyes to the ceiling, and Salma raised her chin.

"Did you invite them?"

She nodded,

Omar held onto the back of one of the kitchen chairs and examined it.

"This Thursday?"

Salma nodded again.

"Very well."

Omar turned to leave the room.

"Is that it? Do you not mind?"

Omar shoulders dropped. He went over to her and took her hands in his.

"You managed to do what I could not. Yes, I am uncomfortable with them coming here. Yes, I wish you had consulted me first, but I see that it is the right thing. We will do it together."

"Have you heard back from Youssef yet?"

"No. It would seem he is intent on denying his past deeds, and ignoring his duties. Nothing has changed there then." Omar drew his mouth into a tight line. He quoted from the Qu'ran,

"Righteous is he who . . . gives away wealth out of love for Him to the near of kin and the orphans and the needy and the wayfarer and to those who ask and to set slaves free."

"My brother has forgotten these words, so it is our duty to uphold them on his behalf."

❖

Ann sighed, lifted her easel and went out. For the first time in all her years in the flat, she didn't stop to listen for footsteps or worry if she had to speak to one of her neighbours. She was too pre-occupied to realise the dramatic change in her own behaviour that day. Sure enough, there was somebody else on the stairs. Francois was making his way down towards her, a case in his hand.

"Salut."

They both faced each other, and took in the art easel, the music case.

"Going to the Promenade?"

Ann shrugged,

"Haven't decided. You?"

Francois lifted his case

"Have to pay for my keep somehow."

Ann pointed to his case,

"What have you got there?"

"It's a clarinet."

They both started walking down to the door. Ann was thinking furiously. When they reached the front door she turned to Francois.

"I wonder if you would let me paint you playing your clarinet?"

The words had come out in a rush and as Francois hesitated Ann started to backtrack.

"It's ok, I don't have to. Just a silly idea of mine." She gave a high-pitched laugh. "Forget I said anything."

Francois nodded and hurried down the stairs.

"You should paint him Ann."

Rachel was standing a couple of stairs above her.

Ann shook her head at her,

"You and your crazy notions, Rachel. It was a moment of madness that's all."

"In fact," Rachel carried on, "you should paint everyone in this building."

Ann stood there open-mouthed while Rachel listed all the residents and the things that made them worthy of Ann's paint-brush.

"And actually, could you do it quite soon? I'd love to see them before I leave."

"Listen, Rachel, I have only just let you and Alberto into my life. I'm not ready for anyone else."

"Well, think about it anyway."

Then Rachel remembered the words Margaret had said to her months before and she said them out loud,

"It might be a good opportunity for you."

Ann had given up waiting for the knock, the face of Alberto at her door, but it happened that day, a week of waiting later. She whipped off her painting smock, smoothed her hair back in its loose bun, twisted her skirt straight and opened the door. He didn't say anything, but just stood there. If he'd had a hat, he would have been twisting it in his hands.

"Hello Alberto."

Ann gestured for him to come in, but he didn't move. She stepped over her threshold and joined him in the hall.

"How are you?"

Alberto sighed and mumbled something in Italian. Ann tutted, and moved to go back in.

"The ticket," he called after her.

"What of it?"

"I would like it."

Ann put her head down in assertion, and marched in to lift it from the table where it had been crying at her ever since the day she had offered it. She passed it to Alberto. He took it from her and examined it for a long minute.

"We must change this."

Ann moved closer to him to see what he was pointing to. She followed his finger to the word 'aller' and looked up at him.

"But I didn't think you would want to come back."

Alberto shook his head and reached out to cup her face.

"I want to come back. For you."

Ann put her hand over her mouth to stifle a sob.

Alberto kept speaking as Ann cried.

"My family are not all in Italy now. It is also here. You are my family. You, Ann."

Alberto stiffly got to his knees and looked up at her. Rachel walked past the open door, looked in and quickly walked on.

He did not look over, but kept holding Ann's gaze. Then, for

the second time in his life he said it,

"Will you be my wife?"

Ann nodded, still crying.

The pair put their arms around each other, and held on as the fragments of grief and loneliness came together, making something whole again in each one.

CHAPTER TWENTY-ONE

Leaving again

Rachel, Francois, Ann and Alberto all came out of their apartments, called by Mamuon's little voice, and drawn by the tantalising smells coming from Salma's kitchen. Ann and Alberto walked up one flight, Francois crossed the hall and Rachel ran down. They all stood outside, smiling at each other. Mamoun skipped round them all, clapping his hands.

"Welcome to my house! Welcome!"

He led them all inside, and gestured to the cushions scattered round a low sunlit table, laid with deep coloured cloth napkins and brightly painted glasses, sparkling in the early summer light. There was no cutlery, the white Europeans noticed with alarm. They all settled themselves around the table, noticing two empty places at one end.

"Welcome. We are honoured to have you here in our home. We are just waiting one moment." Omar looked every bit the confident host as he bowed and smiled.

After a short pause, there was a knock on the door, and Omar moved to open it. It was Florence and Sebastian. Omar kissed each of them, and led them to the table. Sebastian caught Rachel's eye. He was beaming, and she couldn't stop the silly grin spreading over her face too. Alberto was talking animatedly in Italian to Florence, and then to Ann. Then they were both kissing and hugging her, as though she were an old friend. Explanations were made, the tagine and a clay bowl of steaming couscous were set in the middle of the table, and everyone set about serving each other.

Rachel looked from one face to another, seeing a multitude of stories, a multitude of changed experiences. Ann had left her introverted existence, shaken off her painful past and now was starting a new page. Alberto had found that home was here, not just the place he'd left behind. Omar, Salma and Mamoun were celebrating sharing their home with people who they had once feared as their enemies. And they were trying their best to recover all the years of isolation Youssef had inflicted upon Florence and Sebastian. Francois was finding a new family too - away from the oppressive expectations of his parents. Although, Rachel hoped, he would come back to them in time too. She glanced over to him, deep in discussion about the tricky trade of selling sunglasses with Omar. Sebastian was putting his theories into the mix, and all three were listening to each other, agreeing or disagreeing as it suited them. Salma was giving Florence some Moroccan recipes, and tips on marinating the meat so it fell apart as soon as it touched the finger, or the fork. Ann and Alberto were laughing as they tried to scoop up the dinner with their hands. Mamoun was beside them, showing them how it's done.

"You not eating Madame Rachel?"

Rachel turned to Mamoun,

"I will. I'm just enjoying watching everybody."

Mamoun dropped another morsel of lamb into his mouth and nodded. He pointed to Francois and spoke with his mouth full,

"Did you know he was le diable's son?"

Rachel shushed him, but Francois had heard. He made his fingers into horns and made an angry face at Mamoun who fell on his back laughing.

Francois met Rachel's gaze and put up his hands in mock surrender,

"Sorry I didn't tell you. She's not so bad, really."

Rachel pursed her lips.

"I'll let you be the judge of that."

"You haven't met my father. Now there's a man to fear."

Rachel took in Francois' flushed, set face.

"I'm sorry, Francois. Maybe there's a reason he's like that, you know?"

"I wish it were that straight forward. There's no changing him now."

"He hasn't met Mamoun. There's a boy who could change

the heart of a devil."

Everyone seemed to go quiet at that moment.

Mamoun stood up and bowed ostentatiously.

Omar stood as well.

"Rachel, it is your last night here on Avenue de la Republique, and we all want to thank you."

He gestured round the table, including each person.

"We would not be here, together, if it weren't for you."

The table all nodded and clapped their agreement.

"Des lunettes, Madame?"

Omar opened his jacket and flashed a grin at her, his eyes laughing.

Rachel laughed, and put her hands together in apology to Omar.

One by one, everyone passed her a parting gift: sunglasses from Omar, a painting of the beach from Ann, a jar of pomodoro sauce from Alberto, a scarf from Salma, beads from Florence and Sebastian.

"Thank-you so much." Rachel put her head down to hide the emotion.

"What about me?" Mamoun had something in his

outstretched hand. He took Rachel's and dropped it in.

Rachel gasped.

It was a simple gold chain bracelet. Rachel looked down at her wrist, then at the new gift, then at Mamoun. She collected herself, and saw he was waiting for a response.

"Thank-you Mamoun."

She looked at it again and frowned,

"Is this not your bracelet?"

Mamoun grinned and shook his head,

"Not any more, Madame Rachel. It is yours now. To go with the other one, you see?"

Rachel tried to put it on but the chain was too small for her wrist.

She offered it back to Mamoun but he put his hand up in refusal. She took her purse out and made a show of putting it carefully into the zip pocket. Everyone was watching her, everyone could see the tears springing to her eyes. She looked at each face in turn, and managed a smile.

"Thank-you all of you. You have become - "

Her voice caught and she put her fingers to her lips for a moment. She cleared her throat,

"You have become my family this year, and I will never forget you. Any of you."

She met Sebastian's eyes last of all, and held his gaze longer than the rest. Then she sat down and the conversation started up again.

❖

"I'm fine, Alberto - just had one glass too many." Ann was gripping her new fiance's arm as they made their way back down the stairs to their apartments. Everyone was making their way back after the meal, so the corridor was flooded with the lights turned on as they got through their front doors. The stairwell echoed with slow footsteps, calls of 'thank you' and 'goodnight', jangling keys and lights getting switched on. It had become a place of friendship and family now. They were no longer a collection of unconnected isolated individuals. No-one would have to feel alone now. Ann and Alberto stopped at the space between their doors and watched Rachel making her way to the very top of the building. They smiled at each other, knowing that they were together now because of her, that homesick, uncertain Irish girl.

Alberto followed Ann in to her flat, turning on the lights. She lifted the kettle and raised her eyebrows. He nodded. She started filling it at the kitchen sink. She spoke over the running water,

"I've decided to go back to England for a few days."

Alberto looked confused, so Ann put the kettle on the stove and made her way over to get her English/Italian dictionary.

"No, no, I understand, just - why now?"

"I need to visit my parents' graves, and tell them about us."
She looked defiant, as if expecting a challenge to her decision.

'I see - that is a good thing to do."

Alberto wondered whether he should be doing the same
thing with his Mia, or at least telling his daughters about Ann
before they both landed on them in a few weeks time. All of
a sudden he realised that things were not simple when two
people with tangled histories and commitments came
together. They both stood metres apart and felt the tug of the
people they had once been. The kettle squealed and Ann
jumped to make the tea. As she was pouring the water over
she felt two arms come round her.

"Ti amo, Ann."

Ann looked down at the two gentle hands holding her waist,
lifted them up and kissed them.

"I love you too. We can figure this out."

Alberto didn't reply, he just held her tighter, this person who
had filled his void, broken into his grief, solved his loneliness.
He had never expected this. He had never known the one he
needed so badly was so close. He chuckled to himself.

Home had come to him. Right across the hall.

Salma sang as she cleared away the signs of a successful dinner. Omar watched her with a smile on his face.

"That was a good dinner. Are you glad you did it?"

She put down the pile of plates,

"It was all that I've ever hoped it would be. Omar, we've found the family we never had. And friends."

She wiped away her happy tears and smiled at him.

Omar shifted from one foot to the other. He knew he was supposed to respond positively, but all he could muster was two nods. A glimmer of a frown passed over Salma's face, but she said nothing more.

"I'd better be heading to the school." And with that, Omar was gone.

Omar side-stepped the dog mess on the street, stopped to let a rat scurry past and kicked an empty can along the footpath. It rattled, he kicked it harder then he picked it up and hurled it into the middle of the road. A group of Western tourists saw him and picked up speed, looking over their shoulders at him, fear on their faces.

He ducked in to a side street and chose the hidden route to get to work - like his wife's hijab, the shadows protected him from those frightened, distrusting looks he had to live with every single, miserable day. He had mostly stopped smiling at people, as the sight of his white teeth seemed to repel them more than ever. What was there to smile about anyway? Salma could have her little moments where she felt she belonged, but he just couldn't be that way. Of course, there were people who showed him respect - people like Alberto, or even Ann now she had got over her nervousness of him. Some of the police had been generous to him as well. And then there was Francois - that was a surprise. So he knew all too well that you couldn't tar everybody with the same brush. If only more would realise that.

Maybe Salma was right - maybe life was getting better, maybe Nice would feel more like home now they had Florence and Sebastian. He got out his keys, and jangled them with a lighter heart. But wait! He stopped - the door was already open, somebody was still there. It was ten o' clock at night - no-one was ever there at this time. The latest any of the staff stayed was seven, and that was a rare occurrence. His employer had given him a later time deliberately, so that he wouldn't 'unsettle the staff'.

"Allo?" Omar started treading slowly down the main corridor towards the one lit classroom. One of the blu-tacked pictures whispered down the notice-board and dropped to the floor with a small snap. He picked it up and re-attached it. As he was focusing on the poster, a torch light flickered over his hands. He turned and squinted in the bright light. There, torch in one hand, paper knife in the other, was Mme Tessier.

"What are you doing here?"

Her voice was shrill, nervous. Omar decided to forego his no-smile policy and showed his teeth.

"I am the night care-taker, Omar Jabbour." He put out his hand and bowed slightly. The woman just lifted her letter opener between them.

"You are lying, there is no way they would employ someone like you. What do you want? Money?"

Omar sighed.

"No, Madame. I really am the caretaker - I have the keys." He lifted the keys and jangled them. Mme Tessier screamed.

"You teach my son, Mamoun. And I know your son, Francois too."

Mme Tessier shook her head but started walking backwards, still pointing her knife at him.

"Go! Just leave!"

Omar thought about protesting, but looked at her face - fear, morphing into hatred, then anger, made him turn and walk away. He would have to come back early the next morning instead. He hoped it wouldn't cost him his job. He wouldn't tell Salma or Mamoun - he'd think of another reason for getting back early. As he climbed down the steps he found a crack and shoved his keys into it. He'd tell them he'd forgotten his keys. He didn't want them to know the truth.

People never change. Life was always going to be like this. He took his time getting back. He didn't even kick litter around this time, he didn't hide in the darkness, he just walked slowly home, his head down, the dark clouds gathering above him.

Rachel let herself in to the studio and sat on the edge of the futon. She unzipped her purse, and took out Mamoun's chain. Then she undid the clasp of the one Charlie had given her and placed them side by side on the navy cushion. She stared at them both - one calling her back home, one affirming her decision to be away. She had almost forgotten Charlie's -she never took it off so it had just been a part of her that she'd become used to. But. Mamoun's gift had given her a jolt. It had forced her to remember. She sighed and rubbed her temples. The familiar ache for her family, her friends, Charlie, came rising up, and all at once she had to get there.

It was time to go home.

That night she dreamt of him, being there in Nice. In her dream he told her he loved her. When the midday sun woke her, she sat up believing he was there.

There was a knock on the door. She threw on her T-shirt and pulled on some shorts, slipped her feet into flip-flops and walked over. She ran both hands through her hair and turned the latch.

It was Mamoun and Alberto. They both grinned stupidly at her.

"Bonjour Madame Rachel. We just thought you might like one last ice-cream?"

Rachel thought about her unpacked bags, how few hours she had left before her plane.

"Oh why not? I would love to go for an ice-cream with you. Is this the fourth time you've tricked me into getting you a boule? And Alberto - this is a first!"

Alberto shrugged and pointed to Mamoun behind his back.

So the three of them set out for one last walk to the Old Town. As Rachel watched the two walking in front of her, she felt tears springing to her eyes. She rubbed them away, angry that going home didn't mean an end to missing people you love. Mamoun ran back to her and grabbed her hand.

It was another sun-drenched day, and the summer heat was grabbing them in a close embrace. Rachel realised that she was going to be home before high summer began in Nice, and had arrived just after it last year. Maybe she should have prolonged her stay, maybe there was more to see and experience here.

The Old Town sheltered them from the heat of the sun, and tantalised them with smells of African, Italian and Provencal cuisine. Traders were calling to passers-by. Tourists were chattering to each other and stopping to pose for photos, blocking the way though. There was the smell of one day old peaches and apricots rotting at the back of fruit stalls, the scent of charcuterie and olives that Rachel wished she had developed a taste for. She stopped at a jewellery shop but was pulled on by Mamoun.

"You do not need these things - you have two bracelets already!"

Mamoun touched her wrist.

"It is a pity mine doesn't fit." He looked downcast. Rachel bent down to look him in the eye.

"I will always keep it in my purse. That way I will see it every time I spend any money and think of you. I am good at that, I promise."

"Good at what?"

They stopped at the ice-cream kiosk. Rachel got her purse out and lifted the bracelet, showing it to Mamoun.

She looked down at the ten year old in his tiny T-shirt, scruffy sandals and frizzy hair, and realised it was true.

"Good at missing people."

Alberto cleared his throat and gestured to the ice-creams. They set to ordering and the painful moment melted away into passion fruit, chocolate and strawberry delight.

✤

As she hurried back, Rachel started packing in her head, hoping that would speed up the process. The sun had disappeared, and dark clouds were gathering.

"Well, well. If it isn't Rachel from Northern Ireland, running like someone's chasing her."

Nick put away his book and stuck his smoke behind his ear again. He'd been sitting at a table in a street-side cafe but had got up when he saw Rachel.

"How's things, Rachel?"

Rachel tried to hide her frustration at being held up and smiled.

"They're good, I'm just rushing back to pack - I'm going home today."

Nick nodded slowly.

"So soon? What's your hurry?"

"My job's done, my lease is up on the flat and I'm ready to get back."

Nick slid his smoke out and lit it.

"Good for you. Me, I'm only starting to get used to this place, and I'm not for leaving."

He puffed a smoke ring above his head.

"There's nothing calling me back, that's for sure."

Rachel looked at him, and saw a lost-ness in his face she'd never noticed before.

"I'm sorry to hear that."

Nick laughed quietly.

"Why? All the more reason to live it up here."

"Well, enjoy yourself. I need to rush on now." She kissed him goodbye and started to jog away.

"Enjoy home, Rachel!" he called after her.

It took less time than she had expected to pack, and the studio was already pretty clean. At least, without the sunlight exposing any ounce of dirt that was there, it certainly looked clean. She sat in the living space, eating her last fresh croissant and looking about her. It was empty again, just like it was when Margaret first brought her. Rachel slid her feet out from under her, and heard the sound echoing back. She got up to wash her hands and then sat down again. There was the roar of raindrops hitting the skylights now, washing away all the smears from the last shower weeks before. She looked at her rucksack - fuller than it had been when she'd arrived, and definitely more worn. It told the story of new places explored, new journeys completed. Maybe she should have done more- but then, there would always be somewhere else to see. And she needed to go back now.

She put her hand over her chest and breathed out. It was happening again - the empty, lonely feeling that had never left her. This time she knew she was headed for home, but something had changed. She was sad to leave her new friends here. She sighed. Always a place to leave, always friends to miss. She dug out her album, and flicked through all the photos she'd added - the hostel, Margaret, Laura and Francesca in Italy, her school pupil, her studio, Francois, Alberto, Ann, Salma, Omar, Mamoun, Florence, Sebastian.

She paused over his face and did not feel any pangs for him. They were all her family now, and she would miss them equally.

She flicked back to the beginning for the first time in months, smiling at her mum and dad, and Pepsi. There was Phoebe and Jill pulling funny faces. And there he was. Charlie.

Rachel felt her heart flip and she knew.

She knew he was the one she was going back to.

She put her music on, and searched for the song that was going round her head at that moment. She kept Charlie's photo in her hand and sank back, singing along in a low voice, studying his face.

I need a phone call/ I need a plane ride

When the song was done, she stood up, slung her rucksack over her shoulders, picked up her other bag and left the studio, not looking back.

CHAPTER TWENTY-TWO

Home

There was a three hour wait in Stansted terminal before the flight to Belfast was due. Rachel wandered aimlessly, hearing the babble of English all round her. She realised that for the past ten months she had blocked her ears to background conversations to eschew the effort of always needing to understand a language not her own. She walked into Accessorize and considered the hoop earrings. Maybe she needed to look more exotic now; she had been living in the more glamorous Nice after all. She bought a pair and went in to the toilets to put them in. She looked at herself: tanned, slightly more plump (all that patisserie), hair bleached more blond by the sun. The earrings looked good - they made her seem different. She had to have something to show for her time away. She wandered over to the arrivals lounge and sat down in the corner to people watch. People dressed in suits with name placards stood waiting for a colleague they'd never met. Mothers with fractious children waited for daddy. A gaggle of girls flicking their hair and checking their make-up looked out for their boyfriends who didn't seem over the moon to see them when they reached the gate. A very elegant older woman pulled her suitcase to the exit and waited for her 30ish son and daughter to kiss her on the cheek and usher her out. Two overweight men in their sixties had just caught sight of each other and spent the next five minutes pointing, laughing, crying, hugging each other. Old friends Rachel guessed, or long-lost brothers.

Then there was Ann.

"Ann!" Rachel dropped her bag and shouted. Ann saw her and watched her run over.

"Ann! What are you doing here?"

Ann smiled,

"Just one final tying up of loose ends here, before we go spend some time in Italy."

"Is Alberto here with you?"

"No. I decided this was something I needed to do for me. You know?"

Ann looked expectantly at Rachel. They both thought over all the life-altering things that had happened for Ann during the past year.

"Yes, I think I understand. Hopefully that's what I'm doing for me too."

Ann dug into her case, and pulled a folder out, passing it to Rachel,

"I did the paintings you wanted."

Rachel leafed through the drawings - Alberto, Francois, Mamoun, Salma, they were all there. She turned over to the last page and froze: it was her. She was not looking at the painter - she was sitting on the stony shore looking over to the horizon.

"When did you?"

Ann smiled.

"Just one day early on in your year, before we'd even met. There was something yearning about the way you looked that struck me."

Rachel lowered her head.

"But if I'd had the chance, after you asked me, I would have done a very different one. You've changed this year Rachel."

She took the portfolio back.

"Maybe one day you'll find the strength to come back to us again."

They hugged each other then, and Ann went on her way, hoisting her carry-all over her shoulder. She seemed so at ease with being there, going to a place she hadn't seen for many years. It was facing her fears and finding love that had done it, Rachel concluded. Is that what she had done too? She sat down again, and touched her bracelet. She hoped beyond hope that it had been given as a sign of something more than friendship.

She pushed up her bag to lean her head on, put her earphones in and closed her eyes.

I'm just trying to get myself some gravity/ You're just trying to get me to stay/ Sometimes I'm floating away/ I'm thinking about breaking myself/ I'm thinking about getting back home.

Rachel ducked into the toilets to fix her over-travelled, under-hydrated appearance. She sprayed water over her face, ran her fingers through her hair and added lip gloss. She took a moment to study herself. Did she look as different as she felt inside? Was Ann right about how she'd changed? She grabbed all her bags and went out to look for mum. Or maybe dad this time. She searched through the groups and couldn't spot them. Could they have forgotten? People were leaving with their people and she was still standing here. Alone. There were no North Africans pestering her about sunglasses, little boys demanding ice-cream, English artists heading off to the sea for inspiration, French boys running after her to get her number. She let the pain rise up a little but squeezed her eyes shut to stop it taking hold.

"Rachel!"

She spun round and nearly knocked him over with her massive rucksack.

"Charlie, what are you doing here?!" She put her arms round him for a split second then stepped back.

He grinned at her and put his hands in his pockets, looking

her up and down. She lifted her chin, and levelled her eyes with his.

"I offered to come bring you back."

Rachel put her hand up to adjust her bag. She saw Charlie's gaze stopping at her bracelet.

He came close to her again and smiled, raising his eyebrows in silent question.

Rachel let her bags drop to the floor, and reached out to hold onto his arms. The noises and movements surrounding her dropped into silence.

She reached up,

And she kissed him.

It wasn't a Sebastian kiss.

It was better.

It felt like coming home.

One way or another I just wish I had known/To go out walking in the sun/ And find out if you were the one

Epilogue

"Oh, Salma, I'm glad I caught you."

Florence was out of breath from running up the stairs to catch her new-found friend. Salma stopped and turned to face her, eye-brows raised in question.

"Margaret was just here."

Salma looked blank.

"The woman who owns the studio upstairs."

"Oh yes."

"Someone was with her - another student."

"Is she here to do the same thing as Rachel?"

"He, and yes. Looks as terrified as she was though."

Salma and Florence looked at each other and smiled.

"Well, we know what to do this time. I'll go get the curry

on."

"And I'll tell the neighbours."

As Florence made her way across the landing she called over her shoulder,

"And by the way, his name is David."